David Massey

TAKEN

Chicken House

SCHOLASTIC INC.
NEW YORK

All rights reserved. Published by Chicken House, an imprint of Scholastic Inc.,
Publishers since 1920. CHICKEN HOUSE, SCHOLASTIC, and associated logos are
trademarks and/or registered trademarks of Scholastic Inc.
www.scholastic.com

First published in the United Kingdom in 2014 by Chicken House, 2 Palmer Street,
Frome, Somerset BA11 1DS.

Library of Congress Cataloging-in-Publication Data

Massey, David (David Robert), 1960 – author.
Taken / David Massey. — First American edition.
pages cm

Summary: Rio Cruz and a crew of young disabled veterans are teamed up to sail around
the world for charity — but when they are kidnapped by a psychotic African warlord
and his band of child soldiers, the trip of a lifetime turns into a nightmare journey into
the African jungle.
ISBN 978-0-545-66128-7 1. Disabled veterans — Juvenile fiction. 2. Child soldiers —
Juvenile fiction. 3. Kidnapping — Juvenile fiction. 4. Survival — Juvenile fiction.
5. Africa, East — Juvenile fiction. [1. Veterans — Fiction. 2. Child soldiers — Fiction.
3. Kidnapping — Fiction. 4. Survival — Fiction. 5. People with disabilities — Fiction.
6. Africa, East — Fiction.] I. Title.

PZ7.M423823Tak 2014
[Fic] — dc23

2013049168

10 9 8 7 6 5 4 3 2 1   14 15 16 17 18

Printed in the U.S.A.   23
First American edition, September 2014

The text type was set in Chapparal Pro.
The display type was hand-lettered by Nina Goffi.
Book design by Nina Goffi.

I AM THE CAPTAIN OF MY SOUL.

"INVICTUS"
William Ernest Henley

1

DAY 1

MY RUCKSACK THUDS ONTO THE WOODEN PON-
toon and all the stress of getting here falls away with
it. I feel light and dizzy, like I've just ditched the last thing
that anchored me to reality. Beyond the purple shadows of
the city buildings, the rocky coastline of South Africa reaches
out on either side of the marina. I can actually *feel* the sea in
my hair, pulling my curls tighter, and the warm breeze gives
me this seaweed high when I breathe it in. I'd say it's a cool
southwester, gusting at about fifteen knots. Perfect condi-
tions for the direction we'll be heading — almost due east.
Ahead of me, through a jumbled corridor of yachts, golden

light is glancing off the horizon. Already I can feel its warmth on my face.

Back home in Weymouth I'd be looking out at the gray English Channel, blowing on my fingers and watching ragged strands of steam rise through the gaps. Here, I can be still and take it all in. It's like all the random mess that usually fills my mind has been sucked right out of it. Just standing here is spring-cleaning my head! The orange glow of the pontoon lights, dancing on their sagging strings in time to the swell, is beginning to fade as the sun rises, and I watch it dissolve in front of me. One by one the lights go out like a row of dying fireflies. My chest flutters at the sight, and it's partly nerves, but mostly because I'm so *happy*. This feeling — it's like it's my first day on the water all over again. I love the Atlantic. It's sparkling at me like an old friend and pretty soon it will intro-duce me to a whole *new* sea. Somewhere out there to my left, it crashes against the swirling currents of the Indian Ocean. I can't wait to get there.

I take some time just to listen to how the other side of the world *sounds*. After the hustle of the airport and the nail-biting anticipation of the taxi ride, there is an incredible quiet, full of hushed and expectant noises — the constant *tink tink tink* of ropes against metal masts, the soft bump of wood against plastic buffers, and the gulping water that rocks the very floor beneath my feet. This is *awesome!* I'm nine thousand miles from home, standing on the tip of Africa's Southern Cape, and it feels totally right, as though here is where I actually belong.

I look around briefly, wondering where the *Spirit of Freedom* is, and that's when I feel this weird drop in temperature on the back of my neck. Goose bumps ripple up my arms, and when I look down the pontoon, the way I've come, I see a tall figure just standing there, watching me. I almost jump out of my skin. It's an old guy, about forty, with a pockmarked face. He's wearing a gaudy bandana with an old feather tucked into it behind his ear. Around his neck is a twisted leather necklace, and there is a leopard paw, complete with claws, dangling from it. He's close enough that I can see his fingernails are all yellow and splitting, crusted with dirt, and he has a leather pouch slung across his chest that rattles when he lifts it and shakes it at me. The man grins, revealing rows of twisted yellow teeth. He gives me the creeps.

I have to look down briefly to grab the handle of my rucksack in case I need to make a run for it. When I look up again, the guy has gone. I have no idea how he disappeared so silently, because you can't walk an inch on this decking without feeling the vibration through your feet. After a quick scan all around, I call, "Hello?" but nobody answers.

It all happened so fast I'm not even sure if I just imagined the whole thing. After all, I haven't slept a wink since I left home. I haul my rucksack up with both hands and stagger along the decking like the Hunchback of Notre Dame, constantly looking back over my shoulder. Soon the pontoon is sloshing and rocking in time with me, and the rows of boats moored on either side are bobbing away like corks. To calm down, I force myself to think about other things, like: What will the crew be like? I hope I'll fit in. All I know right now is that four of them are disabled. Everything was so last-minute that I don't know what to expect — only that I'm here as support crew. I just hope that doesn't mean I have to help anyone pee.

I'm beginning to sweat now. Even this early, the rising sun is intense and the heat is so dry. At a T-junction where the pontoon meets the sea, I look left to where another, shorter stretch of decking joins mine at right angles. It projects farther out into the bay like a launchpad and, berthed at the end, is the most incredible seventy-foot yacht I have ever seen.

She has a sleek white cabin above deck, a dark blue hull, and a series of three tinted, rectangular portholes set into her side amidships. The whole of her prow is on fire in the orange glow of the sunrise, her hull ripples with restless fingers of light, and she is built for speed. *Spirit of Freedom* is printed in a bold, flowing font on her stern, and in white near the prow is the logo of a bird taking flight, bursting through some kind of glass ceiling. And she's peppered with sponsor names.

This is it. My whole body tingles with excitement. I have never seen such a beauty up close — let alone had the chance to sail one.

I waddle over with my rucksack, dump it by *Spirit*'s stern, and drop to my knees so that I can peek through one of her tinted windows. All I can see is my own reflection. Up close, I look even rougher than normal, if that's possible. My crazy, unmanageable hair, which has even defeated Mum's industrial-strength flat iron, bounces around my ears in a kind of semi-Afro. My eyebrows are a little too wide and my nose is flat. Oh, and my eyes are so brown the only reason you can see the pupils is because there is this weird orange ring around them. All this the result of being a complete racial mash-up. The Rainbow Girl meets the Rainbow Nation — South Africa. The best thing about my face is my teeth. I run my tongue over them and pull my mouth into a goofy grin to get a closer look.

As I'm looking, my reflection shudders. It steadies briefly and then it happens again. So I didn't imagine it. There is this shuddering vibration shaking the decking planks — and it seems to have some kind of rhythm to it, a weird *thud thud thud*, like someone is hitting the boards with a sledgehammer. I scramble to my feet. I can't tell where it's coming from, but I can feel my body jerking in time with it, see the rippling echoes spreading away in the water. Then I catch a glimpse of movement between the moored yachts. It's a while before I suss that I'm seeing the head and shoulders of someone running, a guy. He's tall, and his long, sun-bleached hair is whipping back behind him. He looks like he's about to take on the world.

When he gets to the T-junction, the guy's eyes turn to meet mine and he slows briefly. He has a pair of sunglasses perched on his head, and his T-shirt has a black-and-white picture of John Lennon with the logo *Working Class Hero* underneath. But it's not until I take in the rest of him that I realize why he seems so tall. It's beautiful and shocking all at the same time: The bottom halves of his legs end in shiny black sockets, which are attached to a pair of long, curving black blades. They make him look like some kind of human cheetah.

Suddenly his fingers curl up into fists and he breaks into a sprint. Now he's hammering along the pontoon and he's yelling at me.

"Hey! What do you think you're doing?"

He covers the space between us faster than I would have thought possible. I don't have anywhere to run to, and the pounding vibration beneath my feet feels like it's matching the hammering of my heart. I consider screaming for help. As I take an involuntary step backward, the sole of my deck shoe skids over something, and next thing I know, my arms are flapping like an angry chicken and I'm flopping helplessly into the sea.

The shock of the water is the least of my worries — the worst thing is the gut-wrenching embarrassment of feeling the buckle of my watch strap gouge a long scratch in *Spirit's* hull as I flail about for a handhold on my way down. I surface choking and retching because I've swallowed half of the South Atlantic.

Blades arrives at the edge of the pontoon with a face like thunder. Now that he's closer I can see that he's not much older than me, and that he has a line of freckles on his tanned cheeks.

"You should stay away from the edge of the pontoon," he says, spitting on his thumb and rubbing at the paintwork around the angry white scratch with a furrowed brow. "Fewer accidents happen that way. Oh, and while we're at it, what were you doing poking your nose around out here? What are you, the press?"

I'm mad at him for caring more about his boat than me, and it's not helping that I have to battle my stupid hair out of my face to see him clearly. As a result my tone is more than a little snarky when I splutter back, "No, I'm not . . . I'm Rio!"

He stares at me. "Rio? Rio Cruz?"

"Don't wear it out."

"Or what? You'll scratch the other side of my boat?"

I'm too mortified to reply.

The guy's eyes narrow. "You don't look anything like your passport photo."

"I was twelve!"

"Right. That explains it." There's an awkward silence while Blades squats there watching me. "You know we need support crew to be sure-footed? *You're* supposed to catch *us* if we fall."

Ouch.

"*Normally* I am! When I don't have some madman after me, that is." I tread water, still looking for a handhold. "What were you running like that for anyway? You scared me."

I'm rewarded with this *you're kidding* look. "I see a stranger snooping around *Spirit* at this time of day, so naturally I'm nervous. There are some twisted individuals out there who don't like who we are or what we're doing. We've already had problems. Do you blame me?"

"Oh. No — I don't blame you."

"Good. Over there . . ." He points out a bumper rope I can grab, and walks to it while I swim. "Who let you get so close to the yacht anyway? Didn't security stop you?"

"I haven't seen anyone."

"*No one?* Are you sure?" Blades looks worried now, like he thinks I'm lying.

I stop paddling for a second. "Er, yes. I'm sure."

"I'm just surprised they're not here. The yacht should be guarded twenty-four-seven." He looks around, as if to try to locate the guards, and then he spots something on the floor. He picks it up and examines it between his thumb and forefinger. "I think I've found what you slipped on."

I'm now doing a pathetic breaststroke back to the pontoon and he's watching me all the way. I'm a good sailor, but I swim like a drowning rat.

"What is it?" I ask him, if only to stop him from watching me.

"I don't know. Could be a bone . . ." Blades holds up this little brown cylinder. "It looks really old."

"What's it doing here?"

"Good question. Here, let me give you a hand — I'm fresh out of legs . . ."

That makes me laugh, despite myself.

He holds out a warm, dry hand, which I take, and he hauls me out of the water until I can flop facedown onto the pontoon and attempt to get my breath back. While I try to control my gag reflex, Blades retrieves my bag. When he gets back, he helps me up.

"I'm Ash," he says.

It's a moment before I notice he hasn't let go of my hand. I pull away to pick my bag up and that's when I see that someone else is there, watching us.

A tall, skinny black girl has arrived at the end of the pontoon. She's like some kind of undiscovered supermodel and her makeup looks like it's been put on by laser. Her shiny black hair is pinned up with delicate cherry blossom flowers at the back. The difference between us couldn't be more obvious. I can feel *my* wet hair twisting itself into some embarrassing modern-art installation as she stares at it.

There's an elastic in my bag somewhere — and a towel. I fumble for the zipper on it and can't get the freaking thing open, of course. When I look back up, the girl is letting out a long, exasperated sigh.

Ash waves her over. "Jen! Come and meet Rio."

She doesn't move. Instead her eyes widen and she points. "Ash! There's a huge scratch on *Spirit*'s hull."

"I know." The way his eyes flick at me as he says it gives the game away.

"You *know*?" Jen glares at us.

Ash doesn't answer her, so she turns on me. "Have you any idea how much it will cost —"

"It was an accident. I'm sorry. *Really* sorry. Excuse me," I mumble as I make my way past her and back toward the clubhouse.

"Ugh! Do you mind?"

Somehow I've managed to drip all over her sandals when I pass. My cheeks flush with heat.

"Sorry again! For everything . . ." This is *so* not the start I wanted to have.

"Don't be too long!" Ash calls after me. "The press are coming and we need to get underway."

I don't answer. All I can think about is getting as far from the yacht as I can. Back home would be good, but that's impossible now. So I slip quietly back into the clubhouse, find the toilets, strip off, and towel myself dry before the air-conditioning gives me hypothermia. Shivering, I wring my wet things out over a sink, wrap them in the towel, and shove them back in the bag — right now I don't care if the other stuff gets wet. I change my tank top for a white cotton shirt that just happens to be at the top of my bag. When I'm done I lock myself in a stall, throw the toilet lid down, and squat on it, burying my nose between my knees.

I don't know if I even want to be here anymore. Not if it means having to *interact*. I'm terrible at it, always have been. Next time I go online I'm going to change my Facebook relationship status from *Single* to *Total Screw-Up, Avoid Me*. I should be sailing around the world on my own — just me and the elements. And I just know that girl Jen is going to be everything I don't need. I'm *so* looking forward to developing my inferiority complex — it's just my luck that the only other able body on the expedition looks like a freaking movie star. With minty breath — mustn't forget the minty breath. I can't help letting another groan escape — we're going to be working together for months. Oh, and did I mention that the crew leader already thinks I'm an idiot? But I can't hang on to these thoughts, however bad I feel. Just thinking about being on the ocean — about sailing on that fantastic boat — lifts my spirits.

When I make my way back outside, the sun is up and the pontoon is full of people. I fight the urge to run. Ash is standing behind a navigation console on the command deck of the *Spirit of Freedom*, wearing an orange life jacket with his hand on one of two huge wheels while a bunch of press people shout directions at him. I try not to think about the long white scratch, or the fact that all the cameras are pointing at it. I focus on Ash. His blades have gone — he's changed them for some gleaming aluminum legs that have electronics and little black buttons on the front. With his high-tech prostheses planted firmly on the deck, he looks almost superhuman.

Jen hasn't boarded yet; she's waiting by the ladder for me. "Well? Ready to go?" she asks. I nod, grateful that she seems to have thawed a little, and she introduces me to the support team, who are gathered around the boarding ladder.

Ash's mum — Mrs. Carter — is trying to avoid the cameras and get off the boat. She gives Ash a last hug and clambers down the boarding ladder to reach me. It's nice to see a familiar face. Mrs. Carter came to the UK scouting for potential helpers, which is how I ended up here. I remember that very gentle Australian accent I first heard back in the UK.

"Rio! I'm so sorry I couldn't come and get you from the airport myself — and for all the rush. You must be exhausted! Thank you for agreeing to help out on such short notice."

"It's no problem, really. I can't wait."

"Ash will take good care of you." She tries to get his attention, but he's too busy to respond. "Just be yourself. You're here because you are a great sailor, not just because the insurers insisted on another able body. I've seen what you can do. You'll be a perfect addition to the team."

We don't have time to talk any longer. It's a shame, because she was starting to make me feel better about myself. Ash waves at us and Jen tugs my arm: I have to go.

"Give us a wave, Charis!" one of the press guys yells at the crew as I clamber up the boarding ladder after Jen. The support team pull it away as I step off it and onto the yacht. Up on deck, a square-faced girl with blonde hair raises an amazing prosthetic arm that looks like an extra-long, shiny black gauntlet. Straps secure it around her neck and shoulder. The fingers whir open and she waves at the reporter who shouted. When Jen drops next to her, Charis gives her a hug with her good arm. It has a beautiful Japanese dragon tattoo snaking around the wrist.

I love feeling the hardwood decking give slightly under my feet as I pick my way over to a space on the other side of the yacht. My heart flips. It's like *Spirit* is *letting* me board her. There are padded seats just behind each wheel, but nobody uses them. The other team members prefer to position themselves on either side of the deck.

"This is yours, Rio."

I catch the life jacket that Ash throws to me as I pass him, and lean against the guardrail next to a baby-faced girl in a pink crop top. She helps me with the straps on the jacket. "I'm Izzy," she tells me, grinning. Her long ginger hair is pulled back into a tight ponytail and she's wearing shorts — which is surprising, given that her left leg is punctured, almost from the top of her knee to her ankle, with pins fixed to long metal rods. I wonder how she gets anything on over them. Her big sea-green eyes are amazing, full of sparkle, and I just know we're going to be friends. Sensing that is a huge relief. I smile back.

Next to Ash is a tall guy with Johnny Depp hair and no eyebrows. Obviously a joker, because his T-shirt has a picture of an arm bone and the words *I found this humerus*. But his face is a real shock. It looks like half of it has been reconstructed: The skin is all patchy, with pink and white bits everywhere. It's quite hard for me to look at him for long without feeling like I'm staring.

Ash puts his arm around the guy and tells the reporters, "Marcus and I are nineteen. We were caught in the same blast when our transport was ambushed in Nad Ali, Helmand. Our tour of duty in Afghanistan was probably the shortest in history — just four days and six hours on the front line. As you can see, Marcus came off best."

Nobody knows what to make of the joke except Marcus, Charis, and Izzy, who all laugh. Ash isn't fazed by the lack of response, though. "Charis here is eighteen, she lost her forearm just below the elbow in Kandahar while checking a vehicle for booby traps, and she'll be testing a brand-new prosthesis specially made for her by Touch Bionics, who are also one of our sponsors."

There is a glass of water on the cockpit table. Charis reaches for it and her fingers whir open. Cameras flash. Everybody is expecting her to shatter the glass, but her metal fingers curl and close delicately around it. Charis takes a sip, smiles sassily, and puts it back down without a hint of awkwardness.

"And Izzy." Ash looks at her fondly. "At seventeen, Izzy is the youngest. Like Charis, she joined the army straight from school. Soon afterward she was hit with a double whammy.

She had a bad fall" — Izzy laughs and shakes her head — "from a helicopter in training, proving the military proverb that if something hasn't broken on your helicopter, it's about to. Then, while she was in rehab, she was diagnosed with diabetes.

"So that's the team, as some of you know already, but let me tell you *why* we're here. Why a bunch of misfits like us have decided to attempt a circumnavigation of the planet. We're here for two reasons: one — to show that disability doesn't disable *us*; and two — the most important reason — to raise money for the Hidden Children."

Marcus holds a rolled-up poster by the corners and lets it flop open. On it is a picture of a tangle-haired boy of about twelve standing in some bombed-out mountain village. Behind him, children in filthy rags squat on the ground. The devastation takes my breath away, but it's the boy I can't take my eyes off. He has nothing, but his dark eyes are filled with fierce pride.

". . . kids whose families have been torn apart by war," Ash continues. "Afghan orphans like Husna and the Young Martyrs here, and children in Libya, Egypt, and Central Africa. You can find more information on our website . . ."

As the cameras click I tear my eyes off the poster and let Ash's press talk fade to a background hum while I take the time to look around. Up close the yacht is even more beautiful than she seemed on first impression, shifting restlessly like she's impatient to dip her keel in deeper water, and I just can't wait to have a go at the helm. If she was a typical round-the-worlder, she would need a few more crew, but she's been adapted to sail shorthanded — I can tell by the way she is rigged and by the panels of switches in front of the wheels. In fact, this boat is anything but ordinary. It's the kind of thing you'd expect to see taking rich people round the Caribbean, but stripped back to the essentials. They have even installed a bank of solar panels on the cabin roof.

In the sheltered waters of the bay, the wind is beginning to curl the heads of the waves over. City smells mingle with the salty ocean breeze, and a group of screaming gulls swoops to play above our mast. While I'm getting my life jacket on, Ash asks a couple of journalists to untie the mooring ropes and throw them on deck. Marcus limps all along the side of the boat, pulling up cylindrical white plastic fenders, while Charis grabs them and stows them below deck. She favors her good arm, but looks totally at ease manhandling something that is easily as long as her torso. I find myself watching them while I clip and adjust the straps on my life jacket.

That's it. I'm done.

My heart is in my throat. I've never been anywhere in my life before where I couldn't turn back. For the next seven months I've got to eat, sleep, and drink with a bunch of total strangers. While I fret, Ash starts his safety briefing and the *Spirit of Freedom* drifts gently away from her mooring. We're on our way.

2

WHEN HE'S FINISHED HIS BRIEFING, ASH STARTS the engine. It coughs some silt out of the bilge pumps astern — oily at first, but then clear — and the prop churns the water into a froth that slowly changes from brown to white. If you ask me, it doesn't look right, but I'm no expert. The boats I train in never have engines. Almost immediately we begin to surge forward over the sparkling water into Table Bay, heading for a distant red buoy. The sea slaps and sloshes lazily against our prow, and the *Spirit of Freedom* slices her way effortlessly through it. It's like she's alive and can't wait to get out there — the deck is actually humming beneath my feet.

Jen looks at me and I realize that I'm the only one on board who's grinning like an idiot. When I don't stop, she rewards me with this half smile, a tiny crack in her defenses. There's another red buoy leaning in choppier water, about half a mile from the first. When we get past it Ash will cut the engine, and we'll hoist the sails and get some speed up. At least, that's what I would do.

Behind us, Table Mountain seems safe and solid. The slopes loom above the city buildings, and clouds droop over the top like a layer of icing. Once we get past the tanker and container terminals some way off on our starboard side, there will just be the open sea between us and the distant, low outline of Robben Island.

Bring it on.

Ash is behind the right-hand wheel, occasionally leaning to look past the mast. His touch on the top of the wheel is light and confident. Watching him, I wonder why he isn't as depressed as hell. I know I would be if I lost my legs, but he gives the impression that after he had them blown off he just woke up and got on with his life as if nothing had ever happened. Surely an experience like that has got to knock your self-belief? The guy is either full of himself or nothing short of amazing, I can't decide which. Then I begin to wonder if I'm a little jealous of his confidence — and how twisted it would be to feel that way about someone with no legs.

Looking around I decide that they're all amazing. I feel small, sitting in front of the left-hand wheel where the back wall of the cabin tapers into the teak deck planks, sandwiched between Izzy and one of the stainless-steel coffee grinders.

Her leg frame is digging painfully into my thigh, but there's no way I'm going to say anything. Marcus is sitting on the cabin roof, leaning back on his elbow to take a selfie on his phone. Then he turns to watch the shore slip past, behind Jen and Charis.

Jen's watching the quay through the camera on her phone, waiting for Table Mountain to shrink until it's small enough to fit into a photo. When she's taken it, she tweaks it with Instagram and thumbs a quick text. The wind is whipping her hair across her eyes as she types, so she tucks it back behind her ear. That girl is *so* beautiful — even in a life jacket. I mean, where's the justice?

"How're you doing, Rio?" Ash asks me over his shoulder, after a brief glance at Jen. "You feel up for this?"

It takes me forever to register Ash's question. Part of me is thinking, *He noticed me!* but I tell it to shut up. How am I doing? Seriously — how does he think? These guys have been through things together that I can't even imagine. All that army training, and they're all so at home on the *Spirit of Freedom* already — probably had days to get the hang of her — then along I come and wreck both their yacht *and* their cozy club. I get a sudden flashback of Ash hauling me out of the water, and I think I can actually feel my toes curling by the time I finally manage to tell him, "I'm fine." It's what he wants to hear.

Izzy's cool, though. She squeezes my arm and smiles warmly. "Don't worry," she whispers, leaning in. "You'll fit in. Believe me." Then she puts her arm around my shoulder. "C'mon. Let's get your stuff below deck and I'll give you a tour."

We have to squeeze past the wheels to drop down into the cockpit. Ash glances at me. "Rio — everything is so crazy right now, but I promise I'm going to catch up with you when these guys have got all the shots they need."

I follow where his thumb is jabbing and see there's actually a helicopter sweeping low across the bay toward us, with the logo of its TV station emblazoned across its underbelly and a kamikaze camera guy leaning out of the side. Izzy shakes her head in disbelief.

Behind me, Jen is laughing conspiratorially with Charis, and they keep looking in my direction. Like I care. I follow Izzy as she carefully descends the steps that lead down into the cabin.

"The *Spirit of Freedom* is an old Oyster 72," Izzy tells me when we get down there. "She used to belong to a South African record producer — a friend of Mrs. Carter's. Which is why we're setting out from Cape Town." She gestures around her and grins. "What do you think?"

I drop my bag on the hardwood flooring and stare. *Wow*. To my left, pastel blue leather bench seats surround an oak-topped table. Shafts of sunlight filter through the wraparound tinted cabin windows above our heads. On the right is another leather bench seat and, alongside that, a navigation console with its own chair and cupboard space. The long, rectangular portholes I saw from outside are between the seats, and they actually drop *below* the waterline, allowing green wavy light in to ripple over everything. Set into the paneling above the cupboard is a glowing screen and a rack of equipment. The screen is a chart plotter showing Table Bay overlaid with grids and arrows, and scattered with numbers that change as we move. The radio is just beneath the screen, its curling cable leading to a black microphone that sits in a stainless-steel cradle.

"This is amazing!"

Izzy laughs. "I know. Not exactly roughing it, are we? But it's not all good news. Some of the fittings have been removed. I mean, there used to be a bar and a master bedroom."

"Shame . . ."

"Tell me about it. The guys were gutted." Izzy leads me forward past a galley that makes our kitchen back home look like a shed, and through a door that leads to two tiny cabins. "The one on the left is mine and Charis's, and this . . ." When Izzy opens the right-hand door my heart plummets.

"I guess I'm not sharing with Ash or Marcus?"

She snickers cheekily. "Don't think they wouldn't try!"

Inside is a pair of bunk beds. The top one is much narrower than the bottom one due to the curve of the hull. We open the stowage compartments to check, but I already know they are going to be full of designer exploration gear. I dump my sorry excuse for a bag on the end of the narrow top bunk.

"Don't worry. I'll get Jen to clear some of her stuff."

"No!" That came out a little too quickly, but I'm thinking the last thing I need to be doing right now is winding Jen up. "I'll manage."

Izzy gets it, I can tell. She thinks with her face. "Tell you what: I don't need much, so I'll clear some space under my bunk for your kit."

"Thanks."

Before we leave, Izzy lowers her voice and tells me, "Don't mind Ash, either. He's a little bent out of shape because the sponsors wouldn't let us put to sea without *able-bodied* support crew. It's not you."

"Do you really think so?"

"Really. He didn't even want Jen here. When we're underway he'll come round to the idea."

"What about the rest of them?" I'm worried now.

"We're all fine with it. It's just Ash . . . Ash is very . . . independent."

"Jen doesn't seem to like me much," I confide.

Izzy smiles. "Don't worry. Believe me, she does. She was stoked when she heard that there would be another able body."

"You could have fooled me."

"Jen's like that with everyone at first. You'll get used to her. Besides, we'll have each other." She takes my arm and leads me out, talking loudly again. "Both rooms have a head and the guys have their own, too — that's toilets to you and me, as I'm sure you know. Marcus has named theirs *Dick* — his lame idea of a joke. Soldiers tend to make a joke of pretty much everything." Suddenly the color drains from Izzy's face, and she puts a hand out to steady herself against the doorframe.

"Are you okay?"

She seems to look right through me. "Will be."

We make our way back, stopping at the open-plan kitchen area, where she introduces me to the fridge, one shelf of which is stocked with shrink-wrapped boxes of tiny bottles. Izzy rips one out. Looking over the counter I notice that Charis is in the saloon now. Her prosthetic arm is lying on the table, and she's sitting on the edge of the bench seat rubbing her stump with a towel. When she's done she starts massaging hand cream on it.

"Bloody thing looks better than it feels," she explains. "Gets a little too sweaty sometimes. I have to be careful I don't develop sores." For the first time I notice she's Welsh. She's got the kind of liquid-amber accent I imagine guys must love. All warm and deep. "Every now and again the arm starts to slip a bit, even with the straps. I had to have them fitted so I don't lose it overboard. Big mistake, because now they hold it on too tight. Hurts like hell. I'm getting used to it, though. And the sleeve is supposed to be breathable, would you believe?"

When she looks at me for a response I realize that I'm just watching her with my mouth open.

Charis rolls her eyes and grins. "First-world problems . . . I know . . ." she says to cover my embarrassment, and we both laugh. I think I'm going to like her.

Izzy drops onto the seat next to the radio with something clenched between her teeth. It's a syringe, complete with needle — no idea where she picked it up. She rolls her top up almost to her bra, holding it up with her chin, then she pulls a plastic sheath off the needle with her teeth and spits it into her lap. She stabs the syringe into the foil top of the bottle and draws all the liquid out. Then she pinches a fold of skin on her abdomen. It dents when the needle punctures it, and I look away.

Insulin. So Izzy injects. I feel sorry for her. My gran has diabetes but all she has to do is watch what she eats. When Iz has emptied the contents into her side, she pulls the needle out, puts the sheath back over the end, and drops it into a ziplock bag.

"Sorry, Rio. Felt myself going hypo, must have been all the stress," she tells me by way of explanation. "Sometimes I need a top-up." Leaning back in her seat with a sigh, Izzy pulls her shirt down, clips the bag shut, and places it on the table.

I reach over and pick it up. "I'll get rid of this for you . . . if you want. I am here to help, after all."

"I can't expect you to deal with my sharps, Rio."

Charis smiles but gives me this narrow look, like she's still trying to figure me out. But I'm hopeful. She seems on the level. "Let her help if she wants to, Iz. It's in the toilet —"

"Head."

"Whatever, Iz. Left-hand —"

"Port."

Charis shakes her head at Iz, but she's smiling. "What is this, *Pirates of the freaking Caribbean*? I'm sorry, my mistake. Izzy's bin is in the *head, port* side, Rio. You can only miss it if you're trying to feel your way in at night. Believe me, I've almost peed in it a few times now when it's dark."

I go back to Izzy's room and squeeze into the tiny toilet cabin. Charis is right: A big yellow plastic bin is right next to the toilet seat, with *DANGER — DESTROY BY INCINERATION* plastered all over it. It takes me a minute or two to figure out how it works, then I discover you have to twist the top to open it first and there's a flap inside. I drop the bag in and it clatters into the empty container — the first of many, I'm guessing.

By the time I get back to Izzy in the saloon, Charis has reassembled herself and gone back up on deck. Izzy's eyes look clearer, and she gets to her feet and slides her arm through mine. "Let's finish our little guided tour, shall we? There's not much more to see."

She takes me down a couple of steps and shows me what used to be the master bedroom, now stuffed full of everything six people might need for a circumnavigation of the globe. Spare ropes and sails, packs and packs of emergency rations, flares, and even spare electrical equipment. The door to the tiny engine room is between the storeroom and where the guys will be bunking. Izzy opens the door to the guys' room just to show me how untidy they are. She's right: The room is a total mess, and it smells like old socks and aftershave. Ash's blades are propped up in the far corner like a pair of skis.

We're on our way back to the deck when I notice a dark smear on the wall opposite the engine room door. I wipe it off with my thumb.

Iz asks, "What was that?"

"Oil, I think."

After showing me the mess the guys have left I can see Iz doesn't understand why I'm so bothered about a tiny oil stain, but I just couldn't leave it there. I'm still mortified about that scratch.

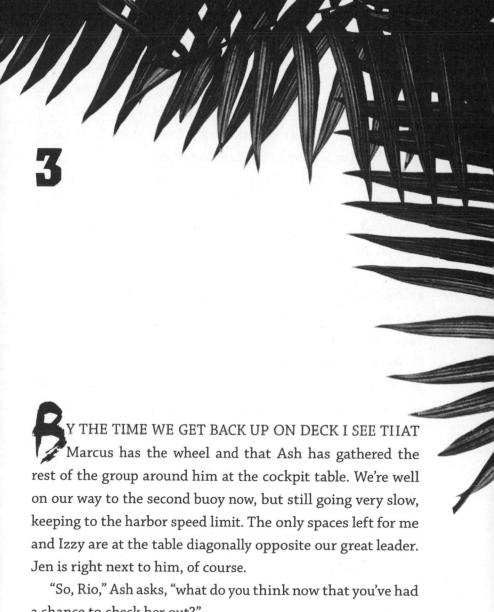

3

BY THE TIME WE GET BACK UP ON DECK I SEE THAT Marcus has the wheel and that Ash has gathered the rest of the group around him at the cockpit table. We're well on our way to the second buoy now, but still going very slow, keeping to the harbor speed limit. The only spaces left for me and Izzy are at the table diagonally opposite our great leader. Jen is right next to him, of course.

"So, Rio," Ash asks, "what do you think now that you've had a chance to check her out?"

All eyes turn my way and nerves get the better of me. I blurt, "The *Spirit of Freedom*? She's *beautiful*."

Jen snorts.

That was too enthusiastic. Way too enthusiastic. I bite my bottom lip and try to pull things back by adding, "A bit OTT, though. All the chrome and leather. I *mean* . . ."

Ash's eyebrows lift slightly and he looks at me with a half smile, like I'm still some kind of joke to him.

"If you think that's bad, you should have seen it before they ripped all the freaking essential bits out. Alcohol is lighter than water — beer's vital safety kit if you ask me," Marcus grumbles from behind the wheel. His lips barely move and he speaks with a mild accent — Newcastle, I think. The skin on his face is too taut to stretch far, but he still manages to offer me what I think is a good-natured smile. His eyes twinkle beneath lids he can barely close.

Ash continues, "Don't mind Marky, he's allergic to the stuff anyway. Oh, and don't ever let him 'friend' you. He's the sole reason both his mum and mine ditched their Facebook accounts. For some reason they both thought he was a complete angel until they saw his posts. A few weeks at sea will sort him out, though."

Marcus shrugs at me. "Don't hold your breath, mate. If eighteen months in the army and getting my freaking face blown off didn't do it, nothing will."

"How about four premenstrual girls on a boat?" Charis wonders dryly.

We all laugh at that one. Marcus rolls his eyes at me. "*Far* scarier than an insurgent with a detonator — granted."

Ash grins at his friend. "Where was I? Oh yes: *Spirit*'s been adapted so that a crew of two can handle her. The mainsail and the jib are self-furling, but we'll still have a few sail changes, and that's when we'll need extra hands. So we're going to start the first leg to Madagascar with three watches and then see how we're managing. Marcus and Charis are taking the night watch, so Izzy and I will be on days."

There's a pause, and Jen looks away from him. Her eyes meet mine for a nanosecond and she surprises me with another friendly smile. The others seem to hang on Ash's every word. I have to admit to myself that there is something very charismatic about him. Something you can't take your eyes off.

"Rio, you and Jen will take the mother watch. That's mainly domestic chores for the other two watches, covering twenty-four hours and getting sleep any time you can."

I try not to look disappointed. Ash seems to sense my mood because he adds grudgingly, "There will still be some sailing for you, Rio, I promise. Mum's told me how good you are, and she's got a keen eye — no, scratch that — she's got a *great* eye for talent." Then, somewhat awkwardly, he continues, "Jen's talent lies with navigation and comms, and she's going to be keeping an online diary of the trip, as well as liaising with the support team in Cape Town."

Jen smiles and gives him a coy little shrug.

"But yours and Jen's primary role is to support and enable the *disabled* crew." He does the finger-quotes thing when he says *disabled*. "Any questions?"

I have loads — but Ash is watching me like he's expecting me to kick off about not being able to sail, and I'm still too worried about rocking the boat — no pun intended — to ask them. Can't even manage a wry chuckle at the thought, because he'd think I was laughing at him. So I just tell him awkwardly, "No. I'm cool. Thanks for having me, all of you. You won't regret it."

"Of course we won't, babe," Izzy chips in. "This whole trip is going to be *amazing*."

"Yeah, as long as you don't keep falling overboard or scratching everything to hell, we'll get on fine!" Marcus adds with a laugh.

Ash obviously told him, then. Or Jen. I think I may have winced. Jen gives Charis a *don't count on it* look, but Charis ignores her.

"That's pretty much it for now, then . . ." Ash says.

Jen and Charis are already getting up. Charis's fingers whine when she straightens them into a salute. "Aye, aye, Cap'n."

". . . except to say that on this leg, we're heading round the Cape all the way to Maputo, then across the Indian Ocean south of Madagascar toward Mauritius. And, judging by the wind, we should make pretty good time."

He's right. The wind has picked up.

Once we've passed the last buoy, Ash kills the engine and points the *Spirit of Freedom* into wind — the opposite direction to the way we want to go. The air from the Atlantic and Robben Island is fresh and clean. I take a huge breath, close my eyes for a second, and wait for it to blow all my worries away. It feels amazing, like taking a cold shower on a blisteringly hot day.

Ash presses a button next to one of the winches, which sets it spinning. Slowly the mainsail rises out of the boom and begins to slide up the mast. It flaps and flutters loudly, stopping about two-thirds of the way up. Ash is keeping it reefed until we're under sail — if he takes it too high and the wind is too strong, the yacht could keel over. The jib goes up next, a bigger sail at the front of the yacht, which unfurls until it slightly overlaps the mainsail. Then, with a spin of the wheel, we lean and come about, turning gradually east until the boom swings out to the left. It clunks into place and the flapping sails begin to fill and billow in the wind.

Suddenly there is a loud slap and the mainsail pulls taut. In response, the *Spirit of Freedom* rises and surges forward like a racehorse. It gives me the shivers, feeling her respond so quickly, and I wish that I was at the wheel. The water at *Spirit*'s prow hisses and foams when we round Green Point, keeping the Atlantic Ocean behind us, and the majestic cliffs of the Cape rise on our left like age-old sentries guarding the passage east. The Indian Ocean lies out there on our horizon, that huge arc of deep, boiling water. We're on our way.

We make pretty good time on our first day, about a hundred and twenty nautical miles, and the wildlife along this coastline is unreal. It is teeming with seabirds, penguins, and fish. A couple of times I even spot the ragged dorsal fin of a great white shark prowling the coves for its lunch.

Nobody can sleep, even though some of us should. In the harsh sunlight, Marcus has to take regular breaks to apply creams to his skin grafts, which is probably why he's mostly going to be on nights. Izzy and Ash take turns to captain the yacht, and Charis spends most of the day either sunbathing or below deck, reading the charts to get ready for her shift. Jen's been talking to the support team back in Cape Town and testing the communication kit, including her funky satellite broadband link. She and I are supposed to feed everyone but we don't even have to bother cooking today, because Marcus jokes that he'd prefer to test the self-heating emergency rations. He's right — they're way better than anything I could have made: chili, pasta, and rice meals that get steaming hot in minutes when you put them in a special pouch and add water. So I allow myself to relax a bit. I'm guessing that the shifts will start working properly as we get farther into the voyage.

Midafternoon, Ash is true to his word. He gives me a few minutes at the helm. When I take the wheel I'm nervous as hell, but all my worries evaporate when I feel how *Spirit* responds to my touch. It gives me the shudders — in a nice way. She has more to give, I can tell, so I trim the boom a little while Ash isn't looking and manage to get an extra three knots out of her. I have this thing with the wind; I can read movement in the air like it's a part of me. I'm not sure, but it might be one thing my crazy hair is good for — apart from slapping me about the face and fascinating small children, that is. It helps me to sense the direction to within an inch.

Ash begins to feel the change. He watches the speed gauge rise while the wind speed stays pretty much static and then looks at me, rubbing his neck. "How the heck . . . ?"

The way he says it makes me laugh. There's a tinge of jealousy that he just can't hide.

"I could tell you" — I shrug, enjoying my moment a little too much — "but I'd have to kill you."

"Izzy, look at this! Rio's a natural." Ash waves her over.

Izzy comes over to look, "Impressive!" she says, tapping the glass of the knotmeter and grinning at me. "Hey, Jen! Why don't you video this for your Internet feed? You can actually see the speed gauge going up."

Jen doesn't even look up from her iPad. Izzy makes a face as if to say, *Don't worry about her.*

I'm so glad Izzy's on board. She's just about to go back to her seat in the cockpit when Charis shouts and points to her left, just off the port bow. She's on her feet now and Jen is making her way forward, too, filming whatever it is on her tablet. Ash leaves us while he checks it out. We're leaning about fifteen degrees to port because of the wind, and the sail is in my way, so it's a few minutes before I can see what all the fuss is about. After a moment or two staring at nothing, I catch a glimpse of a curved gray back arching out of the water up ahead — then another, and another, and another. It's a pod of dolphins playing in our wash! There's got to be at least fifty of them. I've never seen anything so staggering in all my life. They are jumping over the waves, barely making a splash when they arc back into the water.

Izzy screams in my ear. "Dolphins! I love dolphins!"

We watch them play for a while, easily keeping up with us. Several shadows dart under the water next to where we're standing, close enough to touch.

After a while, Izzy asks me, "Rio — what's your star sign?"

"I don't believe in that rubbish."

"Neither do I really. I just find it interesting, especially when I see amazing stuff like this. If Jesus was born under a star, then there's got to be *something* to it, surely? I'm a Leo — open and sincere — trusting, apparently. On my birthday last year, just before my accident, Mum was taking my picture in the garden, and when we looked at it, *Leo* was written in the clouds above my head — in caps. That's when she gave me my St. Christopher."

Iz shows me a beautiful white-gold bracelet. There's a little medallion on it with the picture of this stooped guy carrying a kid on his shoulder. I'm still thinking about the clouds in the photo, though.

"In capitals? How is that even possible? I mean, what about the *E*?"

"Don't ask me *how*. I'm not making it up. Anyway, it made me think, you know — while I was lying in hospital wondering why I survived the helicopter crash — that there could be something else, something bigger than me out there. The accident changed me. I didn't care back then. Now I want my life to mean something. It's when I decided to believe in God; I'd never really thought about it before. I even wondered if my St. Christopher saved me. He is the patron saint of travelers, after all."

I don't know what to say, because no one I know has died and I don't do religion. I mean, I barely scraped by in my Religious Studies class last year. And my existence has been normal, boring, in comparison to Izzy's.

We fall silent for a while, till a dolphin splashes us. It could even have done it on purpose, because it swims sideways for a few seconds with this grin on its face, watching us scream, before flying off at impossible speed.

When we've stopped laughing I tell Izzy, "I believe in something *bigger* — in God, if you want to call it that — I'm just not sure which one. Gran's a Pentecostal Christian and my mum's a Sikh, so I'm just a total mess."

Izzy laughs. "You won't mind me messing your head up some more, then. *Please!* I really want to know. What *is* your sign?"

"Pisces, if you must know. But I really don't want to go there . . ."

She's off on a tangent like she isn't listening. "Uh-huh. Kind, sympathetic. You feel things deeply . . ."

"If you say so." Inside I'm kind of impressed. But you could say stuff like that about anyone and they'd think it was true. I mean, who wouldn't want to hear something like that about themselves?

"Could be something to it, though, don't you think? I just think that we're all born for a reason — to *be* something, to do something incredible before we die."

"But stars don't make us who we are, Iz. They're just *there*."

"I know. But I think something out there *does* make us who we are. Not something, some*one*, and I think he wants us to look for him so he can tell us the reason. God has written himself into the stars and all this *stuff* and he wants us to read it. That's why I want to see a lion before I die — up close. In the wild, as close as we are to these dolphins, I want to look a lion in the eye to see what we have in common. I think I'd feel so alive."

"Not for long . . ."

I'm aware that Ash is back and he's watching us with a big grin. "There's no point arguing with Iz, Rio, especially about religion. When she gets something into her head, she has to see it through. Why do you think we're all on board?"

I turn to Izzy. "You organized all this?"

She flushes. "No. Just had the idea. Mrs. Carter, Ash, and Jen really made it happen."

I watch the rugged black rocks along the coast. "You know that the only lion you're going to see out here is a sea lion?"

"I'm going on safari when we get back to Cape Town."

"Why not just find a zoo?"

"Nope. Not the same. It's got to be the real thing — in the wild."

"Okay, then, Miss Leo." I laugh. "Here's your horoscope. I predict a long and uncomfortable journey ending in an encounter with a wild animal that will almost certainly be the death of you. So, trust me, if you want to see your next birthday, run like the wind."

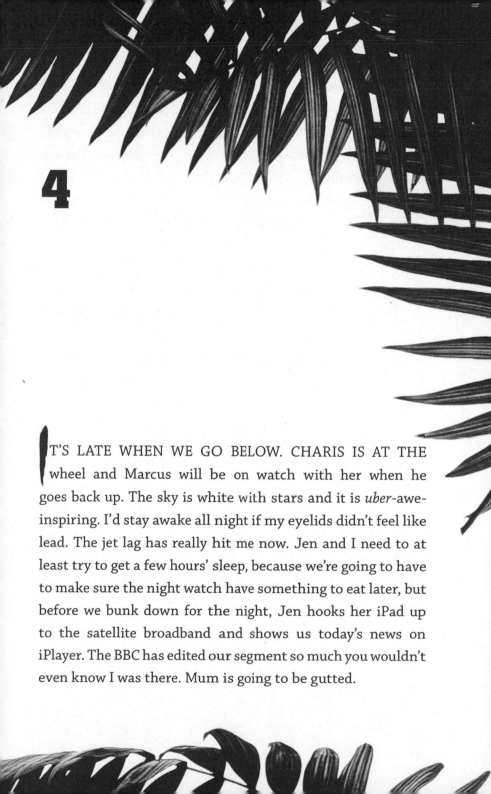

4

IT'S LATE WHEN WE GO BELOW. CHARIS IS AT THE wheel and Marcus will be on watch with her when he goes back up. The sky is white with stars and it is *uber*-awe-inspiring. I'd stay awake all night if my eyelids didn't feel like lead. The jet lag has really hit me now. Jen and I need to at least try to get a few hours' sleep, because we're going to have to make sure the night watch have something to eat later, but before we bunk down for the night, Jen hooks her iPad up to the satellite broadband and shows us today's news on iPlayer. The BBC has edited our segment so much you wouldn't even know I was there. Mum is going to be gutted.

Jen shows us all the *Spirit of Freedom* blog entry next, which also has no reference whatsoever to yours truly. Everyone else is featured, Ash looks especially godlike (I'm surprised she hasn't plastered a soft-focus filter all over him), and there's a link to a YouTube video she's uploaded of our dolphin encounter.

"So . . . what do you think?"

She's asking *me?* I can't believe it. She hasn't spoken to me all day. I'm lost for words.

"It's . . ."

". . . missing something?" Ash finishes for me pointedly.

"Damn right." Marcus. "For one thing, you've only gone and captured my bad side in every shot, like, and for another — where's Rio? She's part of the team, too." He gets his phone out and fiddles with it. "Squeeze in, pet, and I'll get you on here."

Jen elbows him. "I haven't had a chance, okay? None of you have even noticed that I'm hardly on it, either. In case you've forgotten, we're the *support* team. You lot are the main attraction."

"I'll get you next, then. Out here we're a team."

"No, you won't. Get out of the way, Marky. I'll do it."

Ever the joker, Marcus obstructs Jen every time she tries to get around him, so she has to try to take a picture over his shoulder. While he's fighting her off he says, "Put your heads together, man, I can't get you all in."

"Marcus!" Jen is laughing despite her annoyance. "Ash! Tell him!"

I can feel Ash's cheek against mine, rough and hot from a day in the sun. He pulls away slightly and shifts in his seat.

"Look over here, Rio, not at the floor, for God's sake! Work it, baby, work the camera — *rrrrrrr* . . ." Marcus jokes.

I look up and the flash goes off.

Marcus leans back and pinches at his screen, zooming in and out. "Beautiful, like. Very photogenic, Rio. Nice. You want me to send it to your iPad, Jen? You could upload . . ."

She's already on her way to her bunk.

Marcus looks at us. "What's eating her, man? Was it something I said?"

Ash gets up. "Leave it, Marky. Give her some space. Shouldn't you be on deck anyway?"

Marcus raises his hands and shrugs at me. "She needs *space*? On here?" He makes a face at me as he makes his way to the steps. "Welcome on board, Rio. Hope you're thick-skinned as well as beautiful."

My cheeks flush red-hot and I wonder if Marcus needs his eyes tested. Thankfully he doesn't notice. While Ash goes to sit down by the radio I try to work up the courage to face Jen by imagining her lying on her bed in oversized SpongeBob pj's, wearing a green face mask with two thick cucumber slices on her eyes.

Ash checks our position and calls our coordinates in to the Cape Town support team. "Hey, Chris. Yeah." He looks at me briefly. "We've made *really* good time today. Say again? No, just bad static. I'm changing to channel twenty-eight." He twists a knob, looks at his hand strangely, rubbing his fingertips together, before wiping them on the leg of his shorts, leaving an oily smear. "You there? That's a *bit* better." Ash leans forward and whispers to me while Chris is speaking to him, "Rio, can you get me a cloth?"

I find an old rag in the kitchen and leave him rubbing the radio clean. Then I pour a drink and reluctantly make my way forward, only to find that Jen is *still* in the "head." Sheesh! How long does she need? I jump up onto my bunk to wait.

When she finally emerges, the room fills with an overpowering cloud of perfume. I recognize it: JLo Glow. Who wears perfume to bed? She looks softer now that she's peeled away that layer of makeup she hides behind — it seems that getting it off properly is as important to her as putting it on.

"Look, we got off to a bad start . . ." I begin.

"No. *You* got off to a bad start." Jen reaches into a drawer and pulls out a sleep mask. She pulls it onto her forehead and I have to try not to laugh. How is this girl going to cope when things get rough?

"But can't we at least try to get past that?" I continue. "We've got to spend the next seven months cooped up in here."

She sighs. "Maybe. It depends."

"On what? What does it depend on? I'll be your slave . . ." I joke.

Amazingly, my stupid attempt at humor makes her laugh. "You will?"

"Command me."

"Don't be an idiot."

Back to form then, but at least I've confused her by being friendly.

"Rio," she says, "I *really* want this thing to succeed, for Ash. I don't want anything else to go wrong."

"Neither do I!"

Jen snorts. "Okay, then. Prove it to me. Then we'll be best buddies."

"Really?"

"Yes, *really*," she says huffily.

"Thanks."

She exhales slowly before pulling the sleep mask over her eyes and saying, "You're welcome. Now are you going to get into bed, or what? Because I need the light *off*."

Over the next few days we all fall into a routine and I begin doing what I do regularly whenever I go out back home: people-watching. We've been lucky with the weather — mostly sunny — and the seas around South Africa's southernmost tip, Cape Agulhas, are hilly but nothing we can't handle. This is the place where the Atlantic meets the Indian Ocean's strong currents, and it is renowned for its *huge* waves, but it barely troubles *Spirit*.

One thing seriously freaks me out when I first hear it — Marcus sometimes cries out in his sleep during the day watch. I can guess why he does it. A couple of times, when it is really bad, Ash goes below to see how he is. Nobody speaks about Afghanistan in front of me and I don't like to ask, not yet.

Charis and Jen whisper a lot — I'm trying not to be paranoid, but I can't help thinking that a lot of it is about me.

One day, when Jen goes below deck, Charis shows me how her fingers work, how they are triggered by her own arm muscles. In contrast I notice that Ash hardly ever takes his prostheses off, even though they seem to give him grief from time to time.

Izzy is just Izzy. She likes to watch people, too. From time to time even she goes pale and pops painkillers, but her biggest issues are making sure nothing gets snagged in her scaffolding and that she eats at regular times. At first I couldn't work out how she got her shorts on, but then I noticed that they have been custom-made for her. A zipper running from her waist to the hemline has been sewn into them on the side of her injury — very clever.

When I'm serving lunch to the day shift I sit next to her at the cockpit table and ask, "How long do you have to have that frame attached to your leg? Forever?"

"No. About eight weeks. It's pinned to the bones to help them heal straight."

"But I thought your helicopter crash was months ago. How come you need this now?"

"My leg healed with a twist in it and they decided to rebreak it in multiple places two weeks ago. So you can thank *me* for all this . . ." With a sweep of her arm Izzy encompasses all we can see — basically, ocean and boat.

I can't help but laugh at the comical expression on her face. "And how do you figure that?"

"Easy. I'm the reason you're here, baby. Until they decided to rearrange my tibia I was going to be the other able body."

"Hang on — doesn't that mean you're going to have to have that thing removed in six weeks or so?"

Iz grins. "Nothing, and I mean *nothing*, was going to stop me from coming on this trip. We're going to have a brief stopover in Jakarta, where this baby is coming off."

We're quiet for a minute or two and then I decide to share one of my observations. "Ash looks like he's in pain sometimes with his prostheses. Is that normal?"

"Probably. He's just being macho." Iz laughs. "Marcus won't let anyone know what he's going through, either. That's what soldiers do — they just get on with it. With or without limbs . . ."

While I'm people-watching I also start to notice the way Ash is only fine with me if Jen isn't around. I don't get it. The thing is, they look like they are an item but they don't ever seem to do the things couples should do. I mean, they touch — she'll even sit with her arm around his shoulder sometimes, but it's all lacking . . . *something*. But hey, who am I to judge? Both my ex-boyfriends have been pretty pointless. They went right off me the minute they met Gran or Mum and had to decide between joining the church choir or a barrage of questions and the prospect of an arranged marriage. I'm way too complicated for love. I suppose I could ask Izzy or Marcus to dish the goss, but I know they'll wonder why I'm asking. Or worse, they'll assume they *know* why I'm asking. So I don't. I'm not interested in him in *that* way, I just want to know the score.

A couple of times I find Ash sitting in the comms chair with his legs off, recharging them. He's so at ease with me seeing his disability — or at least he seems to be. Sometimes when he sits there rubbing his stumps I wonder if he's trying to freak me out. If so, it's not working. There's just something about the way he is that I can't shake out of my head. It makes me want to spend time with him. The only trouble is, anytime I'm around him I turn into a brain-dead idiot and, when I speak, my words just seem to drop from my mouth and flap around my feet like dying fish.

On day five I'm up at dawn to get breakfast sorted for the day watch, but I decide to head up on deck first because I can hear music. It's quiet, mostly drowned out by the rush of the sea and the wind that has kept us almost constantly under sail since we left Cape Town. But what I *can* catch sounds amazing. Like Ed Sheeran has dropped in to give us a free "unplugged" session, except it keeps stopping and starting. In fact, I'm pretty sure the song is "Lego House."

Charis has gone to get her head down — I can hear her arm humming in her cabin and then falling silent. Marcus is making a couple of drinks in the galley before he does the same. He's wearing a black T-shirt that says *Only trust people who like big butts — they cannot lie*. I try not to encourage him by snickering.

"Where's the music coming from?"

He tickles me in the ribs when I try to squeeze past him. "Someone strangling a freaking cat? It's either that or this thing is haunted. Want a soda?"

"No, thanks."

I go up to the cockpit. Izzy is at the wheel. She nods her head in the direction of the mast and puts a finger to her lips, so I creep around to have a look. Ash is there, Jen's iPad on his lap, and he's leaning against the mast, strumming on the thinnest guitar I have ever seen. It is little more than a neck. Ahead of us is a *staggering* violet-and-orange sunrise. The ocean is on fire. I'm not kidding, you can't tell where it ends and the sky begins.

Ash stops playing when he realizes I'm watching.

"Don't stop."

"I'm just learning the lyrics." Embarrassed, he shows me the iPad screen. There's a video of Ed Sheeran on it, paused. Ash looks like he's about to put it away.

"So — keep learning."

With a shrug he starts playing the guitar again, a throbbing, pulsing rhythm interspersed with this incredible bass line. When he starts singing, his voice is breathy and quiet, but somehow it slices through the background noise. He stops suddenly when he gets to the line about surrendering up his heart, as if it troubles him.

"That's as far as I've got," he tells me, but I know he's just being modest.

"It's beautiful."

"The sunrise?"

"No." I laugh, tucking some strands of flyaway hair back and sitting next to him. "Your voice. Seriously, you should record that."

"Not likely. Do you play?"

My hair falls forward again. "Are you kidding? No. I mangled the recorder when I was younger — until Mum hid it. Borrowed a school violin for a while, but we couldn't afford lessons."

Even his laugh is musical. I'd never noticed. Come to think of it, I'm pretty sure this is the first time I've heard it. He holds out the guitar. "Here, I'll show you how."

The word *no* is on my lips, it really is. But I can't say it, because this is the most he's said to me in five days. Ash puts the instrument onto my lap while I'm wedging my crazy hair back behind my ear again, takes my left hand in his, and positions it, moving my fingers onto the strings one by one.

"What do I do with this one?" I ask, holding up my right hand.

He laughs. "Impatient, aren't we?"

My fingers shake a little when he finally releases them. *Don't think about it. If I think, I blush.*

"That's a chord," he tells me. "C, with an added second." When I do nothing with it he reaches over and strums the strings for me. It sounds *amazing*. It sparkles. I can feel the vibration of the guitar against my chest.

"It doesn't play itself," he says, grinning. "Use your thumb or something." Then he's moving the fingers of my left hand again. "And this is G."

I strum this one myself. The vibration is deeper this time. "You see?"

My mouth is dry. "Easy. Yes. Until I have to move them on my own . . ." I hand the guitar back and he looks crestfallen. "You going to sing 'Lego House' to Jen?"

Suddenly he's serious again and I wonder why my mouth keeps losing any connection with my brain. "What? Why would I sing it to Jen?"

"I just thought . . . Never mind."

He's squinting at me like the sun is in his eyes, he raises a hand to rub them while I'm wondering, *Why do guys always have such insane eyelashes?* "Oh, I get it . . ." He breathes out, long and slow. "Jen and me. It's complicated. Something I need to deal with and I'm not doing it too well, okay? *This* happened." His fingernail clinks against his metal shin as he taps it angrily.

"You don't need to explain, Ash — really." Why can't I keep my big mouth shut? I'm on overload, so I stand up. Don't know where to put myself. "It's none of my business," I say. "Keep playing — please. Nice music, Ash, really. Must go anyway. I've forgotten my sunglasses."

"If you have to . . . You haven't upset me, I'm just mad at myself, at the situation."

I think he's finding my awkwardness funny and I wish he wouldn't. But at least it pops the tension balloon. To make matters worse, I haven't worn my sodding sunglasses since I came on board. Now I'm going to have to try and find the things and wear them for a while — fake Ray-Bans Mum got on the cheap from Poundland. *Just perfect.*

I virtually run below deck and throw open the door to my room. Jen is sitting on the side of the bed, looking startled by my sudden return. On her lap is a folded sheath of lined blue paper covered with handwriting. The envelope by her hand is labeled *To Mum and Dad*. Before Jen can react, the top sheet blows toward me in the draft from the door and I pick it up for her. She snatches it back and flips it over but not before I can make out the words *love you forever, Ash*.

Jen mumbles something I don't quite catch and stuffs the letter under her thigh. When she turns to face me, all the blood has drained from her face. She knows I've worked out whose parents it was addressed to. She's reading Ash's mail? Why?

"Don't tell Ash."

I'm disgusted. The envelope is still on the bed near me. I pick it up and wave it at her. "Seriously? Why shouldn't I? What are you doing with this?"

"He'd never forgive me . . ."

I start rummaging in my bag for my sunglasses. "Could you blame him? It's probably something personal. I can't believe you're even looking through his —"

"You don't understand! I don't do this kind of thing . . . ever . . ."

To my shock, tears well up in Jen's eyes. I sit down next to her, watching her twist the front of her blouse into a knot, undo it, and twist it again, over and over.

"Stop." I pull her hand away gently. "Why don't you tell me what's going on?"

Jen retrieves the letter and places it on her lap again. "I've had it for a few days. It's taken me this long to get the nerve to look, and you came in before I had a chance to read anything."

"Good. But you're not making any sense. Why are you trying to read Ash's mail in the first place?"

"It's not his mail. It's the letter every soldier writes before they go to Afghanistan. You know . . . *In case I die* . . ."

No wonder she's worried that Ash will go ballistic. Who wouldn't? I can't help a touch of sarcasm. "Great. I was worried it was something important."

Jen just looks at me.

"What's it doing on board?" I ask. "He's not in combat; surely he doesn't need to keep it anymore."

Heavy tears drop onto the sleeping bag. "Since he lost his legs, Ash takes this letter everywhere. There's something in it. Something he doesn't want me to see. Recently he's been talking about ripping it up, and if he does, I'll never know!"

"So you went into his cabin and ransacked his things. Nice. That's really going to help things." I give her a dubious look.

"I know it's wrong, but you need to understand — I'm desperate. Before Ash was blown up — while he was still in training — we were talking about getting engaged, but when he came back from Afghanistan he just closed down. I need to understand why, and I know there will be some clue in the letter. I just *know* — he wrote it the day before he went. You think about things differently when you know you could die. You say things . . ."

"Why don't you just ask him?"

"He won't talk about it."

"So you shouldn't look — give me the letter."

Jen's shoulders sag. She knows I'm right, so she pulls it out but she freezes halfway to handing it over. Her eyes are fixed on the top page, which is covered in Ash's loose freehand. We both see what the middle paragraph says before I snatch it away: *Mum, you'll see Jen, and I won't have been able to tell her yet, so don't repeat any of those things I said. It doesn't matter now anyway. Just tell her I love her . . .*

I stuff the sheets back in the envelope before either of us can read more.

All the life has gone from Jen's eyes. She looks at me bleakly and then curls into a ball on her bunk, burying her face in the crook of her arm. Her muffled voice cracks when she says, "Promise me you won't tell anyone."

"You need to make him talk about this. He's going to find out that the letter's missing sooner or later, and this could be the perfect opportunity to get him to open up. Hey, if you promise to try, I promise I won't say anything — how's that?" She doesn't answer me, so I stuff the letter into the end of my rucksack, the compartment that still has a lock on the zipper. Jen lifts her arm off her face and follows my every move. "In the meantime I'm going to lock this away. Don't look at me like that, it's for your own good!"

Jen rolls onto her back and wipes tears off her glistening cheeks. "You're right. I'm being stupid. He was probably stressed when he wrote that. I should talk to him — if we can ever get any privacy on this thing."

I've actually found my crappy glasses in the same compartment. I try them on. For the first time since I've known the girl, Jen actually offers me a genuine, friendly smile — like she's grateful to me. I really feel for her.

I sit on the bed and give her a hug. When we pull away, I pose and look at her from behind my sunglasses. "Well? What do you think — tacky or what?"

"Well . . . they are *way* more shabby than chic. Where do you shop, Poundland?"

Cheeky cow. I laugh with her, but inside I'm all messed up. I'm wondering what I've got myself into. All my life I've been a loner, and now I'm trapped in a confined space, at sea with five other people, getting drawn into emotional stuff I don't even want to think about.

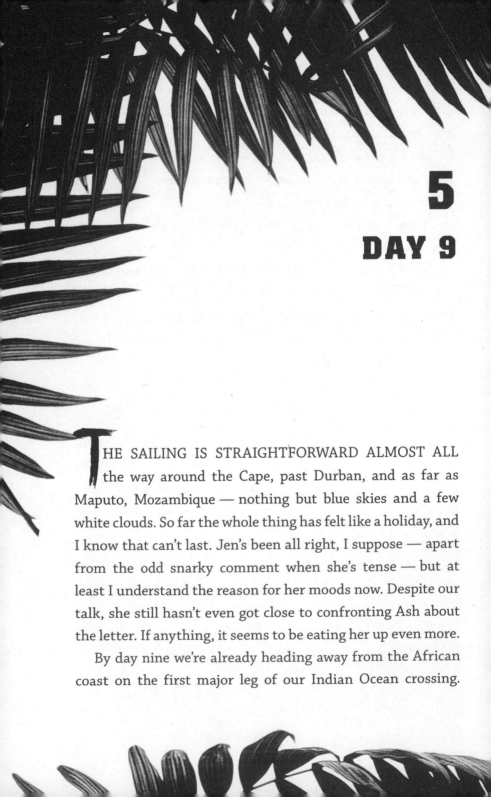

5
DAY 9

THE SAILING IS STRAIGHTFORWARD ALMOST ALL the way around the Cape, past Durban, and as far as Maputo, Mozambique — nothing but blue skies and a few white clouds. So far the whole thing has felt like a holiday, and I know that can't last. Jen's been all right, I suppose — apart from the odd snarky comment when she's tense — but at least I understand the reason for her moods now. Despite our talk, she still hasn't even got close to confronting Ash about the letter. If anything, it seems to be eating her up even more.

By day nine we're already heading away from the African coast on the first major leg of our Indian Ocean crossing.

The wind has been behind us, but the forecast shows an unseasonal low heading from the south toward Madagascar. Ash has been speaking with the support team back in Cape Town, and they estimate that with our current progress we'll be able to make the crossing before the storm hits land, and ride over the top of it past Madagascar and out into the Indian Ocean. I almost choke when Ash mentions pirates, but it's only to confirm that our course keeps us well out of their range.

The radio is still acting up, though. We have to alternate channels constantly, and Ash is reluctant to use the spare this early into the voyage. Mrs. Carter is arranging to send another one to Taolanaro on Madagascar's southeast coast. We'll make land and pick it up in a few days. The favorable wind that has brought us this far has even gusted up to eighteen knots, as if to send us on our way.

Now I'm spending another fitful night sweating buckets and feeling unable to move because it's so hot, and the swell has been getting bigger by the day. If Jen slept any lighter, she'd float up here beside me. I've been trying not to disturb her, but my head is spinning with all the things I know I could be doing if I was on deck. Frustration is eating me alive. I'm virtually an Olympic-standard sailor. When Mrs. Carter met me I'd just won the under-17 Laser Radial championships, and now I'm on the freaking mother shift. You could fit what I know about a healthy diet onto a pinhead, and they're all moaning about my coffee like they think I should be a one-girl sodding Starbucks.

When I sense daylight, I finally get up the nerve to swing my legs off my bunk. We've been sailing with the wind behind us since we rounded the Cape. Enough is enough. I'm going to suggest that we furl the jib and put a spinnaker up. It will mean a bit of hard work, but a huge, billowing sail like that will give us even more speed.

Every morning I've been woken by Ash singing overhead, and I can hear him now. He does it softly so as not to disturb the other watches, but his plaintive tone has found a way to burrow right inside my head. When he's not singing Ed Sheeran, or being convinced by Izzy to play "If Everyone Cared" by Nickelback, he's tackling The Script or Mumford & Sons. Every now and again he plays melodies I recognize from old anime movies like *Spirited Away*. This morning he's given up on all that stuff for some reason and started strumming George Michael's "Faith," just to tease Izzy.

I've been watching him sail, too — and he's so at ease with it. A natural. Sometimes I even wonder what we'd be like sailing together. Gold medal at the next Paralympics in the SKUD 18 class would be just perfect, but I guess his partner would need to be disabled. Oh well. The thought does make me feel kind of warm inside, though.

I drop to the floor and get dressed without breathing. Jen's been finding it hard to sleep, too, since I confiscated the letter and locked it away in my bag. She's taken to wearing earplugs in bed now, in addition to her eye mask, and I just know it's partly so she won't have to tell me why she hasn't found the courage to face Ash about his letter yet. Today I put my bikini on beneath a T-shirt and micro shorts; if I get my way it's going to be hot work. The door creaks when I open it, but I manage to squeeze through and shut it without waking Jen.

Izzy is at the wheel again and looking bored when I get on deck. She loves my idea. "It'll be fun! A bit of real sailing at last. We only used the spinnaker once in training, didn't we, Ash? I'd forgotten the thing."

Ash has already got his shirt off and he's trimming the mainsail manually, rotating the winch by its removable coffee-grinder handle, spinning it first one way and then the other when the gear changes. I try not to notice the shoulder muscles rippling beneath his bronzed skin, but Izzy's constant elbow-jabbing in my ribs doesn't make it easy. I jab her back and we giggle, trying desperately to keep our faces straight when he looks up. He doesn't get what we're giggling about, thank God. When he's finished he comes over and leans against the cockpit wall.

"There wasn't enough wind to do much more than look at the spinnaker when we trained, but I think you're spot-on, Rio. We should try it at least — only we'll need another able-bodied to carry it up. I'll wake Jen and meet you in the stowage area."

All the spare sails are stowed on the right-hand side of our storeroom and it's easy to spot the spinnaker. It's blue, red, and white and is much bigger than the others. I give it a tug but, like Ash said, it's much too heavy for one person to shift.

While I'm waiting for the others I nose around, and that's when I notice that the door to one of the wardrobes isn't fully shut. Not good on a yacht, where everything needs to be secured. When I get close to it I see another oily mark like the one I found when Izzy was giving me the tour, only this one has dried into a crust that flakes off when I scratch at it with my thumbnail. Intrigued, I pull open the door and look inside. This is where our spare radio is kept in its box. I'm just about to secure the door when I notice what was stopping it from closing properly: something small and brown on the floor near the catch. As I pick it up, a shiver of recognition runs through me.

"And I suppose if she asked you to hurl yourself overboard you'd be up for that, too." Jen's best put-down voice outside. "All right, Ash. Stop hurrying me. You can't just wake me up because Rio wants to change a sail and expect me to jump for joy. I'm coming, aren't I?"

I close the cupboard door and turn around just as they enter. For some reason my face flushes like I've been caught stealing. Jen looks at me strangely. "Everything okay?"

"I don't know." I show them my find. "It's another one of these."

Ash frowns. "Strange . . ."

Jen takes it off him. "Let me look at that." She turns it over and over, and then suddenly the color drains from her face and she throws it across the room. "Ugh!"

"What's wrong?" I look at Ash.

He shrugs. "I don't know."

"It's human," Jen says, wiping her hand on her side. "Where did you find it?"

"In here. How do you know it's —"

"Human? I studied enough skeletons and wall charts while Ash was in rehab, believe me. That thing is a finger bone."

"There was another on the jetty in Cape Town," Ash tells her, crossing the cramped space to retrieve it.

Jen looks really worried. "I need to call this in."

"You're right," Ash says. "Though it's probably nothing — one of the engineers might be a part-time sangoma."

"Sangoma?" I ask.

"Some people call them witch doctors."

"That makes us feel *so* much better," Jen says.

My mind goes back to the grizzled old guy I saw on the pontoon in Cape Town. I wonder if that's what he was.

"They use old bones to give a blessing," Ash tells me as he starts hauling out the sail. "It may be nothing. Anyway, let's get this out first and then you can get on the radio while we rig it, Jen."

"Fine," Jen says, but she doesn't look happy.

We manage to get the sail up to the cockpit and onto the forward deck. There is a spinnaker pole built onto the mast, so while Ash and Jen unfold the sail, I attach it to the pole and spare halyard — ". . . it's a *rope*" I have to explain to Jen as I'm clipping it in place. When we've got the sheet attached, Ash winches it up at the same time as he furls the jib. The spinnaker billows out like a hot air balloon and we all feel the surge in power shudder through the yacht. They leave the trimming to me. It is hard work, constantly adjusting the pole, retrimming the sail, and making sure it's catching the wind at the right angle. But it's such a buzz, seeing the foam fizz at *Spirit*'s prow and watching Ash smile at the way we dance over the swell.

By the end of the day we're all exhausted and I haven't even thought about getting any shut-eye before mothering the night watch. I don't care, though. Today has been fantastic. I actually feel like I'm contributing something, and it's been worth it if only so that Ash can see I'm not a complete waste of space.

Jen told us around midday that the support team is investigating our find. When she finished her blog entry she disappeared and she hasn't been back up since. I'm guessing she's finally managed to get some sleep. Around five o'clock Charis surfaces. We've been losing wind, so Ash asks her to help us get the spinnaker folded and stowed while Izzy takes the wheel. It's a lot of hard work, but we decide we'll definitely use it again next time we get a decent breeze. When we're done, Charis busies herself below, plotting the route for the night shift. The wind has become gusty and we're way out to sea between Africa and Madagascar, only making about four knots now. Our southern horizon is littered with tufts of broken cloud.

Ash takes his legs off and sits low down on the transom platform, dangling his stumps in the deep sky-blue water. You could almost imagine that they end in beautiful bronzed feet and he's wriggling his toes. He points at the distant clouds. "See those?"

I kick off my flip-flops and drop down beside him. We're really close, almost close enough to touch, and the water is cool and gentle, tickling the tops of my feet. The sea looks so deep, it makes me feel uneasy. I wonder if it is talking to me. I love the sea, but I'm good at reading it, too. This sea says, *Don't get complacent.*

My eyes are drawn along Ash's sculpted brown arm to the clouds. "That's the leading edge of a weather system," he says.

"Yeah, I know — and this is the calm before the storm," I joke dreamily. "It's still a long way off, though. I figure the wind will pick up again in three or four hours."

While I'm talking I see something amazing, an enormous shadow just below the surface of the water, not ten feet away and about the length of a London bus. A rubbery black dorsal fin clears the swell briefly, and we can see that the creature's back is gray green and mottled with white spots. Ripples of light play over it and we hear a slosh of water where its side breaks the surface.

Ash shields his eyes. "A whale shark! Izzy, stop the boat!" He turns to me, grinning. "Fancy a swim?"

"Out here? I don't know . . ." I'm thinking, *No wonder these guys have bits missing.* They're reckless.

"Come on, Rio. He's just a gentle giant — a plankton feeder. I'll stay nearby, promise."

Izzy is already turning, winching in the boom and spinning the wheel, bringing the *Spirit of Freedom* into the wind.

Ash drops into the water before I can say anything else. He whoops at the cold and waves at me. "Take a chance, Rio! You may never see one of these babies again!"

He's off before I can object, swimming freestyle, and he's next to it in no time, his hand sliding along its flank as it swims past him. A car-sized mouth breaks the surface near me, sucking in gallons of churning water that swirl back out through huge, baggy gill slits. Then I find myself looking into a filmy silver eye. The jet-black pupil flicks in my direction, as if the shark is actually watching me, before sliding back under the water. Without waiting for my reply, Ash dives to take a closer look.

In the end I can't resist the opportunity to see it up close, so I yank off my T-shirt and shorts, tossing them on top of Ash's legs, and jump in. The freezing water sucks all the breath from my body as I sink below the surface. I can see the impossibly long gray shadow of the whale shark arcing around, Ash swimming on his side watching it. The rush of water and bubbles fills my ears. Shafts of sunlight wrap themselves around my arms like some magical curtain that I have to part in order to get anywhere. They break apart between my fingers and turn from turquoise to dark blue beneath my feet until they are swallowed up by the deep. I pull myself upward with my arms and break the surface, gasping. It's *so* exhilarating! My lips are salty, and tingle when the sun warms them. Next thing I know, Ash is grinning at me just a couple of strokes away, crystal strings of water cascading over his face.

"Isn't this the *best*? C'mon!"

I kick out in the cold, clear water and I'm next to him in seconds.

Fortunately for us the shark is feeling lazy and inquisitive. It comes close to the *Spirit of Freedom* again, and I rise on the powerful surge it displaces when its enormous body weaves through the water. Ash grabs my hand and together we dive alongside its ribbed flank, stroking the smooth, cold skin and holding on to one of its fins for a while, letting it pull us along in a sparkling trail of bubbles. For a moment it seems to feel our touch, pausing to hang in the water as if it wants to check us out, and then it is moving again, surrounded by flashing silver-and-gray pilot fish. With one graceful sweep of its tail the whale shark slides forward and my body tingles all over. I can feel its immense power as a wall of water compresses my chest. There is no way we can swim fast enough to keep up with it, so we surface together and watch the tip of its tail slowly slide by. Strands of hair stick to Ash's face and his eyes are full of life. We're both laughing.

He shakes the water off his face and moves closer, framed by the afternoon sun and by the endless blue ocean. There's an intensity in his gaze that I don't remember seeing before. It's like something from the deep has suddenly risen to surface in his eyes, something dark and mysterious.

I just can't move. My heart thuds in my ears. I can't breathe. I'm not even sure I want to, if it means that this moment will end. For a second I think time may actually have stopped. It's like I've been in a sort of prison, this past week on the ship, and suddenly my shackles have fallen off and they're plummeting to the ocean bed. I feel so free, so alive, so drunk with life. Ash is close now. Close enough for his breath to tickle my face. We just float there looking at one another. Nothing else matters. It all just fades away. I know Izzy is watching from the yacht, but she's too far away to be a part of this. It's as if we were out here alone.

Ash pushes back his damp, sun-bleached hair and says, "I've been wanting to ask you something, Rio . . ."

Suddenly I'm nervous, not sure I want to hear him speak his mind but aching for it all at the same time. Even the sea seems to push us apart. I think that's what tips the balance in the end. It's the reason I say, "We should get back," as I watch the whale shark's shadow diminish beneath us.

When I look up, Ash is still watching me, his mouth half open. I think he's going to ask his question anyway but, before he can, I sense something that's *definitely* out of place out here. I turn my head. Above the rush of blood in my ears, the slapping of water on *Spirit*'s hull, the quiet surge of the waves, I can hear something — something rhythmic and mechanical.

Ash floats backward, looking confused. "Rio, what is it?"

"Can you hear that?"

"What? My ears are full of water."

I'm circling now, desperately trying to find the source of the noise, and he's just watching me, his unspoken question lying heavily in the water between us. We rise on the swell, and as the wave crests beneath me I get the briefest glimpse beyond *Spirit*'s stern. What I see makes my limbs freeze in fear, and I can hardly stay afloat.

On the horizon are four black pinpricks, throwing up a foamy white wash. They are racing toward us, and every now and then the breeze wafts the sound of powerful throbbing engines this way.

Ash's face turns pale. He yells, "Iz, bring her about!" Then he grabs my arm, hard. "Back on the yacht, Rio, *now*."

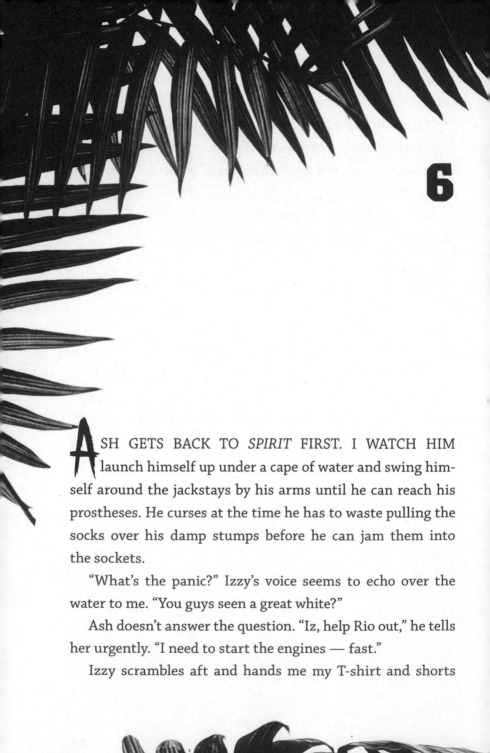

6

ASH GETS BACK TO *SPIRIT* FIRST. I WATCH HIM launch himself up under a cape of water and swing himself around the jackstays by his arms until he can reach his prostheses. He curses at the time he has to waste pulling the socks over his damp stumps before he can jam them into the sockets.

"What's the panic?" Izzy's voice seems to echo over the water to me. "You guys seen a great white?"

Ash doesn't answer the question. "Iz, help Rio out," he tells her urgently. "I need to start the engines — fast."

Izzy scrambles aft and hands me my T-shirt and shorts

while I haul myself onto the transom. I'm breathless after my swim.

As soon as I'm out of the water Ash takes the nearest wheel, presses the starter button next to it, and waits while the engine strains over and over. In the silence it sounds harsh and out of place. For some reason the engine won't catch.

"Ash, what's going on?" Iz asks in the echoing silence between tries. "*Someone* speak to me!"

"There are at least four fast boats coming this way," I tell her, pointing in the direction we saw the launches coming from. She can't see them because the yacht is in a trough and we're behind the sail.

Ash is biting his bottom lip and swearing at the starter button under his breath. "Come *on* . . ." he mutters, banging it again. "Rio, get Jen to raise the alarm."

"I'm on it." I scramble between the wheels, and that's when I notice Jen's face in the cockpit doorway, staring at me and Ash. She has no idea what's been happening, all she can see is that Ash and I are both dripping wet and I'm standing next to him in my bikini. I think, *Crap, what if she saw us through the window, too?* The minute her eyes meet mine, she turns away, elbowing her way past Marcus and Charis, who are climbing up the ladder to start their shift. I race over. Charis looks at me strangely.

"Don't feel you have to do that on my account," Marcus jokes, watching me throw my top and shorts back on. His T-shirt has bloody bullet holes printed all down one side and the slogan *I'm Fine*.

I push him to one side. "Give me a break, Marky. Does everything have to be a joke to you?"

Marcus looks at Charis and makes a face. "Why's Ash trying to start the engine?"

"Ask Iz." I slide down the ladder and run through the galley to find Jen, but when I get there the door to our room is firmly shut. She must have her foot against it or something, because I can't get it open and I know there's no lock. "Jen!" I shout. "Open up!"

Nothing.

"We need you out here."

Izzy clatters through the galley after me and bangs on the door. "Jen, it's an emergency. Ash wants you on the radio *now*." But there's still no response. "Let's go," Izzy tells me, tugging at my arm. "She'll come out now."

Suddenly the door bangs open and Jen emerges all puffy-eyed.

I'm so relieved. "Thank God. Jen, we need you out here. Look, we just went for a swim, okay?"

Jen rolls her eyes at me. "Oh, *please*! Don't give me that BS. You've been flirting with him ever since you came on board. Now get out of my way." She squeezes past me like I'm toxic. "What's the panic, Iz?"

Before either of us can answer, the engine coughs and splutters urgently. It sounds like it might catch, but after a few revs it splutters to a halt again. It strains sluggishly a couple of more times as the battery gives out.

Ash comes skittering back down the stairs with Marcus,

and they both disappear into the engine room. Jen shouts after them, "Ash, are we sinking?" but neither of them answers her. She drops into the comms chair and picks up the handset. A few seconds later, Ash's muffled voice shouts through the engine room door.

"Get on the radio, Jen. Put out a Mayday."

"A Mayday? Why? Why won't you tell me what's happening?" Her hands shaking, Jen lifts the cover off the radio emergency button. "ASH! WHAT SHOULD I TELL THEM?" She rummages in one of the drawers for a laminated sheet and drops it. "I NEED A REASON!"

I pick the sheet up for her and she snatches it out of my hands. "Give me that!"

Seconds later there is a metallic clatter and a thud. It sounds like Marcus must have banged his head because he swears badly, over and over. Then his muffled voice tells Ash, "It's been cut — with this." The guys emerge. Marcus is holding his head with one hand and an oily paring knife with the other. "Someone's punctured the freaking fuel line," he gasps angrily, throwing the knife onto the cabin table. "It's all leaked out."

"When we left Cape Town," I remember, "I noticed that the water behind *Spirit* was oily!"

"And you didn't think to tell anyone? Oh, for —" Jen looks daggers at me but then bites her bottom lip, pulling herself back from whatever she was going to say next. She rubs her face and asks Ash, "I don't understand. Why would anyone . . . ?"

"Pirates," Ash growls, "probably Somalis, but how the hell they've got this far south . . ."

"You're sure?" I ask him.

"We're miles from anywhere. Those four launches you saw, Rio, they aren't on a pleasure cruise — they're heading this way at full speed. There's no way they'd have enough fuel to get this far from land, so my guess is that there's a mother ship just over the horizon."

Izzy looks like she does when she's going hypo. She's fiddling with her bracelet and her voice is barely a whisper. "Without the engine we're dead in the water."

I'm cold as ice — scared — and suddenly we're all thinking the same thing: *The radio has been acting up.*

Jen presses a button and the radio automatically flicks on to the distress channel — CH16. She clicks the handset and starts to speak into it, reading from the laminated sheet. "Mayday, Mayday, Mayday. This is the yacht *Spirit of Freedom*. Our MMSI number is —"

I touch her arm and point at the LED display. She pulls it away like she's been burned. The channel number keeps flickering and changing from CH16 to other numbers. Jen scowls at me as if it's my fault, and hammers at the distress button until CH16 shows again. "Repeat, our MMSI number is two, three, five, five — what the . . . ?"

The channel number has just changed itself to CH27. Jen swears, presses the button one more time, and starts the call from the beginning. "Mayday! Mayday! MAYD — Aaaargh!" When the display flickers to yet another random channel she bangs it over and over with the handset. She's breathless when she hangs her head and tells Ash, "We need the spare."

Ash goes to get it, but when he returns with it I tell him quietly, "There's no point. It's not going to work." Now they are all looking at me, wondering.

"Why not?" Jen is suspicious.

I'm shivering so badly that it feels like my knees will give way. "That bone I found — the one in the storeroom . . ."

They stare at me.

Ash says, "We're wasting time, Rio," and starts to rip the dead radio out of the rack.

He stops when I yell, "Listen to me!" and looks at me tight-lipped, frowning. I can barely get my words out. "I didn't think anything of it at the time — none of us did — but it can only mean one thing."

"And that is?"

I'm fighting back the tears. I *am* a screw-up. Why didn't I think of this earlier? I should have figured it out.

"You'll just be wasting your time. The spare radio isn't going to work, either. Whoever is coming for us — they've been in the cupboard and messed with it."

7

A GUTTERING BREEZE STINGS MY EYES BADLY WHEN I get back outside. It flicks my hair against my face. All I want to do right now is curl up in a ball somewhere and cry like a baby, but I blink away my tears to focus on the situation. My legs are like jelly, and the pitch and roll of *Spirit* amplifies the feeling. I've never felt so utterly lost and scared on the water. The breeze has picked up a couple of knots already and we're beginning to make some headway, but there is no way we're going to outrun the motor launches that are scudding over the swell toward us. The wind is gusting all over the place.

"How long do you think we've got?" Ash to Marcus.

"Five minutes?" Marcus is looking at them through his binoculars. "Does this look right to you?"

Ash takes the glasses and looks. "What do you mean?"

"I mean, are we sure they're pirates? They're wearing military gear — and they've got some serious hardware."

"They're definitely not friendly," Ash mutters, handing the binoculars back, "and they've obviously researched the expedition, knocked out our communications, tracked our position. The only thing of value on here is us, so I'm guessing they'll think long and hard before shooting. We may be able to buy enough time to get an SOS out somehow, to put them off."

Charis is still at the wheel but Ash tells me grimly, "Rio, take over. You're the best — we need all the speed you can get out of her."

I nod and get to it. It's a relief to have something to do.

"Charis, you and Marky come with me. JEN! Forget the radio! Can you use the broadband to get a message out?"

She runs up the steps to the cockpit, waving the iPad. "I already tried. I think maybe half the message went through before I lost Internet access. Stupid thing has been temperamental for days. I wonder if that storm front is interfering with it?"

Ash swears and disappears below deck. "Keep trying. Cell phone, anything. Mayday and position, nothing else, there isn't time. Iz? Gather up all the remaining cell phones we have, see if any of them have got any signal, you never know . . ."

The pirates are gaining on us fast, their powerful launches leaving a foaming triangular wash astern. Amazingly, I find myself worrying about the whale shark not being able to get out of their way. The heaving throb of the motors comes to us on the breeze, their hulls pounding the waves like beating war drums. At a quick glance I'd say there's about five guys on each launch and two of the launches have a huge gun fixed on a stand in the middle. I'm willing the wind to pick up, but it mocks me, gusting all over the place. By constantly trimming the boom and the jib I manage to get the yacht up to eight knots, but we're like an old lady with a walker being run down by guys on motorbikes.

Ash, Charis, and Marcus resurface with armfuls of distress flares, which they scatter onto the cockpit table and benches. Charis's prosthetic fingers hum and buzz frantically, opening boxes of them. Marcus clambers over toward me, squeezes past the wheels, and starts pulling the pins on the can-sized ones that float, throwing them into the sea behind us. They fizz and bob on the water, coughing out plumes of hissing red smoke that begins to rise and form a dense fog. *A smoke screen.*

The smoke swirls around me. While Marcus works, Ash and Charis are opening a dozen rocket flare tubes. When they're done, Ash passes some to Marcus and then comes over to give me a couple. "That's the business end," he says, his face drawn with worry. "You just pull —"

I take them. "I know how to use a flare." My tone is edgy, and I instantly regret it. All I want is for him not to worry about me. He needs to focus.

Ash blinks. "Good. We're going to use these offensively. They'll be more accurate when the pirates get close. Aim at the head — try to blind them. We may be able to scare them off."

I barely hear his words over the thudding in my ears. My mouth is so dry I can hardly speak. "Ash, what if they shoot at us?"

His face softens. "Get as low as you can. If they board us, don't argue, just do whatever they say." Then he turns away, wreathed in red smoke, to take up a position by the port jack-stay with Marcus and Charis.

I reach out to make him stay, but stop myself. As if he's sensed it, Ash says without looking around, "I won't let them hurt you, Rio. We're all in this together, right?"

His words should help but they don't. I feel totally alone.

The smoke screen was a good idea, but it's pretty useless because it hangs too low over the water, sloping away under the breeze. For a few tense minutes all we can do is wait and watch while the pirates get closer and closer. When they are just a few hundred yards away a couple of their guns rattle and spit fire.

I jump a mile at the sound. I want to get off, to throw myself in the water and swim away, but there's no escape. Standing behind the wheel, I'm more exposed than anyone else. I'm almost blinded by my own tears.

"Ash!" I scream. "What should I do?!"

He runs over to stand by me, putting his hand over mine on the wheel. "They want us alive, Rio." His breath is warm in my ear. Then he raises the flare in his other hand and yells at us, "Make it count, guys! Wait for my mark!"

Our attackers howl and scream, trying to intimidate us. They spin their launches, sending waves that hit *Spirit*'s hull side-on, making us roll alarmingly. Most of them look like boys. When I look again, I can see a thin guy with a pock-marked face grinning on the prow of the nearest launch. His leopard claw has been blown back onto his shoulder by the slipstream. The sight makes me want to throw up.

He's the guy I saw in Cape Town.

I flinch when he aims his gun high. It spits fire and rakes our mast with zinging shots, lining the sail with holes. My knuckles are white on the rim of the wheel. The *Spirit of Freedom* begins to roll on the wash when the launches swing alongside.

Ash yells, *"NOW!"*

There's a hissing sound when our first flares shoot off, followed by several screaming discharges, one after another. Smoke trails converge on the launches, but a couple of the flares arc too high and miss. One is on target and hits a boy on the second launch square in the chest, knocking him overboard. A sickening bang and a red smoke trail follow seconds later, but I can see him swimming away. Ash and the others aren't watching. They're already preparing to fire another wave. Ash's next flare lands in the leading launch and sends the pirates into a panic. Their launch swerves out of control while they dance around after it. One of the older ones manages to pick it up to throw it overboard, but it goes off in his hand with a bloody red explosion. The parachute hits him in the face and probably saves him from being blinded. He lets out a guttural scream that cuts right through me, and he tears at his sleeve to wrap his shattered hand and stem the flow of blood.

It is a momentary setback for them. I'm shaking so much that my flares go wide when I let them off. They narrowly miss the second boat and hit the water. It's chaos. There's red smoke and shouting everywhere.

Charis fires her second flare, leaning over the jackstay for a better aim, and it hits another boy pirate full in the face. He falls to his knees, screaming. Seconds later it explodes.

All the color drains from Charis's face. "YEAH, WELL, WHAT DID YOU EXPECT? SOD OFF, THE LOT OF YOU!" she yells, fighting back tears. Suddenly she's shaking like a leaf, too. I don't think she expected to hit anything, because the good arm she aimed with is not the one she favors. Her prosthetic fingers whir into a tight ball and then stretch flat again. She tries to pick up another flare and drops it.

Ash and Marcus have more flares ready, but a line of gunfire rakes the deck and they have to dance out of the way, diving onto the cockpit seats. There's a metallic ping when one of the bullets ricochets off Ash's leg. Charis throws herself out of the way and falls awkwardly to the deck near me, trying not to land on her prosthesis.

I duck between the wheel and the navigation console and pull her under cover, and we crouch there in silence, breathing heavily. Just in case we were in any doubt about their intent, the pirates scream and whoop and fire at the hull again while we are all hiding, the shuddering impacts sending splinters of decking flying.

"OKAY!" Ash yells, waving his arm. "ENOUGH!"

We stay down, listening while the launches roar closer and bump heavily against our hull. *Spirit* leans and pitches. We're being boarded.

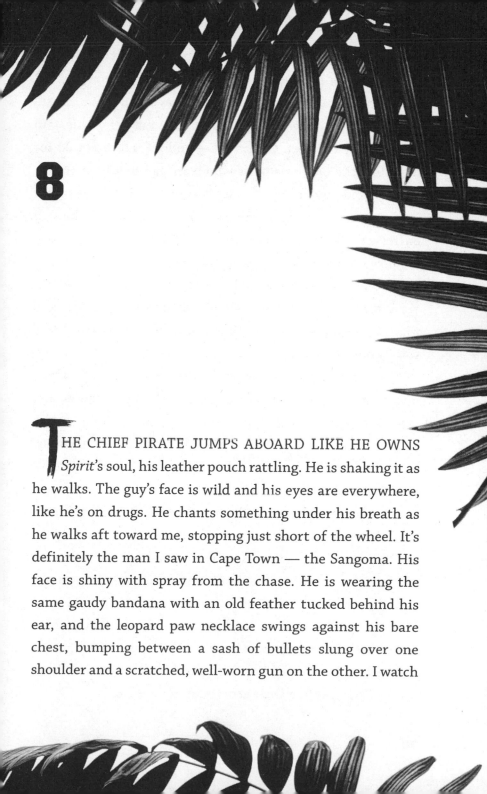

8

THE CHIEF PIRATE JUMPS ABOARD LIKE HE OWNS *Spirit*'s soul, his leather pouch rattling. He is shaking it as he walks. The guy's face is wild and his eyes are everywhere, like he's on drugs. He chants something under his breath as he walks aft toward me, stopping just short of the wheel. It's definitely the man I saw in Cape Town — the Sangoma. His face is shiny with spray from the chase. He is wearing the same gaudy bandana with an old feather tucked behind his ear, and the leopard paw necklace swings against his bare chest, bumping between a sash of bullets slung over one shoulder and a scratched, well-worn gun on the other. I watch as he lets the pouch fall back to his side. He's definitely been on board before. Those bones we found belonged to him.

The Sangoma bares his broken yellow teeth at me, mocking my stupidity while he waves the muzzle of his gun precariously between Charis's face and mine. I'm scared for her. She's the only one of us who managed to kill one of his friends, and judging by the way he scowls at her, he is pretty mad about it. It's scary watching that dark hole in the gun barrel waving at my face, waiting for someone to speak, knowing how unpredictable these people could be.

We move toward the middle of the deck, where the others are being herded in a weird, rattling silence. Ash and Marcus are wary, ready to fight, but it's all pointless. We're totally outnumbered.

The boat lurches again and again with multiple thudding impacts as the remaining launches bump alongside and pirates scramble on board one after another. *Spirit*'s deck shudders under the assault of their bare feet. They're young, all of them, painfully thin and filthy, and their eyes are bloodshot and dead.

The Sangoma barks at Charis and me, "Go with the others!" His voice is cracked and dry.

We edge past him and into the cockpit, where two other pirates have made Marcus and Ash sit at gunpoint on the bench seat. He shoves Charis roughly after me, looking us both up and down when we brush past his legs. Ash is about to protest, but the minute he tries to move, one of his guards shoves him back and forces him and Marcus to lie facedown on the floor, pulling their arms behind their backs.

The Sangoma levels his gun at Charis. When he speaks to her his voice is edgy, manic. "You! You killed one of my men."

I'm afraid to breathe. *Please don't hurt her. Don't say anything stupid, Charis.*

Her prosthetic fingers buzz anxiously, scaring some of the child soldiers, who chatter and point. "Yeah? Well, he had it coming, didn't he?"

Before she can duck or protect herself he decks her with the butt of his gun against the side of her head. The thud is sickening.

Charis shrieks when the blow lands, then falls silent, slumped over the cockpit table. Two of the newly arrived pirates drag her off it and take her astern.

Ash and Marcus try to struggle up off the deck but are beaten down again.

"Try that on *me*, you bastard!" Ash yells.

While the Sangoma laughs at them, we are joined by the guy with the injured hand and another painfully thin pirate carrying a machine gun. The injured man is still holding a filthy, blood-drenched rag over his hand. He stinks of sweat and old clothes.

"Give him first aid," the Sangoma orders me. I'm shunted toward the cabin doorway with a gun in my back. My heart is pounding and I stumble so badly on my way down the steps that the Sangoma, who is following, screams at me, waving his gun.

"*Acheni au mimi risasi! ACHENI!*"[1]

---

1. STOP or I shoot! STOP!

I steady myself on the saloon table, terrified that he'll just shoot me in the back, and I raise my free hand without turning around. I can't stop it from shaking wildly — I don't know what he wants me to do. Jen is still sitting in the comms chair, watching me with wild eyes. There's no sign of Izzy and I'm hoping above hope that she doesn't try anything stupid. My voice is steady, quiet. I'm desperate to keep the Sangoma calm.

"I'm sorry," I tell him, still without turning around. "I slipped . . ." While I'm talking I notice that the small paring knife is still on the table! My hands are shaking so badly I'm afraid I'm going to mess my chance up, but somehow I manage to palm the knife and slip it up my T-shirt before he reaches the bottom of the stairs. I wedge the handle under my bikini top just as the nozzle of the Sangoma's gun bumps painfully against my shoulder blade. He pulls me around roughly by the arm and we wait, face-to-face, for the injured pirate to join us. As soon as he gets down, the Sangoma stands aside and shakes his gun at me.

I try to keep the wobble out of my voice and fail. "Jen, where's the first aid kit?"

"In here." It's in the cupboard by the comms station. She gets it out and passes it to me. Her hands are shaking badly too.

The Sangoma gives me a false smile, revealing a dull gold filling that I hadn't noticed before. There's a horrible light in his eyes. "Quickly, *Rhiannon Cruz.*"

My legs go weak. He knows my name?

The other thin pirate clatters down the steps and the Sangoma virtually yanks him down the last few by the collar of his filthy shirt. He is just a boy, can't be more than sixteen.

"*Kwenda kuangalia!*"[2] the Sangoma grunts, shoving the back of the kid's close-cropped head toward the aft cabins.

The boy disappears beyond the engine room door, which is still swinging open. He looks inside briefly and then goes to check in the guys' bunk room and the storeroom.

I open the first aid kit and hand it to the pirate with the damaged hand. He stands too close to me, virtually suffocating me in a cloud of nauseating body odor, and winces when he pulls the cloth off his hand. Two fingers are missing and the palm is badly burned. It's *disgusting*. All the while, I'm hoping that dirt gets in his wounds so that it gets infected. I can't help myself, though. I point at the alcohol wipes and tell him, "I'm no expert, but you might want to use those first." Even if they try to force me, there's *no way* I'm touching his hand.

For a second it looks like I might have to help him open the packet, but he manages to tear it open with his teeth. He yelps when he wipes the wounds — it probably stings like hell. *Good. I'm glad.* While he's working I take the chance to nudge the knife in my top into a more comfortable position.

Suddenly there's the sound of a scuffle in the storeroom, then a door bangs. It's Izzy. She's managed to overpower the thin pirate and march him back to the saloon with a loaded

2. Go look!

rocket flare gun pressed against his temple. "Tell your men to drop their weapons or I'll kill him," she snarls at the Sangoma.

I'm shocked. It's like some switch has flipped in Izzy and suddenly she's a soldier, taut, controlled, and deadly serious.

To my surprise, the Sangoma laughs and grins at the injured guy. He even takes the time to walk to the kitchen, help himself to a bar of chocolate from the fridge, and walk back. "Go ahead," he says, unwrapping it and taking a bite. "I don't need a boy who can be beaten by a girl."

Izzy is fazed, but only for a second. She pulls the boy tighter, presses the flare gun so hard into his skin that a pale ring blooms around the nozzle. "I'm not joking. I will do this. Drop your gun."

The Sangoma takes another bite and chews slowly, leaving the rest on the table. Then, in one swift movement, he lifts his gun and shoots — a short, rapid burst. It's right by my arm, and I can actually feel the heat from the bullets.

Jen screams.

I clamp my eyes shut, unable to watch. All I can think is, *He shot Izzy! I can't believe he shot Izzy!*

There is a shuffling noise and the spit of the flare gun going off. I open my eyes. Izzy is still standing there, stunned. There is a long smear of blood down the wall next to her and the boy pirate is slumped against it, dead. In the shock, Izzy's finger must have pulled the trigger because the flare hisses and spins on the floor between us. Suddenly it rockets toward me, filling the saloon with thick smoke.

It's chaos as the cartridge ricochets wildly off the walls with cracking impacts too fast for us to see, we're all ducking with no idea if we're getting out of the way or in it. Eventually the flare drops onto one of the bench seats, bounces off it, and rolls to a halt by Jen's feet. There is nowhere for her to run to — it's too crowded.

I yell, "GET ON THE CHAIR!" but I'm too late.

The bang is almost as deafening as Jen's cries, and red smoke is everywhere, billowing upward on the updraft from the hatch.

In the silence that follows, Ash and Marcus are yelling above and I can hear the pirates screaming at them.

"WE'RE OKAY!" I yell back, my voice breaking with fear. "STOP! STOP! DON'T DO ANYTHING STUPID!"

Somehow things calm down. Jen's leg is badly burned and she's sobbing uncontrollably, but the Sangoma won't let any of us take a look at it. "Leave it," he says, knocking the first aid kit out of my hands. "Thanks to your friend we have run out of time. Up! UP!"

The Sangoma yanks Jen up by her arm, and she screams in pain until he slaps her face — hard. Then we're all pushed and shoved up to the deck. They sit us next to Ash and Marcus. Charis is still out cold on the stern deck.

"You okay?" Ash asks us. "What happened down there?"

None of us has a chance to answer. The Sangoma fires his gun in the air and yells at Ash, "DO NOT TALK!" Then he waves some of his men below and we have to sit there while they ransack the yacht, bringing up anything of value and piling it on the cabin roof. They even take our jewelry. One of them holds his hand out for my silver wristwatch and shoves it in his pocket with a yellow grin. All the time they are shouting and bickering. When my bag comes up they savagely rip it apart; it's not worth keeping even as a bag. Ash's open letter tumbles onto the top of the pile when they shake the contents out.

It's a second or two before I realize how bad this looks, and then I glance at Ash. He's stunned, shaking his head and staring in disbelief. He thinks I've stolen the letter — and why wouldn't he?

"That's not what it looks like," I tell him. It even sounds like an excuse to *me*. My insides are tangled like spaghetti, fear twisted up with the realization that now he's going to hate me, too. I look at Jen, but she won't meet my eyes.

"*Kuwa kimya!*"[3] One of the pirates clips me on the back of my head to shut me up. Then he makes us all stand up and move over to the side where their launches are tethered.

Ash wraps his arm protectively around Jen, helping her to stand, and she's crying into the crook of his neck as they walk. I follow, staring at her shoulders. It could all end for us, and Ash will never know the truth. The desperation and hopelessness I feel sharpen the hurt that lances through my heart. I gasp involuntarily and bite back my tears. All I was trying to do was help Jen.

The pirates toss the guy Charis killed overboard and load

---

3. Be silent!

us onto the launches together with their loot, while the Sangoma and a couple of others go back below. I can see Ash's blades on the next boat, in a pile with the iPad and packs of emergency rations. He's in there with Jen and Marcus. Some of the pirates are tucking into boxes of cookies, and one of them has Ash's guitar slung on his back. Izzy and I are sitting in a puddle of bloody seawater with Charis between us. I've got her head on my lap and there is a huge lump forming on it. Her eyes are wide open, and she's moaning, but I don't think she sees us. Her lips are almost white.

When the Sangoma comes back up onto the deck of the *Spirit of Freedom*, Izzy shouts, "My insulin! I've got to have my insulin!"

"Please! It's in the fridge, in packs!" I add.

He walks over with his gun pointed at us until he stands astride the yacht and the launch we are in. "What is all this clamor? Shall I shoot you? Is that what you want?"

"I'm diabetic."

"Pfft!" The Sangoma spits disparagingly. "What of it?"

He's close to me, so I grab a handful of his pants leg, I actually get on my knees, while he and his men laugh at me. "Please — you have to listen. She'll die without it."

"I will use a spell on her . . . cut her . . . she will be well."

"NO! She needs insulin." I stand up, try to get back on the yacht, ignoring Izzy's grip on my arm. "Look, if you won't do it, I'll get it."

"RIO! Let me handle this. They'll shoot you if you make them mad!"

For a second the Sangoma hovers. Then he shoves me so hard that I fall back into the launch. He marches to *Spirit*'s hatch and clatters down the steps, out of sight. When he returns he throws one pack of shrink-wrapped vials at Izzy: just ten small bottles. She looks at it, and when she looks up again, her eyes are all glassy.

I tell the Sangoma, "That's not enough!" and have to duck out of range of the end of his rifle. It clips me painfully on the top of my shoulder and he just laughs.

"Then she will die!"

The pirates start the engines as soon as the Sangoma is on board and we lean into a tight turn, speeding back the way they came. Behind us, the *Spirit of Freedom* rocks on the wash, alone and empty in the vast, glittering ocean, framed by a weary sun and gathering cloud. Suddenly she shudders violently and the sea ripples around her hull like a huge rock has been dropped in it. The sound of the explosion chases after us. My heart is pounding in my throat as I watch, and my chest tightens when I remember that my phone is on there. What will Mum think? She'll be worried sick.

The yacht's prow rises slowly and she slips backward into the water. Iz can't watch. She buries her head behind my shoulder blade. As *Spirit* goes down, I feel abandoned, like someone has ripped the world out from under my feet. Tears stream down my face and drip onto my lips. As if she wants to tell me she knows, there's a sudden rush of air bubbling up from deep inside *Spirit*'s bowels. It gushes out of the saloon door like a giant is blowing over the mouth of a bottle, and a long, mournful wail carries over the waves. The heart-wrenching sound is cut short when the ship is swallowed up beneath a watery green blanket.

The last thing to disappear is the tip of her tall mast. In just a few short minutes all that's left is ocean. There is no sign that the *Spirit of Freedom* ever existed.

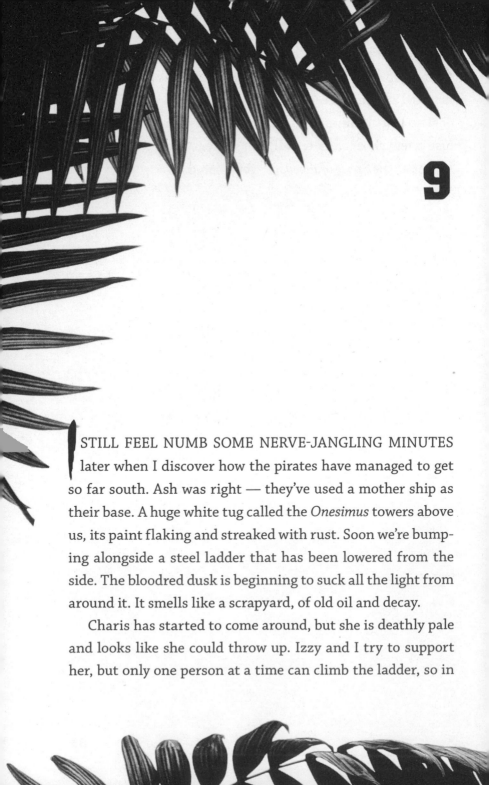

9

I STILL FEEL NUMB SOME NERVE-JANGLING MINUTES
later when I discover how the pirates have managed to get
so far south. Ash was right — they've used a mother ship as
their base. A huge white tug called the *Onesimus* towers above
us, its paint flaking and streaked with rust. Soon we're bumping alongside a steel ladder that has been lowered from the
side. The bloodred dusk is beginning to suck all the light from
around it. It smells like a scrapyard, of old oil and decay.

Charis has started to come around, but she is deathly pale
and looks like she could throw up. Izzy and I try to support
her, but only one person at a time can climb the ladder, so in

the end one of the pirates throws her over his bare, sweaty shoulder, carries her up, and dumps her onto the rolling deck. Izzy and I race after him and help Charis to stand between us. She throws up on the deck. I don't know about Iz, but I'm barely able to support myself.

They don't give us time to even get our bearings. We're taken below at gunpoint and dumped in a dingy room where the only light comes through a tiny window in the door. It is stuffy and airless, crammed with old ropes and rusty parts. The engines begin to rumble and clank, shaking the floor, and dim yellow lights flicker on outside. A few minutes later, Ash and Marcus are brought down and Jen follows them in, limping. She wipes tears from her face and goes to squat in the corner without looking at me.

"Everyone okay?" Ash comes over and hugs Charis, standing back to examine her eyes and the angry lump on her head.

She smiles weakly. "I've got the mother of all headaches, but I'll live."

He doesn't ask about me.

We all slump to the floor, pretty much where we stand.

I wonder, "Jen, do you think the Mayday worked?"

She shakes her head without looking up.

"What are we going to do?" It's Izzy, trying to stay strong.

Marcus has his nose pressed against the porthole in the door, and Ash looks over his shoulder at him. "Nothing stupid, right, Marky?" There's no response, so Ash continues. "The best thing we can do right now is conserve our strength. Maybe see if we can get a message out somehow."

Marcus turns and kicks the door angrily, then comes over to join us. "Bastards . . . ! Anyone manage to bring anything from the yacht? Cell phone, chocolate . . . ?"

"I've got this." I reach under my T-shirt and pull the knife out of my bikini top. My hands are shaking so much it cuts me and I have to swallow a gasp. A warm finger of blood trickles down my sternum, but thankfully it's only a nick, so I don't say anything to the others.

"You star!" Ash's face lights up — until he remembers the letter.

I hand it over. "Look, Jen will tell you — I didn't take your letter," I tell him, with a glance at Jen.

The others look at us, wondering what's going on.

Jen turns away so Ash can't see the guilt that's written all over her face.

"So how did it end up in *your* bag?"

"It's complicated . . ." I'm going to say more, but I don't have the heart to dump Jen in it. It's just going to be my word against hers, and I don't have the strength for a fight. Let them think whatever the hell they want, I'm past caring. Before, I would have wanted to watch her squirm, really, but now? I just can't. Her head pops up, and I try to keep my voice level so Ash won't hear it shaking. "Look . . . we have more important things to worry about. Can't we just forget it?"

He doesn't answer straightaway. Then he turns on me and says, "No, I don't think we can forget it, Rio. I wrote that letter for my parents' eyes only. It was personal — I've never even shown it to *them*! And what else have you stolen? How can any of us know that you haven't been rummaging through our stuff? But do you want to know what the worst of it is?"

I don't answer. I just look him straight in his beautiful eyes and take it, because nothing else matters to me now that *Spirit* has gone.

"It's that it shows you didn't really give a damn about any of us."

My face feels like it's on fire. They're all looking at me, waiting for me to come clean. Somehow I manage to pry a few words out of my mouth. It's barely a whisper, and Jen still just sits there saying nothing.

"That's where you're wrong, Ash. I *do* care."

I go over to Jen, hoping that she'll speak up, and all the while I can feel Ash's eyes on me like I'm his own personal Judas. The others look *totally* shocked and confused, and I don't know how I'll ever be able to speak to any of them again. Weirdly, the only person I feel any connection with right now is Jen.

When I get to her all I can think of saying is, "Let me take a look at your leg."

"No need," she mutters, taking a deep breath and letting her head fall back against the wall.

"Suit yourself."

She looks at me like she's regretting everything, but she can't bring herself to tell the truth. After a while she admits to me in a softer voice, "It's throbbing a lot, but I'm okay if I keep it raised."

"Good." I flop down beside her, trying desperately to rise

above it all, trying not to fall apart. I'm too tired to move away, so I just sit there with Jen, feeling the hum of the engines enter through my back and merge with the growling anger in the pit of my stomach.

Eventually Jen falls asleep. Her head falls onto my shoulder. I have to fight the urge to wriggle from underneath it and let her fall to the hard metal floor. My eyelids are heavy, but my head is full of images of Ash swimming with me, of the sheer power and beauty of that whale shark, and I'm thinking how incredible, how *free* I felt at that moment. I'm not even sure it really happened anymore. Now I'm just left here wondering if any of us will ever get out of this, longing to be able to plunge, like the shark, into the deepest, darkest ocean, where no one can reach me.

I don't know if the aching desperation I feel is playing with my head, but I think I might be in love with Ash, I really do. If we ever get out of this, I want him to know who I am. I want him to tell me what he was going to say back in the water. In the end I think if someone knows you — I mean *really* knows you — they'll take the time to understand the stupid things they think you've done.

But I decide I'm not going to tell him it was Jen who took his letter, ever, and the decision sets inside me like concrete. For one thing, I remember the look on her face when she saw me in my bikini with Ash. She's hurt inside, and I'm not about to hurt her more, however much she hacks me off. That girl stuck with Ash the whole time he went through rehab, and I respect her for that. As far as I'm concerned, it's up to her to be honest with herself.

The minute I make up my mind, it's like cold water has been poured on the hot ball of anger that has been knotting up my bowels. It seems to take forever, but eventually I fall into a fitful sleep.

I wake up sprawled on my side. It's hot and I'm dripping with sweat, and for a second all the horror of the last few hours hits me like a hammer. I suck in a breath like I've been punched, then try to swallow the sound I make. Desperate to calm my rising panic, I check that the others are still here, trying to slow my heartbeat while I count them. The others are sleeping restlessly in the shadows, and Jen is limping up and down the room with her hand on the far wall, tears streaming down her face.

The sound of distant laughter seems to ooze out of the steel walls. It sounds wild, drunken — edgy and dangerous. I wonder if they're taking drugs. My chest tightens at the thought of what they might do to us if they're stoned.

I can't keep the panic out of my voice. "How long have I been asleep?"

"A few hours. Go back to sleep," Jen whispers.

"You okay?"

The old glint flashes in her eye for a second. "No, I'm not! Why would I be?"

I fall back on my elbows and take a breath. "I was just asking . . ."

Jen bites her bottom lip and her shoulders sag. "Rio, I'm sorry. You didn't deserve that."

"No, you're damn right I didn't. Why didn't you say anything to Ash? You left me out to dry."

"Because I want things to be like they were."

I laugh. I can't help it.

"What? What's so funny?"

"We've been kidnapped by lunatics with guns, Jen. You're priceless."

Jen's face cracks a little.

"How's the leg?"

"It's hurting . . . badly. I just need to keep moving, to take my mind off it. I'll be fine, really."

"What do you think they'll do with us?"

"I'm trying not to think about that. Get some rest."

I can't, though. I'm too awake now, and wracked with worry. The side of Jen's left leg is badly blistered from the ankle to just below her knee, and the angry skin is lined with beads of pale yellow fluid. All I can think is, *What if it goes septic?* None of us has any idea how long this could go on for — and I don't even want to think about how Izzy will cope with so little insulin.

We are left for hours in stifling heat before a couple of the pirates chuck a few of our emergency rations in along with an old plastic bottle filled with water. The engines grumble constantly, flat out, and the only way to tell that day has dawned is when the yellow light outside our door clicks off.

Nobody has much to say. We're all dripping with sweat, thinking about search and rescue and whether anyone will come after us. Ash has his right leg off, examining the ankle joint. There is a rough tear in the metal at the back where the bullet hit. He puts it down and squints as he rubs his stump.

I ask, "Is it hurting?"

"No more than normal."

"He's having phantom pains." Jen flashes me a look that lets me know she understands all of this stuff. "He's feeling it more because the painkillers have worn off. Why don't you just *tell* her, Ash? It's okay to be in pain. It doesn't make you less of a man."

"Give it a rest, Jen," Izzy snaps, her teeth clenched on a needle cover. Suddenly I'm scared that we're all falling apart under the pressure. I don't remember Izzy snapping at anyone before.

Iz is going as long as she can between shots, injecting with the syringe she had on her when we were taken. You're supposed to change the needle, but she's using the same one.

Ash slips his prosthesis back on.

"Sod it." Marcus — like he's just thought of something. He hits the floor — he seems to like hitting things at the moment. "My skin creams!"

Nobody comments. What's the point?

Marcus exhales into the silence. "Someone'd better find us soon or I'll end up looking like Tutankhamen."

"Shh!" Charis's head snaps up and we all listen.

Someone has a radio on and it's in English. The only trouble is, it's a long way off and some of the pirates are speaking over it. We can only catch bits.

"Voice of America . . . UTC . . . East Africa . . . news."

Amazingly, someone turns it up.

". . . on board their yacht, the Spirit of Freedom. *No Mayday signal was sent out and investigators have ruled out bad weather. Currently the authorities are working on the assumption that there may have been a catastrophic failure in the yacht's hull."*

"Or that they were taken by freaking pirates, you arse-hole!" Marcus yells, banging the wall.

The pirates laugh. They heard him.

"Marky, shush!" Charis hisses. We're all desperate to hear more.

". . . of piracy has not yet been ruled out, although it is thought to be unlikely so far south. The South African coast guard says that their search perimeter will be extended today, but that if the search for the young adventurers enters another night, it is not likely that there will be any survivors."

10
DAY 12

WE'RE SITTING CROSS-LEGGED IN A ROW AT THE top of a sandy white cove beneath a line of tall palms and trees with round, dark leaves. After the gloomy room on the *Onesimus* we're all blinking back the tears because the light reflecting off the white sand is so painfully bright. I'm scared witless, but I'm grateful that at least I'll feel the breeze on my back before I die. Our arms have been tied behind us with frayed nylon rope, and it's *really* sharp. We all smell rank.

Judging by that light outside the door on the *Onesimus,* we were at sea for two days and two nights — that's about

forty-eight hours. The engines were going full out, so that's probably about twelve or thirteen knots, which means we've traveled about six hundred miles. So by my reckoning we're in Tanzania, and that's *miles* away from Somalia. I'm wondering if any of the others have worked it out, too, and I'm thinking, *Crap — no one will ever think of looking for us in Tanzania.* Why on earth would Somali pirates bring us here? Surely they'd want to take us to Somalia.

I twist my wrists to ease the pressure on them. Already they are wet with sweat, but the rope scratches and leaves them feeling so sore that I have to give up. The pirates won't let us talk, so we have no choice but to wait here, listening to the hiss and crash of the breakers at our backs and the loud hum of hungry-sounding insects ahead. While we're waiting for God knows what to happen, this huge black *thing* flies at my face from nowhere, buzzing loudly. It lands in my hair and burrows in it for what seems like ages. I want to scream but I'm too scared, and I just have to wait for it to crawl out, spread its wings, and clatter off.

The sand we're sitting on is burning hot, but we don't dare move. It's still early but the sun is almost unbearable on my back. I glance at Marcus's mottled neck to my left and find myself worrying about sunburn; already his skin looks taut and angry.

In front of us is a disheveled, ragtag army dressed in jungle camouflage gear and carrying guns and machetes. There's another ten of them besides the pirates who took us, and most look as though they can't be much more than teenagers, like us. One or two have short African hair but the rest of them wear it longer, in lines of thin, stringy braids tied with colored thread and beads. Their faces are mega hostile, and they watch us with restless, narrowed eyes. One has a congealing black line where his upper lip has had a chunk torn out of it, exposing three of his upper teeth. Part of his nose is gone with it, leaving a curving black hole. Two of the pirates are carrying the gear — stolen from the *Spirit of Freedom* — from the launches and into the trees ahead of us. Ash's blades seem to puzzle them.

Suddenly the soldiers go mental. They shriek and trill and scream, firing shots into the air. The sound is primal. It sends shivers down my spine. We all look at one another, wondering what on earth is going to happen. The unruly ranks of boys part like a wave and a tall, thin man strides over the crest of the sandbank ahead of us. He is wearing tight, beaded braids underneath a green military beret, and is much older than the others. His face is lined and he's got a pistol in his hand. I decide that it's a statement: It's all he needs.

The Sangoma is unpredictable, crazy, but this guy is something else again. He walks proudly with a straight back, wearing his camo jacket like it's some kind of business suit, and he has a dark charisma, a fatal calmness that rivets your attention. I just know that this is someone who is capable of doing *anything*, and he won't think twice about doing it.

Following him is a blank-faced child soldier — a girl of about fourteen, with a potbellied toddler clinging to her leg. Bizarre. She clutches a machine gun that dangles around her neck on a length of frayed, twisted string, and she wears a necklace of cream-colored beads. When she gets closer I see that they are teeth. Maybe they are from her victims.

The two strange newcomers approach, lifting a spray of sand as they walk that clings in a fine white layer to the girl's bare legs. An awful, expectant hush descends. All I can hear is the pounding of my heart and the crash of the breakers. The toddler shows me a gummy grin. For some reason young kids latch on to me. I think it's my funny hair. Now is *so* not the time, though. I'm out of my mind with fear, shaking so badly I can barely stay upright.

"I expect you are all wondering why I have brought you here," the man says. He speaks with tedious precision, and his vowel sounds are clipped and angry, just like the pirates'. None of us reply. I notice that his eyes constantly flick up at the sky. Is he worried about aircraft? That's good, isn't it? I wonder if we are near civilization.

"You may have heard of me. My name is Moses Mwemba."

I don't have a clue. But by the looks the others are shooting one another, I'm guessing they do.

"You are prisoners of the Lord's Resistance Army."

The soldiers trill and whoop again at the name, and the sound goes right through me. I get the feeling that there isn't much keeping them from tearing us limb from limb just for fun.

"That's bad," Izzy hisses in my ear. She bites her lip when one of the kidnappers shoves her in the back.

I whisper, "So they're not Somali pirates?" and get the same treatment.

Izzy shakes her head.

Mwemba continues, "You will be released unharmed in a few days' time *if* your government agrees to our terms. In the meantime you will follow my instructions. Do not test me." He looks at us through heavy-lidded eyes. "If you do what I tell you to do, you will be safe. If you do not . . ." He shrugs.

"You should save yourself the trouble," Ash tells him angrily. "The British government doesn't pay ransoms, and the minute you make your demands they'll be down on you like a ton of bricks."

Mwemba laughs, but anger twists his smile into a snarl. "You really think so?" Hissing waves fill the silence while he scans us. "I believe they will think differently — on account of your particular *needs*."

I'm shaking so badly I can barely lift my head up. What Ash just said is news to me. Our government won't pay a freaking ransom? We're screwed! My own fears have to wait, though — I need to say something. *Avoid eye contact. Whatever you do, Rio, avoid eye contact.* My throat is dry when I speak.

"Mr. Mwemba. You have to let Izzy go."

"Rio!" Izzy's face flushes and she twists to flash a look at me. I give her one back.

The guy covers the ground to me faster than I could have imagined. He leans over and screams in my face. "WHO SAID YOU CAN SPEAK? *DID I SAY SO?*"

I can't help the tears. They tumble down my cheeks and spray my arms as I shake my head and whisper, "No. No, sir. You didn't."

He goes calm almost as fast as he flew off the handle, and stands upright, scanning us. "Which one of you is called Izzy?"

She lifts her head next to me, slowly, proudly. "Me."

Mwemba's soldiers laugh and point at her leg frame. He just asks her, "Can you walk?"

She nods.

"Then there is nothing wrong with you."

"But there *is*! She has diabetes," I tell him, before Izzy has a chance to nudge me. Then, to her, "They can't just ignore it, Iz."

By the way his jaw clenches I can see that Ash is not happy with me, either, but he backs me up before Mwemba has a chance to scream at me again. "She needs insulin if you want her to live long enough to get your ransom." He inclines his head toward the Sangoma. "Your friend here wouldn't let us bring it all."

Mwemba rounds on the Sangoma, who stumbles backward as the LRA leader takes a couple of steps toward him. His breathing is ragged and he clutches his pouch of bones.

"Is this true?" Mwemba hisses dangerously. "Did I not tell you to bring *everything* they might need?"

He stutters, "I . . . I will heal her."

Mwemba screams back, *"MSIWE WAJINGA! KWA UCHAWI?"*[4] pointing his pistol at the Sangoma's forehead.

---

4. Do not be stupid! With magic?

There's a rhythm to the strange words that leaves them ringing in your head, like he's taken a beautiful tune and sung it off-key — filled it with hate. Whatever he's said, it's *bad* for the Sangoma.

I don't know about the others, but I feel sick. Black spots float in front of my eyes and I don't know if I'll be able to stay upright. It looks like this Mwemba guy is even worse than the Sangoma. I'm sure he's going to pull the trigger, so I look away. I force myself to focus on the palm fronds swaying against a sun-bleached blue sky and try to imagine that I'm somewhere safe, that none of this is happening. All the while I'm waiting for the bang. When it doesn't come I look again.

The Sangoma's forehead is beaded with sweat. Lines of it trickle down his cheeks. Mwemba has decided not to pull the trigger, but you can tell he wants to. Instead he swings his arm suddenly and shoots the pirate with the injured hand, who is standing next to the Sangoma. He just *shoots* the guy — right between the eyes.

Maybe I should have expected it, but the sound is like an electric shock, pulling every muscle in my body taut in an instant. I almost topple sideways. There is a sickening thud; the guy doesn't even have a chance to cry out. Inside I'm screaming hopelessly, *Please, God, I want to go home. Please — let me go home.* My heart is pounding so hard I can feel it in my throat.

Breathing heavily, Mwemba lowers his smoking gun and turns to look at Izzy with half-lidded eyes. His voice is deadly as he waves his pistol at her and tells his fighters, "*Mzigo kila mtu isipokuwa hii msichana.*"[5]

The child soldiers are suddenly *really* jumpy, forcing all of us, except Izzy, to get to our feet and walk toward the trees. I'm not leaving without Izzy, so I stand my ground until the girl with the disgusting teeth-necklace shoves the nozzle of her gun in my gut. There is no pity in her bloodshot eyes. When I still don't move, she pulls her gun back and shoves me hard with the side of it. I stumble backward, keeping my eyes on Izzy. Mwemba is placing a heavy hand on her shoulder so she can't move. She doesn't lift her head, and her lips move silently. The sun pulses off the St. Christopher bracelet behind her back.

Ash, Marcus, Jen, and Charis are straining to see her, too, and Ash angrily shunts his guards out of the way. He almost gets past them until one of them hits him between the shoulder blades with his rifle butt. He falls to the sand.

"Get off him!" Jen screams behind me. I hear a loud slap, and she whimpers but says no more.

The soldiers are getting more and more edgy, and groups of them shove and hit Ash and Marcus until they begin to fall back. I'm *so* scared. What is happening? What's Mwemba going to do to Iz?

Ash is still struggling as two of them drag him to his feet. The veins in his neck look like they will burst, and he rages at Mwemba, "If you harm one hair on her body, I'll rip your heart out . . . !"

---

5. Load everyone except this girl.

Next thing I know, a rough hand grips my arm. I turn and find myself looking the blank-faced girl right in the eye. She drags me up the beach.

"We can take care of her," I say hoarsely. "We'll find a way. Please. You have to stop him."

The weird child just shoves me at a couple of soldiers and watches them drag me away.

Mwemba raises his gun and places it against Izzy's temple.

Her eyes close.

Ash, Charis and Marcus are going mad, fighting the LRA soldiers, but there's no way they can do anything. They're just getting beaten up. I feel limp and helpless. What's wrong with me? Why did I even say anything? Izzy is going to *die* here, and it will be my fault.

Suddenly my legs won't support my weight and the soldiers have to hold me up, drag me like a sack over the sand. Everything in me has shriveled up, I'm gasping for air, I want to tell them to stop but only a pathetic croak will come out. There's nothing I can do but watch Mwemba's finger close on the trigger and pray to Izzy's God that she won't feel anything.

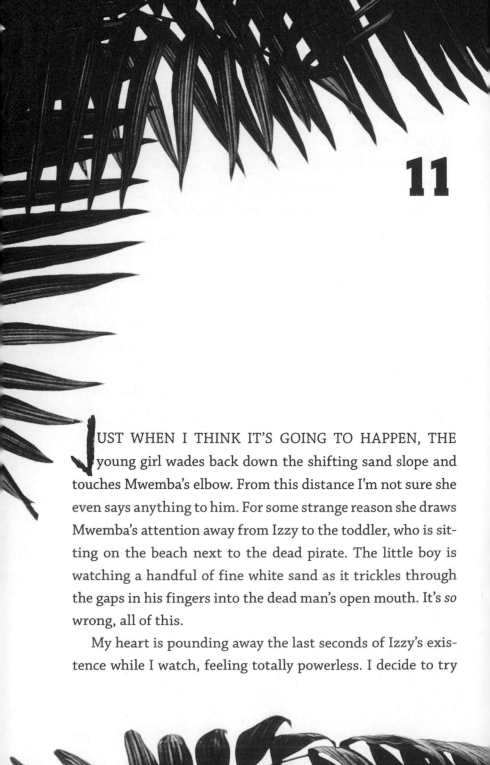

11

JUST WHEN I THINK IT'S GOING TO HAPPEN, THE young girl wades back down the shifting sand slope and touches Mwemba's elbow. From this distance I'm not sure she even says anything to him. For some strange reason she draws Mwemba's attention away from Izzy to the toddler, who is sitting on the beach next to the dead pirate. The little boy is watching a handful of fine white sand as it trickles through the gaps in his fingers into the dead man's open mouth. It's *so* wrong, all of this.

My heart is pounding away the last seconds of Izzy's existence while I watch, feeling totally powerless. I decide to try pleading with Mwemba one last time. My mouth is still so dry I have to force the words out. I shout, "Please — isn't there a hospital or something? They might have insulin. You could take the rest of us and leave her there!"

To my relief, Mwemba's grip on the pistol loosens slightly. He ignores me and looks at the dead-faced girl. They just stand there locked in some weird, unspoken agreement. When she places her hand on his arm the tension seems to drain from his face. He flicks a catch on the side of his gun, holsters it, and shouts back at me, "How long can the girl last?"

"I can speak for myself," Iz says weakly.

Mwemba waits, but she's too exhausted by her ordeal.

"Not long," I tell him vaguely. I don't want the freak to think about shooting her again, but I need him to get a move on if he's going to get help. It could be just a day or so before she goes hypo.

Without speaking, Mwemba hauls a shivering Izzy to her feet and shoves her roughly at the girl. "TAKE HER!" he barks.

As usual, she doesn't bat an eyelid. My guards are still pulling at my arms, but somehow I manage to yank myself free and run back down the beach toward Izzy. She virtually falls onto my chest, white as a sheet and shaking uncontrollably. Her pupils are wide and as black as night. I can't hug her like I want to because of the stupid rope, but I manage to get my face next to hers and whisper, "You okay?" before we are separated.

Izzy nods. She actually smiles at me, and lifts her arm with its St. Christopher. "He's looking after me," she tells me, so quietly I can barely hear her.

My cheek is wet, crusted with sand. I have no idea what just made Mwemba think again. Somehow I don't think it was me, but for a second I'm almost grateful to him.

The girl points her machine gun at my chest, and her face is as mean as ever. Whatever is going through that kid's head right now, it's not remotely friendly. She rattles her gun at Izzy and me, lifting it so I can see her finger closing on the trigger. I climb the bank next to Izzy, unable to help her, following the others toward a sandy ridge beneath the trees. It's hard, walking up the slippery sand slope — the sand is so dry it slides away under your feet so that you have to take three steps just to go forward one. It's even harder trying to do it with your hands tied. Izzy has the worst of it, though — she almost knocks me over a couple of times when she staggers into my side. Her leg frame digs painfully into my thigh, but somehow we stay upright and make it to the top.

On the other side of the rise there are three vehicles: a beaten-up flatbed truck, an old jeep, and a battered but relatively new red Toyota open-backed SUV. There are bullet holes in all of them. I'm taken to the tailgate of the Toyota and we have to clamber onto the back of it with three jumpy LRA guards watching our every move. Not easy when your legs won't move and you haven't got the use of your hands. In the end we're half lifted on backward and dumped like sacks of potatoes.

Izzy is so worn out that her legs give way when it's her

turn. She has to be shunted up so that she can shuffle along on her butt until she's next to me, where she collapses with her head on her knees. When she has had a chance to catch her breath, she looks up at the nearest guard and tells him, "I need to inject." Then she half turns to show him her tied wrists.

Mwemba, on his way past, overhears. He barks at the boy, "Tie her hands in front."

When Iz is released, her hands are shaking so badly she can hardly fill her syringe. I really want to help, but somehow she manages to do it alone under the spiteful glare of the boy soldier. Once she finally empties the contents into her side she is bound again, this time with her hands on her lap, shivering violently. I rub her shoulder gently with mine, desperate to give her some comfort, still unsure whether or not she blames me for what just happened. I know *I* do.

To my relief, Iz looks up and smiles weakly.

Our guards are all so thin and young that, if it wasn't for their weapons and how hyped up they are, I'm sure we could easily take them on. I strain back over the side of the Toyota and I can just see Ash and the others waiting to be loaded onto the flatbed between rows of heavily armed LRA fighters. Marcus waits for Charis to get on, but she stops abruptly. Some of the child soldiers shriek and chatter wildly when they see the fingers of her metal hand close. One or two of them even back away from her, and I think she takes some strength from seeing them scatter. Her arm hums. She spins around and faces Mwemba.

"Don't think you're going to get away with this," she tells him bravely, and her beautiful Welsh accent is heavy with anger.

"For God's sake, don't wind them up again!" Jen hisses at her.

Marcus limps alongside her and leans heavily on the tailgate of the truck. "Don't fret, Jen. These little bastards don't scare her, that's all."

"Well, they scare me."

Ash is going to be the last one up.

"Not him!" Mwemba beckons, and one of the child soldiers points his gun in Ash's face. Mwemba waves his pistol between Ash and Marcus. "We will keep these two apart."

Ash doesn't even flinch. He just stares at the kid and watches the gun barrel wave him away from the vehicle. He's so calm under all this pressure. I'm willing him not to play the hero, just to do what they want, but it feels like ages before he makes a move. When he does, I find that I have stopped breathing.

By the time he gets to us, Ash is grim-faced and he drops angrily onto the floor opposite me. Three of our four weedy young guards keep their weapons trained on him, and he just glares up at them.

Through the narrow cab window I watch the blank-faced girl and the toddler climb into the backseat. To my amazement, she actually takes the time to strap the kid in! Mwemba gets into the passenger seat and the Sangoma slides behind the wheel. Ahead of us, the truck splutters a bitter-tasting black cloud of smoke, and then the Toyota wheezes and shudders into life. The gears crunch and whine. Seconds later we're lurching away from the coast, throwing up choking billows of dust, skidding up the incline toward a series of rocky, scrub-lined hills.

The Sangoma's driving is terrible. I watch him spinning the steering wheel through the cab window. Unlike the truck in front, we skid and lurch everywhere, but Mwemba either doesn't care or just puts up with it. After a while I decide that Mwemba actually likes being driven. It's like he's the general and the Sangoma is his sidekick.

Izzy's shoulder keeps jabbing into mine while we bump along. Each time it happens I am reminded that but for the grace of God, she wouldn't be here. It feels good — such a *huge* relief to feel her touch. There's no way I could have lived with myself if we were driving away from here leaving her cold, still body on the beach. I look at Iz, just sitting there with her head bowed. If she never spoke another word to me I wouldn't blame her.

Ash is sitting opposite us with his legs straight, and the steel of his prostheses feels cool against my calves. On the *Onesimus* he spent a lot of time looking after Jen. I'm not sure he even notices me anymore, and the thought burns inside me. I have no idea how to make him think better of me. Not without heaping more pain on Jen.

His eyes meet mine briefly, then flash at our guards. "I'm sure you meant well back there, Rio, but with these guys it might be better to think first and speak later, for all our sakes."

"*Thanks*, Ash." I almost bite his head off. "I'll have a side order of guilt to go with the freaking *fantastic* day I'm having." Gran's favorite Jim Carrey line seems to sum up all my hurt. "I thought if I spoke up they'd let her go." Even as I say that last sentence I can hear how stupid it sounds, so I follow up with, "Do you think I wanted what just happened?"

"Of course not. That's my point. If you'd just rein in that tendency you've got to meddle in things that you should leave well alone, then we may just get through this. You might like to be especially careful around any psychopath you see carrying a gun." He jerks his head at the soldiers, and four guns rattle nervously in response.

My chest tightens and I can hardly speak. "Is that what you think of me, Ash? That I *meddle*?"

"*Stop!*" Izzy lifts her head and her face is gray. "*Both of you!* The last thing we need is to be fighting each other."

Ash looks away, and I watch the turquoise sea sparkle between the trees behind us for a while, trying hard to swallow my pain. Obviously that *is* what he thinks. When I turn back, he's watching me. Maybe he's rethinking whatever it was he was about to ask me back there in the ocean, a lifetime ago.

I'm trying not to cry. "What are they going to do to us?"

Ash shrugs angrily. "Don't worry — they'll keep us safe, for the moment. But Mwemba had better watch his back, because if we ever get out of here —"

"You'll do what, Ash?" Now Iz is losing it, blinking away waves of tears. "Take a life for a life? Kill them all? Well, don't you *dare* think you'll be doing it for me. You'll just be as bad as they are, and nothing in this stupid world will ever change. If I'm going to die here, please, God, let it count for something, something good. I'm *begging* you, Ash. If they —" She fights to speak, has to take a deep, gulping breath. "Just promise me — both of you."

Neither of us answers. I'm thinking that the others are all so strong. They've faced death before, and all I can do is try to look strong even though I'm scared witless.

Izzy is trying hard to fight it, but her face begins to crumble. *"Why won't you promise me?"*

The desperation in her voice is heartbreaking. Ash wants to comfort her — we both do — but we can't move. One of the guards pushes Ash back against the side of the truck with his gun when he tries.

Ash glares at the boy soldier. "All right, Iz. Whatever. If it will make you feel better."

I lean in. "Iz, I promise. What, though? What are we promising?"

"If they kill me," she gasps after a painful silence, "if I die — however it happens — I don't want you to take revenge. I don't want either of you to waste your lives thinking about it. No eye-for-an-eye crap. Not even on Mwemba, Ash. Not for me. Try something different. Love those who hate you. Like Madiba did — in the end."

Our guards look at one another, but they don't stop us talking. I think it's because they recognize the name.

"Iz, who is Madiba?"

"Nelson Mandela. After twenty-seven years of hell Mandela came out of jail ready to forgive those who put him there. He even set up this thing called the Truth and Reconciliation Commission to try to fix the mess apartheid left behind."

"How can someone *do* that?" Personally I can't see it working in this situation. Whatever Izzy says, I don't think I could ever forgive these people if anything happens to her.

"Hate just leads to more hate. We've got to break the cycle — it's the only way." She wipes her nose on her arm. "Look at these soldiers, for God's sake! They were kids once."

I turn to the soldier opposite and he gazes right through me like I don't even exist. The goose bumps on my arms tell me Izzy's right. He can't be more than fifteen. I shake the thought out of my head: Whatever they are now, it's not kids. Nowhere near. They are more like zombies.

Ash sucks a breath in through clenched teeth. "Iz, you're not going to die, all right? But I can't promise about him. He was going to kill you."

"Don't worry," I say, just to make her feel better, "I'll stand in the way if Ash tries anything."

Iz rewards me with a weak smile. "Thanks, Rio."

Her words, and that smile, release some of the tension that's been pounding in my head. She doesn't blame me for what happened, even though I blame myself. I smile back. "How much insulin do you have left?"

Iz holds up three fingers. Her hands are still shaking. "Enough to last till tomorrow morning. At a push."

"Three? How come —" But I remember, as I'm asking the question, that she used six on the tug, and the vial she's just used makes seven. Izzy looks away.

Ash's face is lined with worry. Things are bad. *Really* bad, and we're totally helpless.

I watch the landscape open up, and nerves cramp my insides as we get farther and farther from the sea. The terrain is lush and green, especially to the right, where I catch glimpses of a wide, muddy river. Tall palm trees shoot up way higher than the others, and the ground beneath them is tangled with bushes and tall brown grasses. We seem to be following a dirt track at not much faster than walking pace, because of the huge potholes and weatherworn ruts in it. Every jerk and bone-jarring drop goes right through us, and the whole thing is made even more uncomfortable by the fact that there is nothing to hold on to.

Izzy smiles wryly at some secret thought. When I give her a *What?* look she tells me, "You got my horoscope right, didn't you?"

"Did I?"

"You predicted a long, uncomfortable journey . . ."

When I remember the rest of my words — *ending in an encounter with a wild animal . . . death of you* — I say firmly, "I still don't believe in that crap."

We fall silent and watch the bush pass by. I can see the flatbed bumping along in front of us with Jen, Marcus, and Charis in it. Tall steel hoops on the back, which must have once held some kind of canvas cover in place, break branches and shower them with leaves. Even though our SUV is lower, we often have to veer away from the deep tread left by the truck, and sometimes our guards are surprised by low branches that swing over the cab at them. There's even a snake hanging from one, and it panics the boys. In the confusion Ash looks like he might try something, but he thinks twice about it when the LRA kid next to me gets unnerved and shouts at him, waving his machine gun violently in his face. Will the jolting ride set it off? I wonder. The thought of what might happen at any moment is terrifying. I look away, trying not to think.

On our way we pass a small troop of potbellied baboons that look over their shoulders at us. A large male and his mate bark loudly, and two babies scurry to jump onto the backs of their mother, their tiny fists clinging to tufts of yellow-brown fur. The pair sit and watch us warily for a moment, but when they decide that we are not a threat, they wander off lazily in single file, their pink backsides disappearing into the bush.

Izzy is watching the baboons, too, and she smiles when one of the babies stands on its mother's back to watch us, loses its balance, and falls off.

"Do you think we'll see a lion?" I ask her.

"I hope so," she whispers.

None of us can talk for some time after that. I'm too worried I'll say something else that will remind her she doesn't have long unless something changes. Ash just sits there being moody. There is one thing that I need to know, though. I keep getting glimpses of the beaded braids and stiff back of the rebel leader. He gives me the creeps.

"Who is this Mwemba guy anyway?" I ask Ash in a low voice. "You've all heard of him before?"

He shoots me a look and answers my question reluctantly. "The Americans, us, and half of Africa are after these guys. The Lord's Resistance Army began in Uganda. They said they wanted to rule the country according to the biblical Ten Commandments, but they've broken every one. They torture and mutilate innocent people, abduct children. When they can, they take kids and turn them into soldiers — or slaves for the leadership . . ." One of the kids looks at Ash and I wonder if he understands English. Ash watches the kid and indicates with a tilt of his head. "If our guard here even *thought* about leaving, he'd have to risk losing a few limbs, having his nose or ears cut off, or — if he's lucky — being killed. Am I right?"

The boy looks away.

"Some of them get to like the lifestyle, though. Their leader is a nasty piece of work — part Catholic, part witch doctor. A guy called Joseph Kony. Moses Mwemba is Kony's second-in-command. His nickname is Shetani."

One of the LRA kids smirks at Ash. His face is deadly and his voice flat when he says to the other soldiers, *"Hii mvulana nyeupe anadhani yeye anajua kila kitu."*[6]

They all laugh. Like with Mwemba, the rhythms are so infectious I almost feel I should understand what's being said.

---

6. This white boy thinks he knows everything.

When he sees my face, the kid who spoke points at Ash. "White boy — think he knows *everything*."

When they've finished their little joke, I ask Ash, "And what does *Shetani* mean, exactly?"

It's a while before he replies. "You really want to know?"

I nod.

"It's Swahili for 'Satan.'"

12

SOON THE GROUND FLATTENS OUT AND OUR CONvoy gets some speed up. I feel like I've been dropped into a tin can and some giant hand has decided to pick it up and shake it. As I feared, one of the boy soldiers riding on the tailgate almost loses his balance, and his gun swings wildly and goes off with an angry rattle. His friends laugh at him, but I'm terrified until he manages to steady himself. My shoulder blades are so badly bruised they're too tender to lean against the side any longer, and I find myself having to balance against every wrenching impact with my stomach muscles. If I ever get out of this, I'll have abs like iron.

After several exhausting hours, the trees start to thin out and are gradually replaced by lower ones with much flatter tops, spaced out between wide areas of tall, dry grass. Coughed up from the wheels, clouds of dust and grit shower us constantly now, and everywhere looks like typical African safari country, all flat grasslands and scrubby bush. I can actually *taste* the place, crunch it between my teeth. Here, the branches of the few trees strong enough to survive are all twiggy and twisted, and it looks like they are holding all their leaves up as high as they can get them. It's not long before I get why. I can spot small groups of giraffe gliding between the branches, their long necks swaying back and forth, stopping from time to time to pull at great clumps of leaves. If I wasn't being kidnapped, the whole thing would be *so* cool, but the reality is that the farther we get from the sea, the more my stomach knots and twists.

Ash is still watching everything keenly, like he's making a mental note of every rock and bush. It must be the soldier in him — looking for opportunities — but I'm thinking that, if his thoughts are as obvious to the LRA kids as they are to me, then we have no chance. Every now and again his eyes meet mine, and they are heavy with disappointment. I wonder if I will ever find out what he was about to say when we swam with the shark. I long to be back in my bunk on the *Spirit of Freedom*, listening to Ash sing, his voice floating over me. When I find my thoughts drifting to the curve of his neck, I shake my head clear. Better to focus on other things.

I notice that the tall palms don't seem to care where they

grow. They look down on the shorter giraffe-bait trees like they can't believe how stupid they are. Sometimes we pass enormous, solitary baobabs, so wide and twisted that they look like they must have been planted when God was a kid. Once or twice, when the track turns to the right, I manage to get a glimpse of the others in the back of the truck, or at least of Jen and Charis. It looks like Marcus is lying across their legs and they are trying to shield his vulnerable skin from the boiling sunlight. Jen's face is gray.

I don't know exactly how many hours pass like this, but our kidnappers seem to have no intention of stopping for a break. The faces of the boy soldiers are watchful, and they constantly scan the sky. If you ask me, it's because they think that, sooner or later, someone back home is going to put two and two together and come looking for us. I'm hit with a wave of panic. Mum probably thinks I'm dead right now! She'll be in pieces.

To take my mind off Mum I try to figure out which way they are taking us. Once we got clear of the thick vegetation near the coast, the land flattened out and we traveled quickly. Judging by the way the sun eventually begins to lower and set ahead of the lead vehicle, it's got to be west — inland. My heart plummets. Every hour takes us farther from the ocean, farther from the life I know.

It's dusk when we finally come to a halt in a cloud of dirt and the engines fall silent. My whole body feels like it's never going to stop vibrating and, as I allow myself to collapse back against the side of the truck, my muscles decide they can de-stress and start to throb angrily. We must be at least a hundred miles from the beach by now, maybe a hundred and fifty. In the sudden silence, I long for a clean ocean breeze and for an endless expanse of cool turquoise waters. Everything is covered in gray dust here, and is brown and withered by the relentless sun. After just a day under its glare, the skin on my face is taut and dry. I can only imagine what Marcus must be feeling right now.

The doors to the vehicles click open and thud as the cabs empty. Metal springs creak and shudder under the weight of the soldiers jumping off. While it cools down, the Toyota makes *tink tink tink* noises and smells like burning rubber. The metallic noise reminds me of the marina at home in Weymouth and the sound of the yachts in Cape Town. My chest tightens with painful longing.

While the boy whose gun went off chatters with another of our guards, I search for something familiar to calm the panic rising in me, but everywhere I look the horizon is identical. Endless grassland and prehistoric trees are framed against a burning sky, and above my head to the east, stars are begin-ning to shine through the darkest bits as if the sun is leaving a trail of sparkling crimson, gold, and blue dust for us to fol-low before it sets in its ocean of fire.

Moses Mwemba and the Sangoma order their soldiers into positions beneath a small group of trees. All around us, crick-ets trill at stadium-gig volume. The soldiers are on edge, but their leaders seem really confident considering we're pretty exposed out here. I'm guessing it's because they think there's no way anyone would look for us in Tanzania. If Jen's Mayday was heard, which I doubt, everyone will think we're with Somali pirates.

Our LRA guards shove us off our vehicle and take us in single file to sit under a wide tree. I'm sandwiched between Izzy and Ash. We lean back on our elbows almost simultaneously, grateful to be able to stretch our legs. Izzy fiddles awkwardly with her syringe and somehow manages another injection with her hands tied. It takes her a while to puncture her skin, and she winces with the pain. The needle must be getting blunter. When she has finished, Iz pockets the syringe and then holds up a finger, looking right through me with wide black pupils.

One left.

Ash looks like he's about to say something to me, but before he can, a group of soldiers arrive, speaking Swahili in short, staccato bursts, pushing the others along. Charis and Jen drop next to Izzy, while Marcus lowers himself to the ground by Ash in the shadiest spot he can find. His face is red and sore.

"Marcus is in a bad way." Charis — stating the obvious.

If you ask me, Jen doesn't look too good, either. She is limping badly when she arrives, almost hopping. The skin on her leg has gone gray and is crusted with yellow pus.

Ash inches over and nudges her gently. "You okay? How's the burn?"

She smiles at him and leans her head onto his shoulder. "How weird is this?"

"What do you mean?"

"You — having to look after me."

I have to turn my back on them. The letter thing seems pathetic right now, with things the way they are, but I'm still stung. I try to swallow the hurt and focus on Marcus. Charis is fussing over him.

When Marcus speaks, his voice is muffled, strained, but still tinted with humor. "Look, you mad Welsh woman. Stop worrying. Pretty soon my lips will be so tight I won't be able to ask you to bugger off, so take the hint now — okay?"

I still can't look at Ash and Jen, so I ask Charis quietly, "How bad is he? Is it sunburn?"

She shakes her head. "A bit. His biggest problem is that he can't sweat like we can through his skin grafts. They're drying out and he's overheating."

"I've been through worse." Marcus lifts his head so he can see me around Ash's chest. "Your cooking, for instance."

"Ha-ha," I attempt a laugh. I love his spirit. The poor guy's going through hell.

"I just can't believe we've been kidnapped by a bunch of kids," Marcus chunters on. "It's going to annoy the hell out of me if they just run around aimlessly like noobs, shooting at anything that moves."

Curiosity gets the better of me, and I ask out loud what I've been wondering ever since we set sail from Cape Town. "How did it happen? You and Ash, I mean. I know Iz was the helicopter crash, and Charis was searching for an IED, but what about you two?"

Marcus doesn't answer. My question seems to knock the life out of him. He looks at Ash.

It's a while before Ash speaks, and he doesn't look at me. He turns so that he can see Marcus. "We were on patrol in Nad Ali. Our first week — eh, Marky? What were the chances?" His voice is husky.

Marcus laughs. "Judging by our lives to date? All I'll say is, we should seriously consider playing the lottery."

"Our driver, Ed, was smoking while he was on duty. It was against the rules, but nobody said anything, because it's rough out there and people find ways to cope. Marky and I didn't really care — in that situation, *we* were the newbies. That's not the way you fit in, is it? To betray your friends?" Ash's eyes flick at me.

My cheeks flush with heat and I bite my tongue so that I don't say anything I might regret.

"Ed always kept a roll-up behind his ear. Anyway, as we were approaching this village, we went over a bump. He dropped his cigarette and took his eyes off the road — off everything — to look for it. He didn't see an insurgent step out of a house carrying a rocket launcher, didn't take evasive action. Next thing I know, I'm coming to in a ditch in the middle of a gun battle, it's raining red-hot metal, and Marcus is burning like the Olympic torch."

"Just my way of attracting attention," Marcus jokes grimly. "Bloody worked, too."

It's a miracle that Ash isn't completely screwed up. I can imagine what that must have felt like now — the fear, thinking you are going to die. I look at Jen, but her face is hard and drained of emotion. She must have heard this story a hundred times.

"When they told me something had happened to him, I threw up," she says to me. "I didn't know what to expect."

I'm not sure Ash even hears her. His voice sounds like it is leaking out of some parallel universe. "For some reason I couldn't stand up, so I crawled over and managed to drag Marcus away from the wreck and put him out with my jacket. The effort took it out of me, though — I started seeing black spots, and that's when I noticed the trail of blood I'd left. I didn't think it was possible for anyone to bleed so much and stay conscious."

Nobody speaks for a while.

I'm glad I finally plucked up the courage to ask, though. A fire for life burns in Ash, and it's contagious. After surviving that, it will take more than a few madmen to put it out. If anyone can help us get through this, it's going to be him.

After a while Izzy tells me, "We all met at Headley Court Hospital, in rehab. Nothing builds a team like months of pain and a few slave-driving Ministry of Defense physiotherapists."

Jen stares at the ground, pulling up her knees and resting her forehead on them. Her voice is muffled. "I'm glad you all got so much out of it."

None of us speaks for a while after that. Marcus groans a few times; even though he makes a joke of it, he's really suffering. Most of the LRA soldiers are getting something to drink. Mwemba barks at one of them, who grabs a jerrican, walks over, and throws it at us. It lands with a heavy thud by Ash's legs, half buried in the dirt. One of the three guards left to watch us comes over and unties me, Charis, and Izzy. It feels so good I almost thank him.

He points his gun at the can and then at the guys. "Give it to them," he grunts at us. The barrel of the gun is shaking.

Izzy ignores the casual sexism, unscrews the lid, and looks inside. "It's water, thank God!"

Our guards watch, shaking their heads as Charis and I use half of it to douse Marcus's face and T-shirt. The girl is with them. She looks up. I've decided I'm going to call her the Empty Child from now on. Her big dark eyes and motion-less face are disturbing because they make me feel that when she looks at me, I don't exist. She might as well be wearing a mask like that horrible kid in *Doctor Who*. That thing gave me the shudders, and she's having the same effect. She is feeding the little boy from one of our foil pouches, and the kid has brown goo all over his face and hands. When the girl stops to watch us he demands more, but even he stops and chuckles as he watches us throw our water over Marcus.

Mwemba's not happy that the Empty Child has been help-ing the boy to eat. He yells at her when he walks past and knocks the pouch from her hands. When he has gone she picks it up and carries on. Her attitude makes me smile, but I get nothing back.

The tension falls from Marcus's shoulders as soon as he begins to feel the cooling effect of the water. "Sweet Jesus, thank you, thank you, thank you. If we ever get out of this, you're both invited to a return shower at my place, man. A bring-a-towel party — or you could both forget the towel. It's up to you."

Any other time I'd let him know what I think of his offer. Right now we both just laugh.

"You're such a tart, Marky," Charis says. When she sees that the Empty Child is now standing to get a better look at us, her face darkens. "What are *you* looking at?"

When the girl doesn't move, I ask her, "Do you even have a name?"

Nothing.

While Charis attempts to stare her out, I point at my chest. "I'm Rio."

The girl doesn't blink. She just rearranges the machete in her belt and walks off.

"Charming," Charis mutters. "Seriously, Rio. I don't know why you're even trying."

I get back to cupping water in my hands so that Izzy can wash the bits of her leg that are punctured by her frame, and what's left I pour over Jen's leg to soothe her weeping yellow burn. Flies are everywhere, attracted by the smell of sweat and decay. The flesh around Jen's burn is red and angry. I'm no expert, but even I can tell that something about it doesn't look right. She dabs gingerly at it with a strip of material she's torn from her pink tank top, and when she has finished she throws it into the grass, hoping it will draw some of the insects away. Finally we pass what's left of the water around to drink. It is metallic and oily, but it's like a taste of heaven, and we even manage to save a little to cool Marcus off with later.

When we've finished with the water, our guards tie us up again. My wrists are so tender now that I have to bite my lip when the ropes go back on, but at least they're tying our hands in front. Just us girls, that is. They leave poor Marcus and Ash trussed up like turkeys. The insects seem to multiply as the sky begins to darken. Poor Jen is being plagued by them. I'm still wondering about how to keep her leg free from infection when I notice a green plastic box in the cab of the jeep. I get to my feet and start toward it, willing my legs to work despite the guns that swing in my direction.

Ash jumps up. "Rio! For God's sake!"

I can't bear it. He thinks I'm a liability.

The three LRA guards scramble to their feet and point their guns at me, too. The Sangoma is squatting by the side door of the jeep, rattling his pouch of bones and throwing them on the floor. Every now and again he moans softly and tugs at the feather in his bandana. I notice that Mwemba throws him a scornful glance while he is arranging his defenses for the night. So, the LRA leader doesn't approve of the magic. What on earth keeps these two together? As if he senses that I'm watching, the Sangoma turns to look at me, and his lips part in a sneering smile.

"In there!" I shout at him. "Is that a first aid kit?"

He reaches in through the open window and pulls the green box out. Without answering, he spits on it and throws it over to our guards, watching as one of them picks it up and brings it to me. With a last dark glance in my direction the Sangoma returns to his pile of old brown bones. He prods at them with his finger, singing in a low monotone under his breath.

I shake the plastic box at Ash. "No need to worry — see?"

Ash ignores my rebuke. "You comfortable?" he asks Jen. "You can lean against me if you want. Try to get some sleep."

Jen's sitting there with her head back. She manages to shake her head, but she's clearly suffering.

There's something inside the first aid box, but it's too light to be anything much. As I'm walking back to sit with Jen I flip the plastic catches and take a look, balancing the box on top of my bound hands. It turns out to be an adhesive dressing that will only cover part of her burn, but it's better than nothing.

"What do you think?"

She actually smiles at me. "I think that's going to hurt like hell when it comes off."

"Your choice," I say, watching her trying to fend a few annoyingly persistent flies off her leg.

"Give it to me."

I watch while she opens it with her teeth and gingerly puts it on.

"I've been thinking" — Jen's voice is strained as she smoothes the dressing into place — "about Marcus."

"Oh?"

"I saw a few aloe plants on the way here. They're used to make aloe vera for skin creams and such."

"Yeah, but we've got no way of making —"

"Don't need to," Jen interrupts. "If we can get some leaves and split them, we can use the gel inside like a skin cream. It's got to be better than nothing."

"What do they look like?"

"Like a greeny-purple cactus. Thick, pointed leaves, quite long."

"I've seen those!" I look around and see nothing but brown grass.

"They tend to grow in rocky places," Izzy adds.

"Guys!" It's Ash, whispering.

Our guards are distracted. They're talking together in low voices about whatever it is the Sangoma is doing with his bones. He has started a deeper chant now, and the eerie drone of his voice carries surprisingly far.

"We need a plan," Ash continues. "They're obviously taking us somewhere nobody will *ever* find us, and if we don't make a move soon, then we might as well be dead."

Marcus sits up. "We're all ears. Or at least I will be soon, if my face shrivels up any more."

Ash and Marcus are scaring me. "What about all the guns?"

"Don't worry about that now. All we need is to wait for an opportunity, for them to drop their guard. Charis, Rio's knife is in the side of my sneaker. If you fiddle with my prosthesis, like you're adjusting it, you could slip it out."

"I'm closer than she is," I croak. This whole *Rio is a liability* thing is getting on my nerves now.

Jen shoots me a look. "Keep your voice down!"

Unbelievable! She's jealous about me fishing a knife out of his shoe.

"Look," Ash sighs. "I don't care who. Just be quick."

Looking back nervously at the guards, I shuffle closer and slip my fingers down the side of his shoe until I feel the cold metal blade. "Got it."

When his eyes meet mine I find myself looking away. We haven't been this close — face-to-face — since the swim. The warmth that was in his eyes then, the question that hung between us, seems like a distant memory. I pull the paring knife out between my thumb and forefinger. Ash clears his throat, slides his cheek past mine, and I can barely hear his voice in my ear when he says, "Thanks . . ."

I don't want to, but I pull away. I take a quick look at Jen. She's watching us with a furrowed brow. "Now what?"

"I need you to cut through the ropes, Rio — mine and Marky's." He twists. The guys still have their hands tied behind their backs. "Just make sure you make it look like we're still tied up . . ."

Charis slides over to us like she's just thought of something and hisses, "No, wait!"

We're both dumbstruck.

She reads the question on my face and tells me, "It's too dangerous. They'll find out —"

"There's no time for this," Ash mutters angrily. "Go for it, Rio."

Charis holds my hand. "Trust me. You don't need to use the knife." She holds her bound arms out meaningfully for us both to see, making her prosthetic fingers purr open and shut, open and shut. When they stop she's managed to make them give the finger and she's grinning like the Cheshire cat.

We all laugh when we understand what she's trying to tell us. We're almost hysterical and have to choke it back before it gets out of hand — and gets the attention of the guards. I slip the knife under my waistband, reluctant to give up on it just yet. We allow ourselves to relax and enjoy our moment of triumph. None of the soldiers has realized that even when they tie her wrists together, Charis can just slip her arm off.

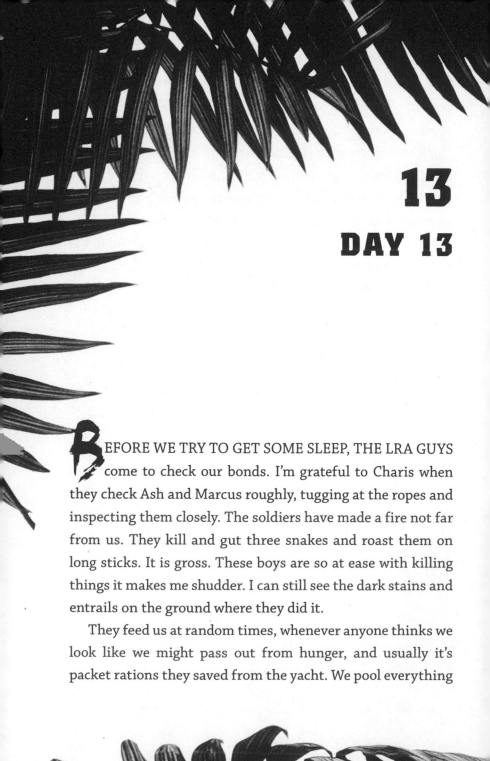

13

DAY 13

BEFORE WE TRY TO GET SOME SLEEP, THE LRA GUYS come to check our bonds. I'm grateful to Charis when they check Ash and Marcus roughly, tugging at the ropes and inspecting them closely. The soldiers have made a fire not far from us. They kill and gut three snakes and roast them on long sticks. It is gross. These boys are so at ease with killing things it makes me shudder. I can still see the dark stains and entrails on the ground where they did it.

They feed us at random times, whenever anyone thinks we look like we might pass out from hunger, and usually it's packet rations they saved from the yacht. We pool everything they give us and split it up. Tonight's meal consisted of peanuts and raisins, cold spaghetti Bolognese, and rich butter cookies. There is hardly anything left of our rations now.

The LRA boys speak in hushed tones, constantly checking to see if Mwemba will shout at them to shut up. They seem to be nervous about the gathering dark. I wonder if there's some settlement nearby and they're afraid that they'll be spotted. Then distant howls and barks echo across the grasslands as the night hunters emerge from their dens. So *that's* why the soldiers are nervous. The sounds send a shiver down my spine. Who knows what wildlife is out here?

Ash is leaning back against our tree and Jen has managed to fall asleep on his shoulder. He smiles at me for the briefest moment, and his eyes glint in the flickering yellow light. My eyes sting so badly that I have to turn away until I can control my emotions. It's the first time he's smiled that way since everything went mad. The saddest thing is that I think he only smiled because he forgot to be angry with me.

Sleep is almost impossible. My wrists are sore, the ground is hard and lumpy, and I'm so high on adrenaline that my heart feels like some huge, fluttering moth trapped behind my rib cage. Ash's guitar twangs in the shadows on the other side of the fire when one of the LRA soldiers attempts to tune it and snaps a string. Soon after, he strums a chord anyway, and several of them start to sing quietly in really close harmony. The bass line is strained because they are all so young, but it is a painfully beautiful sound, full of rise and fall and lines that end in long, mournful notes. Every now and again one of the kids clicks with his tongue or trills. Ash bangs the back of his head against the tree we're leaning on and looks away. When he looks back again he starts to hum a rebellious counter-melody under his breath, and I get goose bumps. As I listen, I imagine Ash is singing for me, and his voice is the promise of another world that is too far away for me to reach.

A weird longing crushes my chest, so I turn my attention to our captors. The Empty Child and the toddler always seem to be separate from the others. Even now, she is sitting on her own some way from the fire and the main group of LRA fighters, shrouded in darkness. The toddler is sleeping in a ball with his head on her thigh. If ever one of the LRA soldiers needs to pass by, they give the Empty Child a wide berth, as if she's going to jump up and pounce on them the minute they drop their guard. Even Mwemba seems careful around her. I wonder why.

"That's one disturbed kid," Ash whispers, and I notice that he's stopped humming and is looking at me. I wonder how long he's been doing that. "She can't be any more than — what — fourteen?"

"I know. I've been trying to figure her out ever since the beach," I reply. "There's something different about that one. I call her the Empty Child."

Ash shakes his head and gives me a wry smile. "Like in that episode of *Doctor Who*?"

I nod.

"The kid in the gas mask, I like it. You sure it's a girl?"

"Pretty sure."

"I'll take your word for it." He watches her for a while. "I think she may have some hold over Mwemba."

"What makes you think that? She won't even look at him."

"The baby. There's no way a guy like Mwemba would let that toddler live. He's too much of a liability — slows them down — another mouth to feed. It just doesn't make sense. She's *way* too young to have a baby that age, so I reckon they found him. Or they're going to train him when he grows up."

Like some kind of bizarre pet? I shudder. "Poor kid. You really think so?"

Jen mutters, "Did you see what that little brat was doing with the dead guy on the beach?"

She's awake, then.

"I know," Ash says grimly.

Jen takes over our conversation. "If you ask me, Mwemba has the same eyes as her — only his have more life in them."

"Or death," I mutter.

Ash shrugs. "The other LRA guys resent the kid — I've seen a couple of them kick the boy when the girl's back was turned."

A chill rattles through me. It's hard not to hate these sour-faced boy soldiers sometimes. I have to keep reminding myself how young they all are. "Ash?"

"Yeah?"

"Do you think they'll let us go — you know, when they've got whatever it is they want?"

He lets his head fall back against the tree again and closes his eyes. "We're not sticking around long enough to find out."

His words aren't very comforting. And he didn't answer my question. Somehow I don't think escaping is going to be that easy.

Some sixth sense makes the girl turn her head toward us, and the firelight flickers in her dead eyes. We clam up. She pulls her machine gun closer to her leg and turns to watch the fire, letting out three loud, barking noises. It's like some kind of signal to the other child soldiers, because they answer her with screams and shrieks that send shivers down my neck. When it dies down one sound remains, like a fading trickle of water: the toddler's gurgling laugh.

I'm woken at dawn by the drone of the Sangoma's voice, chanting in the bushes somewhere. Through a low mist, I see a shadow dancing on the other side of the blackened circle, which is all that remains of the fire. I sit up and stare. At first it doesn't look human, but then I decide it could be the girl with the toddler on her hip. The shadow dance seems to go on for ages, but by the time the sun has burned off the mist whoever it was has gone. All that is left are a few scuffed scratch marks in the dust, and the girl is back with Mwemba.

Mwemba is checking his reflection in the sideview mirror of the Toyota. He straightens his collar and smooths the creases out of his cargo pants. When he's satisfied, he checks his pistol closely and blows dust off it.

They get us moving after a breakfast of yet another slimy, tepid spaghetti Bolognese from our emergency rations. After she has eaten, Iz injects the last of her insulin and throws the syringe away. She stands up as if she's seizing control of her life, and says to the nearest kid with a gun, "Right. Let's get this show on the road." Like she has some say in the matter.

I'm insanely worried about her, but I feel so proud. She's got this indestructible spirit that makes you feel like there could still be hope. Maybe she's right.

We're loaded onto the same vehicles as yesterday, and our kidnappers follow a rough track that climbs slowly through the grasslands for hour after tedious hour. I wonder if we are leaving the plains. Midmorning, a herd of buffalo raise their heads and shake their coat-hanger horns at us, unafraid. Like yesterday, I make sure that I watch the sun as we travel, constantly checking its position. I'm desperate to work out where they are taking us. The heat is unbearable again, and soon we are all sweating like pigs. My top is drenched and there is no wind to cool it. It makes me worry about how Marcus must be feeling, but we are powerless to help him. I know Charis and Jen will be doing whatever they can — I just hope it's enough.

As the day wears on, the sun peaks above our heads and begins to lower to our left, which means that we are heading northwest now. White vapor trails hang tantalizingly in the sky far above us. I imagine the cool, air-conditioned airplane cabin up there, meals on trays and tiny cans of Coke dripping with condensation. A couple of times we even glimpse people walking in the distance, but when they see the guns and uniforms they run.

It must be well after three in the afternoon when the track suddenly drops into a wide brown river valley. If I'm right about our direction this could be the Katuma River, and that would mean we've come nearly all the way across Tanzania. It's a crazy guess based on a picture I once saw in a magazine, but it makes me feel like I know something important, something that might help us.

Izzy and I are thrown helplessly into the legs of one of our guards when the Toyota dips suddenly. I'm drenched by a surging wall of water that breaks over the wheel arch. Soon it's sloshing around us, inches deep.

The Sangoma guns the Toyota through the river way too fast. God knows what he's thinking. My T-shirt sticks to my back and it feels *disgusting*, like things are wriggling under it. *Please, God — let it just be water.* All I can do is twist and tug at it, but I have to give up in the end. Just as we can see the opposite bank, the flatbed truck in front of us makes this horrible choking, cracking noise, lurches, and comes to a stop about halfway out. The Sangoma tries to find a way around the truck and gets the Toyota stuck in even deeper water. It floods in waves over the hood, and steam hisses out from the sides in a white cloud. The gears crash and we're drenched again in muddy spray from the wildly spinning wheels. We lurch backward and then forward. The Sangoma crashes the gears again and again until the engine splutters and dies with a shudder that rattles through every rivet. When he turns the key now, there's just a dull, metallic click. After a few tries, he gives up and hammers at the horn in frustration. It doesn't make a sound.

Doors open on all the vehicles, and the LRA soldiers wade around to force us off at gunpoint into the water. Thankfully they untie us first so we can use our arms for balance. When Ash tries to rub his wrists a little too eagerly, the boy with the split lip barks at him and hits his forearms apart with the barrel of his gun.

Ash holds his hands up and yells in his face, "Take it easy!"

Split-Lip doesn't take it easy. He yells back, spraying spit, and lets off five or six shots into the water by Ash's legs. Scared witless, I jump down and wade over to Ash, pulling him back by his arm. I couldn't bear it if they shot him.

The rest of the LRA kids keep scanning the water for the slightest movement. It's a free-for-all, with the young soldiers pushing and shoving each other to get to the safety of dry ground. Muddy water comes up to my waist and I can't see anything in it. The last time I was in water it was clear as crystal and magical. This is hell. I'm trying not to panic about crocodiles or snakes — all I want is to get out. The dirt and parasites in this warm soup will have a field day with Jen's burn and Izzy's leg pins.

Ash and I help to get Izzy out of the Toyota, and with one arm under her thigh and the other behind her back, we manage to hold her high enough to keep her leg out of the water. Parts of the leg frame go right through her skin, so God knows what might happen if those bits get infected. By the flatbed, Charis and Marcus have got Jen between them. We all start wading to the bank.

Mwemba shoves past me, yelling at the driver of the lead truck, who is scrambling in panic out of his cab. The boy is terrified, especially when Mwemba gets there and snatches his gun away. He yells some more and then, to everyone's relief, he just shoots at the empty cab, shattering the windshield and the mirrors, puncturing the doors. There's confusion at the back of the truck because the others are still trying to get off and there are so many. Several soldiers throw themselves over the sides and into the water.

The Empty Child wades behind me, keeping her gun above water. Her little boy has his arms wrapped around her neck and is hanging there with his face by her ear.

"Ow!" I stub my toes on a rock and have to let go of Iz.

"You okay?" Ash grunts, holding her up on his own.

I nod, and they carry on ahead while I wait for the pain to subside enough to start walking again. The Empty Child jabs me in the shoulder with her gun and I push it away. "I'm coming. You don't need to keep pointing that thing at me."

The girl's face doesn't move, so I turn and we wade on side by side in knee-deep water. As soon as the level drops to our calves there is a *plop!* behind me. The toddler squeals excitedly and races past, splashing as he goes. Ahead, Ash is already helping Izzy up the riverbank. It is steep and crumbly where the water has worn away great chunks of the sunbaked dirt into a small cliff. She has her arms wrapped around his neck and somehow he's managed to get her onto his back now. He's struggling, though, and walking really awkwardly, like he can't bend his knees. Just as they get to the top, he loses his grip and they both fall backward. Izzy has no choice but to let go and land awkwardly beside him. She slips back down the bank and sinks knee-deep in mud.

Suddenly there is panic in the deeper water behind us. A couple of straggling soldiers fire their guns at something, and the filthy water turns red. The girl is the only one who doesn't seem totally fazed. She just stands knee-deep in the river, scanning the surface with her gun. Everything goes quiet for a second or two, and then my heart leaps into my throat as a gigantic brown-and-gray hippo rises on a massive surge of muddy water. Its bristly mouth is gaping wide, and it is bellowing in pain. Blood flows down its shoulder and its eyes are wide and white. It is as mad as hell, enraged by the bullets. Before the soldiers nearest to it have time to react, it charges at them, closing its mouth on the nearest one, cutting short his scream with a bloodcurdling crunch. It shakes its head, and the body spins and floats away facedown in a spreading, muddy red halo. The others scatter. Everyone scrambles in panic up the bank like fleeing wildebeests.

I grab the Empty Child by her sleeve. "Where did your kid go?"

I don't know why I'm expecting any answer. Maybe it's because, for the first time, some human emotion is written on her face. It's fear. She still doesn't answer. She's frantically scanning the chaos for him.

I catch a glimpse of the toddler first, beyond a group of panicked boy soldiers. He's ducking under the front wheel arch on the near side of the truck, trying to see around the tire. Inexplicably he turns and yells.

The enraged hippo's ears flick forward and its head swings around.

There's no time to think. I'm already running toward the toddler when it charges.

The girl must think I'm making a run for it. Her machine gun clatters behind me, whipping up a line of spray, but I ignore the bullets and run like hell at the kid, my legs slowed by the treacherous pull of the river. I'm just thinking I'll never make it when a roll of water gives me an unexpected boost. Mwemba's pistol shots crack over my head from the riverbank again and again, and just when I feel my arms close around the child's warm belly and yank him away from the truck, something hard hammers into my legs like a freight train. I'm thrown forward, closing my eyes and pulling the boy into a ball against my chest, expecting to die.

14

THE KID SCREAMS ANGRILY. HE KICKS AND STRUGgles in my arms but I'm not letting go. For a second everything is quiet. I can actually feel the hippo's dying breath on the back of my knees. It lets out a deep, rumbling gurgle, and water swirls around my legs. When I open my eyes I find out why the hippo was so mad. There's a calf trapped under the truck. It bleats at me weakly. The axle of the truck is snapped and the whole weight of the vehicle is resting on the poor thing's back. There's no way it will live.

My eyes fill with tears and I whisper, "I'm sorry . . ."

When I look over my shoulder, its mother's head is just by my leg, riddled with bullets. Her enormous mouth is wide

open and a ragged, bloodstained section of camo jacket is impaled on one of her brown teeth.

The Empty Child arrives and yanks the kid from my arms, shaking and prodding him to make sure he still has all his bits. She slaps his leg and throws him up onto the bank, where he collapses in a heap and bawls his head off.

"You're welcome," I mutter at her.

Somehow the girl hears me. She tilts her head, a movement so slight I don't think anyone else will have noticed, but I do. In some weird way she's thanking me.

By the time I clamber up, the toddler has subsided into gasping sobs and he follows my every move with a pair of watery brown, accusing eyes. I make my way through a crowd of agitated teen soldiers, shaking so badly I can barely walk. One of them grabs my arm, shakes me, and shouts at me, putting his gun right in my face before literally dragging me back to the others. Mwemba is still screaming at his men as they duck and dodge past him to get to safety. He strides over to the far side of the truck. There is a single pistol shot and the pathetic bleating of the hippo calf stops.

Marcus throws his arm around my shoulder when I reach him. "Did you know how close that momma hippo was . . . ?"

I nod, unable to reply.

"I thought you were done for," Charis mumbles, looking away for a moment.

Even Jen is close to tears. We have a group hug with Ash and Izzy until our guards separate us and tie the guys' arms behind their backs. Thankfully they bind us girls in front again.

"Rio — you were amazing," Ash tells me, his eyes shining.

I want him to look at me like that forever, but it's not going to happen. He turns and walks awkwardly alongside Izzy. Fifty yards or so from the riverbank we are left beneath a few twisted trees, guarded by a small party of agitated, squabbling LRA fighters who stand behind us and rattle their weapons. Split-Lip seems to be in charge, but he's got his work cut out. The guerrilla boys are totally freaked by what has just happened, and I can see why. Mwemba is stiff with rage, shoving his panicking soldiers back into the river, gesticulating at the two salvageable trucks. He waves his pistol and rants at the Sangoma, who is waiting by the Toyota. The witch doctor beats the kids up some more when they get to him.

"Those kids aren't soldiers," Marcus mutters, "they're a joke. And there's no way those trucks are going anywhere."

I sit down between him and Ash.

Ash asks, "Iz, are you all right? I'm so sorry I dropped you. I think my batteries gave up — either that or the water has shorted them."

Izzy tries to clean the mud away from her leg with spit. "You couldn't help it."

Remembering those charging sessions I saw on the boat, I wonder, "What do the batteries do?"

"These legs have powered ankle joints," Ash explains, kicking them off angrily. "Stupid pile of crap."

"Be careful! You still need them." I pull them closer and straighten them up unnecessarily.

"Yeah, I do, don't I? Great observation, Rio. I need them and they're useless." He rubs one of his stumps against the other leg and sighs loudly. "Without the batteries the ankle joints will be too stiff. My stumps are killing me already. I can't go much farther on them."

"You want me to massage your legs for you?" I really want to help him and it's all I can think of.

He gives me a *you must be kidding* look, but when he registers my worry he shakes his head, frustrated.

"We need you to be strong," I whisper.

Ash falls back on his elbows. He takes a breath and anger flashes across his face. "And how would you like me to do that, Rio? I'm missing half my freaking legs! I need batteries, for God's sake." He picks one up and hurls it at our huddled group of guards. They dodge it and Split-Lip picks it up, making some joke about it that makes the other boys laugh.

Ash glares at them and his face darkens even more. His outburst leaves me feeling winded and confused. I have to tell myself it's just the frustration — not *me* — but I'm not sure I believe it.

The toddler runs over, screaming, and tries to put the other of Ash's prosthetic legs over his stumpy little foot. He steadies himself by placing a hot grubby hand on my knee. When the Empty Child arrives the toddler points at the metal leg and drags it to her. She makes him drop it, and he runs to me for comfort. The girl chases after him and pulls him off me roughly and shakes him until he stands still. She is about to leave until I wave her back.

I kick at the useless prosthesis with my foot. "Broken — understand?" Ash's blades should still work, though. Maybe I can get the girl to find them.

She lifts the boy by one arm and sits him on the same hip as her machine gun, still dead-eyed. He tugs at her necklace until she bats his hand away. I point with my bound hands at the steaming truck: Ash's running blades are still inside, leaning against the tailgate. "He needs *those*."

She doesn't even respond; she just walks off while I'm talking. I want to scream at her.

"You know," Ash says, rewarding me with a wry smile, "in some ways you are a total mystery to me, Rio Cruz. But I've got to hand it to you — you're one determined girl."

"Maybe I just have hidden depths." And I'm thinking, *Which you'd know if you took the time . . .*

He rubs his chin. "I think you do. But you shouldn't hide them so much. You really shouldn't." He glances meaningfully at the LRA kids cleaning mud off their guns. "Life's too short."

That leaves me speechless. I'm not hiding *anything* from him — completely the opposite — if only he could see it. Part of me hoped Jen would own up to stealing the letter eventually, but it doesn't look like she ever will.

"I didn't mean to take it out on you," Ash continues. "It's just frustrating sometimes. I forget there are some things I just can't do anymore."

"I understand."

"Speaking of hidden depths," Ash says, shielding his

eyes from the sun, "something's been bothering me about you — a lot."

Now what? "Oh?"

"Like, why you'd steal my letter. I mean, if you're going to take something, there were plenty of things in my room that were way more interesting. Like the diary it was in, for instance . . ."

"You keep a diary? You don't seem like the type —" The words are out of my mouth before I grasp what I'm saying. Ash's eyes narrow, but I don't care about my mistake — he's been thinking about me. Suddenly I feel warm inside.

He smiles. "And you don't strike me as a thief."

"I'm not," I say, feeling a huge load lift off my chest.

Ash's eyebrow lifts. "So why don't you tell me what really happened?"

I don't get the chance. Jen limps closer with a prize-winning scowl souring her beautiful face. Don't ask me how, but she can even make a limp look amazing. Behind her, in the river, Mwemba has given up on the kids and is waist-deep in water with the Toyota's hood up, inspecting the damage. The Sangoma is keeping his distance, chanting and waving his pouch of bones at them. Suddenly Mwemba slams the hood shut and wades back to shore. He shoves the Sangoma aside and the witch doctor looks our way, watching Izzy through narrowed eyes. He's been watching her a lot today, and it worries me. I wonder if he's beginning to think she's a liability.

The Sangoma has had his eye on Jen, too, but for a different reason. If she has noticed anything, she's bravely trying not to let on. If we forget the letter — and that's a *big* if — I think I actually admire her. It's like she's made of steel or something. Her dressing is coming off her burn and her legs are covered with drying mud, but she still has the poise of a supermodel.

"What the hell have you two got to smile about?" Her angry face is reserved for me. "You're enjoying this?"

"No." I help her to sit down, stealing a glance at Izzy. "I'm just glad we're all alive."

"I *really* need to eat," Izzy moans. Her head is in her hands and she keeps shivering. My stomach is growling painfully, too, but our scrawny captors don't seem to have much left to give us.

My eyes travel from Izzy to where Mwemba is talking to the Sangoma. He's pointing. I'm sure that the guy is taking us somewhere where he thinks he can get insulin for Izzy. Why else would he have chosen not to kill her? I remember what Ash said on the boat — *they want us alive*. That means we're worth something to them. I just hope for Iz's sake that we can get there in time now that the trucks are useless.

"I'm going to ask these jokers to find us something to eat," Charis complains, getting to her feet. As soon as Split-Lip hears her arm whir he covers her with his gun. "Hungry!" She glares at him, rubbing her tummy.

Split-Lip's gun waves up and down.

I pull Charis's arm. "Leave it. After what happened with the hippo, they're too wired to care."

To our surprise, the Empty Child turns up with Ash's blades. She throws them on the ground and watches Ash crawl over to them on his knees. It must be humiliating for him. Her toddler has a handful of bananas. He tears one off and is about to hand it to me, but the girl snatches it away. He dumps the rest of the bananas beside Ash's blades, totters over to me, smiles, and plants a wet kiss on my lips. Then he runs off with a throaty laugh.

I watch the girl spin on her heel and grab the kid's chubby arm. He squeals loudly and squirms, but she won't put him down. She takes him away, clamping him to her side until his squeals morph into a full-blown kicking tantrum.

"Well, I never!" Marcus laughs. "He likes you, and she's jealous."

Mwemba made his guys abandon all the trucks. I'm worried sick about Izzy now — walking is the last thing she needs, and I have no idea how far it is to get wherever we're going. The land is still mostly sunburnt grass and bush, but it seems to be constantly rising. We follow snaking compacted paths that, judging by the number of withered trees that have had their bark stripped to virtually head height, must have been made by elephants.

I never thought I would be sorry to leave the Toyota behind, but I don't need to walk far to find out that things are going to be *much* worse on foot. For a start, the flies can get at us now, and we're constantly bitten. Some of them are huge. I can actually feel them puncture my skin like pins. It's gross. I have to grab one by its writhing body and pull it out. Soon itchy lumps grow and harden on my legs, arms, and neck, and I can't scratch them. They're driving me insane.

Ash's blades are a mixed blessing. He can walk amazingly well in them, but the feet are quite small, so he has to watch his step. They sink in loose dirt and are hard to control on uneven ground. I like to see him in them, though. They make him look powerful, superhuman. Watching him walk up ahead gives me hope. It's stupid, I know, but he looks like he could take on all of these jumped-up kids, armed or not — and I still can't help feeling hopeful about the fact that he's been thinking about me. Then I'm back with the whale shark for the briefest of moments, thinking about what could have been, if the pirates hadn't screwed it all up. What was he about to say? But there's no point daydreaming now. When I pull myself out of it I notice that the LRA soldiers seem unnerved by Ash, too. His blades really worry them — especially the Sangoma, who shoots dark looks at him and mutters under his breath.

An hour away from the river, the toddler appears by my side and warm, sticky fingers grab on to the frayed hem of my shorts. He walks beside me until the girl sees him and yanks him away.

Mwemba is like a human walking machine, constantly goading on his soldier boys by shoving them in the back or slapping the backs of their heads if they show any sign of lagging. In turn they hit us with their guns and scream insanely at Iz when she falls. The bastards won't let any of us help her up, either. Mwemba forces us on at a stupid pace, especially considering that the ground has been rising slowly since we left the river. We seem to be leaving the plains and entering an area of thick, scrubby bush and tangled trees. Curious primates chatter and look down on us from high in the branches.

Charis and I have Jen limping between us, while poor Izzy insists on staggering on unaided. She is sweating buckets and gets uber-testy whenever Marcus offers to help her, pushing him away. It's so unlike her. But after a few hours, she has to admit defeat, loop her tied hands over Marky's neck, and let him carry her on his back.

Ash shouts at Mwemba, "How much farther do you think we can go on like this? Look at her!"

Mwemba grins. "If you are that concerned about saving her, you will find the strength." He unclips his pistol holster. "He may drop her if you wish and I will end her pain."

I want to punch him in the face.

Even this late in the day it is crazy hot and none of us feel like we can walk another step. The kid soldiers have no choice but to watch helplessly while we collapse in the first shade we can find.

"Look what God sent us." Iz smiles, but she can barely talk. Her lips are cracked and sore, her pupils black and wide despite the sun. She's not thinking about herself, though. Izzy drops to her knees by a small aloe plant growing by a rock. She starts pulling at it, but it's too tough for her, so Charis lends her good hand and manages to yank away three long, fleshy leaves. I pull off a few more so that we have a good stock and shove them into the back pockets of my shorts, much to the amusement of the soldiers. They're stripping bark off a low bush and chewing it, pushing at one another to get at the best bits until Mwemba pistol-whips a couple of them.

The aloe plant is tough, but Charis makes light work of it with her bionic arm. When she splits the leaves open they're full of clear jelly that doesn't smell anywhere near as revolting as I am expecting. It smells like the inside of a freshly peeled potato skin. Charis gives Jen some to smear on her leg. When we lather handfuls of it over Marky's skin grafts the toddler gets curious and scrambles nearer to help. Thinking we're not looking, he scoops up a handful to eat, and spits it out. It's a second or so before his chubby little face crumples and he bursts into floods of tears. The Empty Child jumps up and brings her gun to bear on us until she sees me holding up my gel-covered hands.

"It's okay," I tell her, "I've seen people drink this stuff. Don't ask me why."

Her face still gives nothing away. She lifts the screaming toddler, shoulders her gun, and walks off.

I'm just wedging a few more spare aloe leaves into my pockets when Iz gets to her feet, staggers past me, and throws up in a bush. She won't let me near her, though, and I'm paranoid in case Mwemba sees what's happening and decides to shoot her. Iz wipes her mouth with the back of her hand and gives me an apologetic smile; then, to my surprise she holds out her St. Christopher bracelet and tells me flatly, "I took this off when they untied us. I want you to have it."

"No! No way!"

"Really — I mean it. I don't think it can follow where I'm going."

"Iz. Stop talking like that. I don't like it."

She huffs at me and dangles it in the space between us. "It's okay, Rio, really. Take it when I'm gone, then, but you're going to have to put it back on my wrist now."

I hate her giving up like this. I just shake my head at her. "With pleasure. There's no way I'm taking your bracelet. It's going home with you."

"UP! UP!" The Sangoma arrives, waving his arms at us, totally wired. He's been chewing bark with the others. All the soldiers seem much more talkative now, in fact, and one or two of them shove one another and let out laughs that are borderline hysterical. They're not joking, though. It sounds dangerous, like a fight could break out.

Our rest is over. They prod and pull us to our feet and start off again at a renewed pace. This time they fall into a loping march with us jostled in the middle, and they sing and rattle their guns while they jog. After a couple of hours, what's left of my flip-flops disintegrates and I have to kick them away and carry on barefoot.

Ash and Marky do their best taking turns to carry Iz, but they are constantly whipped by the soldiers if they start to flag. Charis and I are supporting Jen, who is limping really badly now. Anger at her still gnaws away at me, though: Ash thawing a little toward me has just made the whole letter thing feel really raw again. In fact, the only way to stop it eating at the back of my mind is by reminding myself that these lunatics with guns are my enemy, not Jen.

A couple of times on our journey, groups of migrating meerkats join us, scampering by our feet and stopping to stand up and watch for predators. It's quite touching. When a warthog charges out of some undergrowth, snorting at them, I don't know whether to laugh or cry.

I'm breathless, but I tap Jen on the arm and point. "Look, it's Timon and Pumbaa."

"What?"

"*The Lion King.*"

Iz is clinging onto Marky's back. She manages a laugh and starts singing "Hakuna Matata" under her breath.

Marcus laughs and sings the warthog line with her — operatic style — so loud that the LRA guys all shut up to listen.

The song is contagious. It's totally out of place, but it feels like an act of defiance to sing. Even Jen joins in with us once she's picked up the words. I jog alongside them, stroking Izzy's arm, and I hold on to Izzy's good leg, desperate for her to feel the contact, but I don't know if she can anymore. Her skin is all clammy and cold.

When some of the LRA guys join in to sing harmonies it really pisses me off. I wish they'd shut up. This is *our* song. Half of them sound like they're stoned. Then it dawns on me as I watch them that *Hakuna Matata* must be Swahili. *Stupid me.* Then again, it never would have occurred to me that I'd hear the chorus to a happy kids' song sung by a bunch of boy soldiers high on tree bark.

When I see the state Iz is in, I can't stop the tears from streaming down my face. I want her to live. I want her to see her lion. But right now I don't know if she ever will.

As darkness falls we reach the top of a low hill and drop to the ground, exhausted. The stitch in my side is crippling, and I want to take huge gulps of air, but I can barely breathe. Over the crest of our hill, a warm yellow light glows from behind a thick clump of trees. It's a small compound with a couple of single-story buildings. A few of our guards whisper uneasily. If the place has electricity, it can't be too far from civilization. Ash and Marcus are exchanging meaningful looks, but Mwemba either doesn't notice or doesn't care. I think I can see a road leading up to the main building. It's not much more than a dirt track, but it looks more used than anything else we've been on so far.

We've climbed quite a long way since yesterday, and the vegetation has changed again. My feet are sore as hell from walking on stones and sharp dry leaves. There is much more variety in the plant life here and the air feels heavier, like we're getting near to water again. We are — I can sense it. Mwemba made us all stop when he spotted the light, and his soldiers have all fallen silent. Some of them have pockets of the bark they stripped earlier and they start chewing again. Soon they are fidgeting with guns or knives, chanting with the Sangoma in barely audible tones. Only the Empty Child is still. She's just squatting calmly, peering at the ground and drawing in the dust with her finger, pushing the toddler away when he tries to stop her.

I nudge Ash. "What's she doing?"

"No idea."

We're all desperately worried about Iz. It must be a full day now since her last insulin injection. She's spent the last couple of hours muttering incoherently. It can't be long before she slips into a coma.

There are a couple of soldiers near us. One of them is Split-Lip. Suddenly Mwemba strides over and snarls at them. His voice is chilling. *"Nenda kuzunguka nyuma. Kuhakikisha ni wazi."*[7]

Split-Lip shows his teeth in a spine-chilling grin. His friend flinches at the sound of Mwemba's voice, and they both pull long machetes from their belts and set off at a jog down the slope toward the light.

---

7. Go around the back. Make sure it is clear.

15

MWEMBA GIVES HIS SPIES TEN MINUTES AND THEN the rest of us follow. The LRA kids all have their weapons drawn and ready — mostly long knives. Ash is carrying Izzy on his back now. Sweat is dripping from his forehead and I can see the pain he must be in. The impact of twice the normal weight on his blades is killing him, but he's determined not to show it.

Close up, the building turns out to be a clinic. It has whitewashed mud walls painted with a red cross and a simple grass roof. Outside there are rows of tables and benches with grass canopies. The soldiers make us sit down out of sight behind some trees, but I can just see past the trunk of mine and through one of the two large windows.

There's a stocky black guy inside, short hair, about thirty or so. His friendly face is illuminated with warm yellow light. He's wearing a white coat and is packing small plastic tubes into styrofoam boxes on a table. Some tinny-sounding dance music wafts over to us while he works. I think there are at least two women in there with him, because I get occasional glimpses of a shoulder near the window, and a plump woman with a colorful headdress walks behind the guy into the other room. He grabs her hand as she passes, twirling her in time to the music. She laughs, and her voice sounds warm and happy.

Just beyond the corner of the building is a mud-splattered SUV. It is olive green and the white lettering above the grill on the hood reads *Médecins Sans Frontières*. Split-Lip and the other scout appear near it. They duck around the fender and jog over to Mwemba, keeping to the shadows and crouching low so that they're not seen.

When he gets back to us Split-Lip holds up four fingers. *"Wao ni juu yao wenyewe."*[8]

It's the first time I've heard his thin, nasal voice, and I'm almost shocked at how young it sounds. He has trouble with the *W*s, though, and has to lick back saliva as he talks.

Mwemba's lips twist slowly into a chilling smile and he waves at the Empty Child. I don't like the way he looks at her.

---

8. They are on their own.

His eyes are black pools. It's as if he knows that she, of all of them, will understand *exactly* what he wants them to do — like he owns her soul. She has already placed the toddler behind a tree and is squatting to examine the blade of her machete, almost like she's praying to it. The Sangoma is preparing, too. When the four of them are in front of him, Mwemba tells them quietly, *"Msiharibu daktari."*[9]

Daktari — that's got to be *doctor*. The way he says it gives me the creeps.

They slip back into the darkness and, whatever they are planning, I just know it's not going to be good. My heart is pounding so badly it's giving me a headache. I think I should shout to warn those people, but I'm too scared.

It looks like Charis is thinking of doing something. She's twisting her fake arm, slowly working it free, perhaps so that she can release her ropes and make a run for the clinic to warn them. It will be certain death if she does, because the LRA kids have such itchy trigger fingers. The ones watching us never lower their guard; they flinch even if we bat an eyelid. Charis is prepared to risk everything, to blow the only advantage we have, but I say nothing.

Ash catches her eye and shakes his head. Charis glares back at him but, to my relief, she stops. He's probably the only person she would do that for. As Ash quietly slips Izzy to the ground, his neck pulls taut and he suddenly yells, "RUN!" at the top of his voice.

---

9. Do not hurt the doctor.

The guy in the white coat appears at the window briefly and then disappears.

Marcus joins in. "Run! Get the hell out of there!"

Instantly three of the LRA kids are on Ash, raining down blows with the stocks of their guns. He tries to fend them off with his shoulders, but with his hands tied there's nothing he can do to stop them. Marcus stops shouting before they get to him. His grafts don't need any more abuse.

Mwemba barks at his boys and it takes four of them to force the guys to their knees.

"They're unarmed, you bastard!" Ash says breathlessly. "Innocent civilians!"

"Their suffering will be brief," Mwemba replies.

Inside I can hear the box of vials crash to the floor. There is shouting, the doctor's voice. A scream is cut short, glass breaks, and there is a horrible thudding sound. Two female voices, thin and desperate, pleading with the soldiers, grow quieter as they are led outside from the far end of the building. Then there is another long, piercing shriek, followed by another with words jumbled in it, and wild rustling sounds that seem to go on forever. When they stop, there is total silence. Even the crickets shut up. I think I'm in shock, because I'm shaking like a leaf and my vision is blurred with tears.

Soon the Sangoma appears at the window and trills exultantly, a huge smile on his face. Behind him, the man in the white coat is shoved facedown on the table he'd been working at. A trickle of blood runs down the side of his head. On Mwemba's order we are pulled to our feet and marched around the building to a door at the back. Two soldiers manhandle Izzy, dragging her between them. She's barely conscious now. Just before they take us inside, the Empty Child emerges from the opposite bushes, standing in long shadows cast by the triangle of light from the open door. She is holding a long, dripping machete in her hands and she lets it fall to the ground. The toddler runs to her.

I want to throw up.

She just drops to her haunches, pushes the child away, and draws the silver blade through the grass to clean it, flipping it from side to side. The girl knows we're watching her and she won't look up. Split-Lip and the other boy emerge behind her, all sweating and breathless, and the Empty Child stands up and gives one of them the wiped machete. Then she stands there like a zombie, playing with the string of her necklace. Even the toddler can't get her attention. For some reason Split-Lip won't meet her eyes when he walks past her. I think he's scared of her.

I don't see any more because I'm shoved through the door with the others into a room with three low, empty beds. The doctor has been moved onto a chair. His eyes widen with shock when we are shoved inside. He watches closely as the soldiers lower Izzy roughly onto one of the beds, and Jen limps in and drops onto the next one.

Mwemba stands over his new captive, holding his pistol loosely. "The girl is diabetic. Do you have medicine for her?"

The doctor nods in the direction of the other room. A name tag on his pocket says *Dr. Mayanja*. When he speaks, he has a

French accent. "Insulin? We keep a small stock in there. You are fortunate. We have very little else, because of the clinic today. What have you done with Marta and Mary?"

The names of the nurses drop like ice from his lips.

He gets no answer to his question. Mwemba wipes beads of sweat from his forehead and shakes his braids out of his face. He jerks his thumb at Izzy. "Can you help her?"

The doctor looks at the bed, too scared to get up. "How long has she been hypoglycemic?"

Mwemba prods me over to him.

I almost trip but the doctor steadies me with his warm, firm hands. I tell him, "Most of today."

"You are the missing teenagers?"

There is a loud slap when Mwemba hits the poor guy with the back of his hand.

I nod, and the doctor rubs his cheek and smiles at me as though the LRA leader isn't even there. He's not going to give in to the intimidation. "What is your name, dear?"

"Rio."

"You are very brave."

"I don't think so."

Tears are streaming down my face, because five minutes ago he was dancing with Marta or Mary. He knows they're dead. I'm sure he also knows there's no way Mwemba's boys will let him live when we leave.

The doctor looks up at Mwemba. "How is the little boy? Your master, Kony, said that you would never return. You dare to go against his wishes?"

The LRA have been here before.

Mwemba pulls out his pistol and marches over to Izzy on the bed. He puts the barrel against her head again. I'm remembering her request and thinking of my promise to her. A decision hardens inside me: I'll kill Mwemba if he harms her, whether she wants it or not. Ash and Marcus struggle with their guards, but there are too many.

"That is none of your concern. I do not have time for words! If you cannot help her, then she is no use to me," the LRA leader says flatly.

"Leave her alone —!" Ash is silenced with a punch to his stomach. He falls to the floor, winded, but none of us dares move to help him.

"Do not be so impatient!" The doctor is trying desperately to remain calm but he can't help letting anger crack his voice. "I may be able to help her. Let me try. As I said, I have some insulin in the storeroom."

Stuffing the gun back in his belt, Mwemba struts back, yanks the doctor up by his collar, and tells the Sangoma, "Go with him. Get the drug."

The witch doctor is playing with his pouch of bones. For a second it looks like he may say something, but fear widens his pupils and he thinks again. He ducks around Mwemba and takes the doctor to his storeroom.

When they return, the doctor sits on the bed next to Iz. He's brought some wipes and a box of medical stuff, and is so gentle with her when he cleans a spot on her filthy arm to inject the insulin that I want to hug him. Then he checks her pulse and shines his pocket light into her eyes before taking the time to wipe away the dirt from her face and neck.

"How long will it take?" Mwemba is impatient.

"I don't know how long. This girl has been through a terrible ordeal and she is dehydrated. If you want to keep your captives alive, then you need to stop behaving like animals and treat them better."

Mwemba barks at the Sangoma, "Get water!" and he disappears. Outside, a tap runs and splashes into a tin bucket while the doctor examines Jen's leg with a worried frown.

"This is infected. It is swelling."

The blood drains from her face but Jen does her best to sound brave. "I'm fine. I think it's getting better."

He gives her a steady gaze. "I'm glad *you* think so. I have no more antibiotics until tomorrow . . ." The doctor falls silent: He doesn't know if he'll *see* tomorrow. Sweat gathers on his forehead while he cleans Jen's burn and rebandages it. Despite his words about the antibiotics, he hands her two bubble-wrapped pills when he's finished. "These are all I have. It is not enough, but it will have to do. They are strong — take one a day."

The Sangoma and a couple of the soldiers return with water for us. It's clean and clear and tastes like honey.

"Did you see those meerkats?" Izzy lifts herself up suddenly and coughs up yellow bile, spitting into a tissue. Her eyes take a while to focus. "Where are we? I feel funny."

I have to stop myself from screaming with delight, and I hand her my water. She glugs it back and holds the cup out for more. The doctor peers in her eyes again and takes her temperature. Then he listens to her chest carefully with his stethoscope and takes her blood pressure.

Behind us, the Sangoma speaks to Mwemba: *"Kuna njia mbili redio katika gari."*[10]

Redio — that's got to be something about a radio. I wonder if the car has one and they're worried that the doctor will use it.

Mwemba waves at his soldiers. "Watch them," he says, and follows the Sangoma out. Guns rattle at us, but we ignore them.

"Have you always had arrhythmia?" asks the doctor.

Iz looks at him. "No, never. My chest does feel fluttery, though."

I ask, "What does that mean?"

"Your friend —"

"Izzy."

"Izzy has an irregular heartbeat. It might be nothing, but it could be the result of the stress her body has been under. She is showing signs of what could be autonomic neuropathy, a cause of diabetic cardiomyopathy. It is very serious. She needs to stay here."

The doctor doesn't get the chance to elaborate; I jump out of my skin at the clack of automatic gunfire, several rounds, accompanied by the dull ringing sound of holes punched in metal.

"Sounds like they've decided not to use the car, then," Ash says grimly.

---

10. There is two-way radio in the car.

Mwemba strides back in with the Empty Child at his side. He waves his pistol at the doctor. "We are leaving. Give the rest of the drug to her."

The doctor's calm almost crumbles. "Izzy needs to stay here," he tells Mwemba through gritted teeth. "She is not well."

The LRA leader hauls Izzy to her feet. "She will come with me."

There's no point arguing. I shake my head when the doctor looks like he's about to answer back. If he carries on, they'll kill him, too, and I can't bear the thought of that. I notice the Empty Child studying me and wonder how you go from hacking innocent people to pieces to ice maiden without batting an eyelid. She makes me sick.

Her little demon patters into the room and grips her leg, looking up with huge brown eyes and calling, *"Dada, dada!"* He wants to be picked up. It sounds weird — he can't think she's his dad.

Dr. Mayanja's hand is shaking when he lifts it to pat the toddler on the head.

"Hello again, little fellow. Yes, your sister will protect you."

The little boy is her brother? So *dada* must be Swahili for *sister*.

The doctor doesn't get to say anything else, because Split-Lip walks in behind, carrying Ash's broken prostheses. The Empty Child takes the box of insulin that the doctor hands her and then Mwemba has him tied up and gagged.

"Your life is spared because you helped the boy," the LRA leader says coldly. "When you are freed, call Reuters news agency and tell them we have the missing teenagers. If they ask for proof, show them these." He waves his arm, and Split-Lip lets Ash's legs clatter onto the floor at his feet. Mwemba digs in the breast pocket of his fatigues and fishes out a bunch of crumpled photographs, which he tosses onto the doctor's lap. The top one is of me in Arrivals at the airport back in South Africa, looking stressed out and disheveled. "And these. Tell them *Moses Mwemba* demands five million US dollars in unmarked bills for the safe return of the young people, and medication to keep this one alive." He points at Izzy. "The boy with no legs — 'Ash' — will die in five days if they do not do as I say. I will be in touch soon to tell them where to leave the money."

16
DAY 14

WAS WAY TOO TENSE TO THINK STRAIGHT AT THE clinic, but as soon as we march away from it and that lonely yellow light melts into the trees behind us, I find myself totally freaking out about the nurses they murdered.

"What the hell did you do to them, you *animals*?" I roar at the girl and Split-Lip while we walk. "What's wrong with you?" Neither of them will look at me. I'm so mad, I even try to take a swing at Split-Lip with my arms, but the ropes tear at my wrists and take all the power out of it. Split-Lip laughs and catches my fists. He slaps me in the face. It stings like hell but I don't care. Every time one of the LRA scum looks at me now,

I see red. After what I witnessed back there, I'm also sure that the Empty Child is not just the youngest. She's also the most dangerous.

Izzy is only able to walk slowly and Mwemba doesn't do anything to speed her up. The LRA leader has even let Izzy walk with her hands untied. What Dr. Mayanja said seems to have had an effect, and I'm *so* grateful to him. I hope he's going to be okay.

While I'm thinking, there's a long, rumbling roar in the distance.

"Iz . . ." I whisper.

Her eyes are still glassy. There's no way she should be walking anywhere. She wraps her arm around my waist and lets her head rest in the crook of my shoulder as we walk through the bush bathed in shadows and silver starlight. "Yes?"

"Did you hear that?"

She nods and waves the wrist with the St. Christopher on it in front of me. Her face lights up with a smile. "You were right. I should have had more faith."

Ash is walking ahead of us with Jen. They've heard the roar, too. Charis and Marcus, to my right, don't even lift their heads. I've grown used to it, but suddenly I see what a mess we all look. Our clothes are bloody and torn. I wonder what my hair must look like. It feels like a mat. Having Izzy back feels good, though. It felt lonely without her optimism.

"Someone's definitely looking out for you," I agree, with this weird, light-headed relief washing over me. I point to my left. "If you still want to say hello to your lion, I'd say we need to go in *that* direction."

"Now you're coming round to my way of thinking," she jokes. "A lion's not so scary when you've had a gun in your face now, is it?"

"True."

We walk all through the night, and our path is lit by the brightest stars you can imagine. The silver crescent moon lying on its back is too lazy to compete with them, but it does light our way with a sliver of ghostly light. The sun has long gone in but its heat still oozes from the ground beneath my bare feet. We find ourselves crossing wide fields of maize and other crops that I have no name for. Short, fragrant mango and citrus trees are dotted along the thin, weatherworn paths that we take every now and again, as if they were planted by people walking this way many years before us. Mwemba allows only the Sangoma to gather fruit as we walk. The LRA leader is jumpy, and I know it's because there are people nearby, but no lights puncture the darkness. My heart flips when I think I see the angular black outline of a thatched roof, but as we pass by and I turn to get a better look, it turns out to be a bush.

Just before daybreak the soldiers let us rest for a couple of hours, hidden in a thick patch of shrubs, while a much thicker mist than yesterday rises from the undergrowth. Monkeys scream and chatter in the denser patches of bush and overhead, and the place is alive with creaking, hissing noises. Through the leaves, the morning sky is blue and cloudless. I notice that the girl has gone, and I've almost given up looking for her when I catch glimpses of that strange gray shadow again, broken by leaves and branches. She seems to be jumping. This time I can even hear her soft voice punctuated by a thudding sound and a tiny gasp for breath as she lands. I wonder what she's doing.

After the farmland we had to cross two tarmac roads in the night, and I'm thinking we may be near civilization now. With regular injections through the night, Iz is almost back to normal, except that the whites of her eyes look yellow to me and the beds of her nails are purple. She seems to be way more out of breath than she should be, too.

Our rest is far too short, even for the boy soldiers. Some of them get up muttering under their breath. Unconcerned, Mwemba gets us moving again, and now it is Jen who is beginning to slow us down. Her leg is badly swollen and she spends most of her time hopping. The dressing is peeling away from a huge oozing lump on her calf — infection is beginning to take its toll on her despite the pills that the doctor gave her. To top it all, she's sweating badly, like she may be developing a fever.

Last night, Ash's eyes were everywhere, searching for an escape opportunity, but the roads were deserted. Today, he is walking slightly ahead of us with his head bowed.

I want to lift his spirits but I don't know how. All I can come up with is a lame, "Are you okay, Ash?"

"No, I'm not. Why would I be?" he snaps back. Then, when he sees my face, "It's not you."

He's frustrated because there are never any decent chances

to break away and, the longer we go on, the less likely it is that any of us would be able to get very far even if we tried. I know he's desperately worried about Iz and Jen. None of us would even *think* of running without them. To make things worse, the LRA kids never seem to tire or drop their guard.

In the afternoon we cross another track and, after wading through a swathe of tall brown grass, we reach a group of rocks shaded by a few trees and low thorn bushes. While we're sitting there in silence, the sound of an engine comes out of the distance. A cloud of dust rises in a thin column heading this way. Suddenly the soldiers shove us into a tighter group and make us sit on some boulders while they scan frantically for cover. Several of them raise their guns in the direction the vehicle is coming from. My heart leaps. A shiver of hope rises in me.

Mwemba barks angrily at his unruly kids and points to a patch of scrubby bushes and long grass behind us. The Sangoma and a couple of others rush to where we are sitting on the rocks and force us to the ground behind the cover of the bushes. After what happened at the medical center when Ash and Marcus cried out, the soldiers aren't taking any chances. A filthy rag is shoved in my mouth and tied behind my neck, and Split-Lip kneels astride me with his gun pointing at the back of my head. The others are getting the same treatment, and as the roar of the engine gets closer, I can hear excited voices. Some weird insect tickles my calf and I choke on a scream. When whatever it is bites my leg, I squirm, panicked. Split-Lip pushes my shoulders into the ground. I freeze.

"Over there! By those rocks. I swear, honey, that bush moved!" An American voice — a woman.

The vehicle squeals to a halt, not far away. Nobody gets out. If it's a safari, they'll have to stay in the trucks.

It's a chance for us, though, and Ash struggles violently, almost toppling the Sangoma off his chest before the guy gets him under control.

I love that he won't give up.

"There! Did you see that? It moved again."

There's a murmur. It sounds like they're not going any-where for a while.

Somewhere by my head a gun rattles. I can't move my head much but I can see enough. To my amazement, Mwemba slowly rises to his feet, smiling.

There is a scream.

Another voice asks, "Mommy, is that a poacher?"

From where the tourists are, he must look spine-chilling, like the devil in combat fatigues rising from a sea of waving grass. Cameras click, bleep, and then fall silent when they see his gun. Mwemba just laughs at them. He shakes his beaded braids out of his eyes, whooping and trilling, firing automatic rounds into the air as the safari truck turns tail in a cloud of dust and floors it. Hot, empty shells rain down and bounce painfully off my back and arms.

When the tourists have gone, Split-Lip pulls me to my feet and the others follow suit, but when the Empty Child tries to pull Izzy up, she's a dead weight. She's clutching her chest and groaning with short, hissing breaths. The toddler is pulling at the side of her open mouth, trying to wake her up.

Suddenly I'm hearing the doctor's words in my head: *cardiomyopathy . . . very serious*. It's her heart.

"Get off her!" I scream at them, and the little boy looks at me and bursts into tears. The girl flicks the safety catch on her gun and raises it.

Mwemba angrily shoves her gun aside and between them they try to pull Iz up. He kicks the toddler out of the way and they manage to get Izzy upright. He's really rough with her, though — like she can help this. Sweat is pouring from her forehead and she's gasping for breath, white as a sheet. Then, suddenly, the breathing stops. She just sits there, staring for a second, and slowly flops forward, her eyes as wide as saucers. The Empty Child stops her from falling sideways and hitting her head on a rock.

I can't help myself, I'm screaming, *"IZZY!"* at the top of my voice, as if she's going to hear and come back. Then at Mwemba, "Let go! She's having a heart attack, for God's sake!"

The others are yelling, too, straining against groups of armed kids, shoving them out of the way. The soldiers are dangerously agitated, shouting at me and waving their guns angrily — I'm trembling but I don't care if they shoot me. Ash and I manage to shoulder our way past them and, when Mwemba stands aside and waves his pistol, they do nothing to stop us.

I shove the girl out of the way and feel Izzy's cold wrist for a pulse. Nothing! I tell the girl, "Untie me!" When she does her usual zombie act I scream and wave my wrists right in her stupid face. *"Freaking untie me!"*

Without blinking or wiping my spit off her face she pulls out her machete. For a second I think I've had it. I try not to close my eyes. If she's going to kill me, I want her to know I'm not going to run or hide. But instead she stoops and cuts my ropes. Then she stands up and steps away to watch, pulling the screaming toddler to her side by his arm.

Mwemba won't let Ash get any closer, just me. Gently, I lift Izzy's face and lay her on her back. For a while I try breathing for her, mouth-to-mouth, pumping her chest, and putting my wet cheeks next to her face, praying that God will let me feel the soft echo of her breath. For one fleeting second I swear she says the word *love*. That would be *so* Izzy. But, as her pupils widen to black, I realize it was just a last breath of air seeping from her lungs.

"Come back, Iz," I plead into her ear, watching my tears splash onto her forehead. "We're in a safari park. The lion king is waiting for you. Come back."

There's no answer. Not even when I sob, *"I love you — thank you for being my friend,"* again and again into her lifeless ear.

The bastards don't give us any time to be with her, but before they drag me away from her body I manage to unclip her St. Christopher bracelet. After that they won't let me touch her. They won't let us bury her, either. All Mwemba will allow is a little time for Charis, Jen, and me to pile rocks around her to protect her body from wild dogs and vultures.

The moment we're done they tie us up again. I just stand there looking at that pathetic pile before we're all shoved on our way. It's like all the life has been sucked out of me and, as I stumble forward, the color drains out of the world.

When we leave I shout, "I'm not going to forget you, Iz!" and I keep my eyes on her grave over my shoulder for as long as I can, walking on tiptoe until all that is left is the reflection of the sun on the pale stones. When even that is hidden, I'm blinded with waves of tears that just won't stop, and a terrible pain like nothing I've ever known squeezes my chest every time I try to gulp for air. Charis is next to me helping Jen to walk. Both of them are sobbing their hearts out, watched from behind heavy lids by the Empty Child. Ash's face is wet and streaked with tears that he can't wipe away. Marcus breaks my heart: He has no tear ducts, there's no release for his pain. All he can do is let out these gut-wrenching moans and gasps, shaking his head in anguish while Charis tries to comfort him.

Right now I'm not afraid to die. It would be a relief.

As we trudge away, Jen throws up in the bushes a couple of times and I'm terrified to hear that she's developing a rattling wheeze. It feels like Izzy's God, if He ever existed, has deserted us. Either that or He doesn't care. Maybe He never cared, letting us get kidnapped in the first place — and allowing the others to be blown up in war zones before that. For Izzy's sake, I'm trying hard not to hate Him, but her St. Christopher medal feels like it's burning the palm of my hand, as if she's telling me not to give up on Him. I hate it and want it all at the same time. Eventually I have no choice but to turn my head back to the path and try to give a damn whether or not I take another breath.

I don't know how any of us keep on walking. No one talks, not even the soldiers, and the girl watches us even more closely than usual. I'm close to losing it at her, but instead I just bite my lip, drop my head, and watch the tears roll down my nose, where they fall to darken the dirt at my feet.

A couple of hours later we trudge past another stand of trees, where, in the shade, three lionesses stretch out and yawn. My insides knot up with this raw ache the instant I see them. The feeling is so powerful it almost knocks me to the ground. I want to rant at God, but the pain of it has sucked all the breath from me. It's as if we're just being mocked now. If only she'd lived another couple of hours, Izzy could have seen them!

I need to stop. I need to fall to the ground and curl up, but two of the soldiers see me stumble and hook their arms under mine, dragging me along. We leave a wide berth when we pass by the lionesses, and one of them lifts its head to watch us. That's when this amazing lion appears on the highest rock and stands there. He shakes his mane and roars angrily at the LRA soldiers and at the endless blue sky. I'm not scared of him. Not anymore. I look right into his sad, pale eyes for ages — until he stops roaring and turns his back on me.

By nightfall we're standing on the top of a wooded hill, looking over a vast black expanse of water. If I didn't know better, I would think we've reached the sea, but that's impossible. A warm, damp breeze rises from it and slips through my dirty, tangled hair. It's like meeting an old friend again. I want to get down there and splash water on my face. Maybe then I'll wake up from this nightmare. In the darkness, though, the valley is a wide black mouth waiting to swallow us without a trace. I can't see the end of it.

Everything feels hopeless to me now. Small clusters of lights flicker far away to our right: ordinary people in their ordinary houses living ordinary lives. Above our heads, the stars just wait there and watch us suffer like they have since history began. My eyes are so wrung out from crying that it's almost painful to look up at them. I wonder whereabouts in the heavens Leo is. *Hiding from me, that's where.*

I become aware that I'm still clutching Izzy's bracelet like I'm holding on to her. I slip it around my left wrist and Jen, seeing me struggle with it, limps over and closes the clasp for me. The soft warmth of the metal reminds me that Izzy is cold now, and my chest contracts in a groan. I just can't help it. I don't know what to do with the pain.

"*Tanganyika,*" Mwemba growls under his breath at the Sangoma, scanning the endless water. "*Ambapo ni wao?*"[11]

I'm good at geography — all part of being a sailor — and I know that Tanganyika is a huge freshwater lake that separates

---

11. Where are they?

Tanzania from the Democratic Republic of the Congo. Over the restless black water is the poorest, most unstable country in Africa. The Sangoma is straining to see, too. He points to a rocky inlet about half a mile away. There's a flickering orange light over there, a fire. Mwemba reacts angrily. He waves us on, and soon we are standing on a sandy beach hidden from the blaze by an outcrop of rock. The sand feels cool and soft under my throbbing feet. I don't want to move another step.

Another eight child soldiers are waiting for us by their fire. They scatter in panic when Mwemba arrives raging at them and kicking it out, scattering red embers everywhere. Sparks fly up into the darkness, morphing into gray flakes that flutter away on the breeze. Four large fishing boats are moored a little way out and we are made to wade out to them. As we near the boats, I can't help but wonder what happened to the fishermen who used to own them, because I'm pretty sure that they don't belong to the soldiers. I close my mind to the thought. The water feels clean and cool. I want to slip beneath the surface and wash away my pain, but I know that can't happen. The lake can draw the ache out of my legs, but right now it can't *begin* to touch my heart.

We are all in a sorry state. Izzy's death has sapped all the fight from us. Some of Marcus's skin grafts have begun to weep along angry red stretch marks. Ash is in constant pain but he hides it well; the only way I can tell is by the way he shifts his weight on his blades. Jen can barely walk at all, and the cold water seems to give her some relief. She stands knee-deep in it, in a trance, until Charis tells her that it may not be safe and gently ushers her forward. Of all of us, Charis and I are holding up best.

I'm hauled into the middle of one of the boats with Ash and forced to lie on my back next to him on a lumpy pile of netting. It smells fishy. The boat rocks wildly because the LRA soldiers are trying to clamber aboard, fighting for places on the bench seats. Several times they almost capsize it, until Mwemba beats them into some kind of order. The last one into our boat is the Empty Child with her kid, and she sits where she can keep an eye on us.

It would have to be her, wouldn't it? The heartless bitch. For a moment I wonder if she's studying me.

She sits in the prow with her gun on one knee and the toddler on the other. Her black eyes glisten.

When everyone is on board the four boats, they start the motors and we're off across the water, traveling slowly because they're trying to follow one another out into the deep without lights. The soldiers are nervous on the water, but to me it feels good.

Ash's arm feels warm against mine and I'm grateful for the touch, it's the first contact I've had since Izzy . . . His breath touches my ear.

"You okay, Rio?"

I nod, even though I'm *not* all right. Unable to stop the tears from flowing again, I bury my face in the crook of his shoulder.

He rubs the top of my head with his chin and then rests his cheek in my hair. "Remember the whale shark?"

How could I forget? I try to laugh but end up sobbing harder. I don't know why I'm alive, or even if I *want* to be. Desperate to be back there, in the ocean, where I felt safe, I close my eyes and remember.

"Ash, what were you going to ask me?"

He is silent long enough for me to know that I'm not going to get an answer to that one. Not until other things are sorted out. *If* they're ever sorted out. And it doesn't matter anyway, now that Izzy's dead.

Eventually Ash says, "I don't remember," but I know he does.

We're quiet for ages after that and then, for the first time in days, his husky voice — quiet and breaking with emotion — starts to sing Izzy's favorite song, "If Everyone Cared," into the night.

The Empty Child turns her head, but it's too dark to see her face.

Before I can choke on another agonizing breath I'm back on the *Spirit of Freedom* after our swim. Nothing bad has happened, and I'm imagining lying in Ash's arms watching the sun sink into an ocean set on fire with crimson, orange, and deep, deep yellows. Izzy is at the wheel. Ash is singing to me and his voice is strong and unafraid.

I try to join in, but can't. He stumbles over the words, and I wet his neck with my tears and listen to his voice vibrating in his throat and chest, even more beautiful because it is wrung out and dried to dust by sorrow.

Holding up my wrists, Izzy's St. Christopher catches the dancing reflections of the moon off the water, and I focus on it until all the other noises around us fade away to nothing, until I feel like I could reach back in time to the yacht and touch Izzy's hand, until it's just me and Ash out here under the stars, and we're floating away from this crazy nightmare on a song.

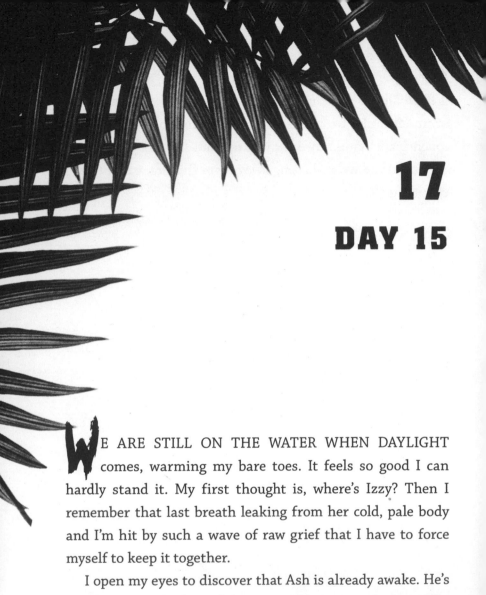

17
DAY 15

WE ARE STILL ON THE WATER WHEN DAYLIGHT comes, warming my bare toes. It feels so good I can hardly stand it. My first thought is, where's Izzy? Then I remember that last breath leaking from her cold, pale body and I'm hit by such a wave of raw grief that I have to force myself to keep it together.

I open my eyes to discover that Ash is already awake. He's watching me. Neither of us managed to get much sleep. The netting was hard and uncomfortable, my back aches, and my head feels like it's going to explode. I can't stop thinking about Iz lying out there in the game reserve, about what might be happening to her. *Please, God, let those people we saw call the police.*

The Empty Child and her soldiers won't let us sit up in case of prying eyes. So there must be other boats on the lake, and we're going much faster in the daylight. I remember seeing a picture of Tanganyika in the in-flight magazine, a long finger of water in the middle of Africa, running virtually north to south. It is huge. Above us, little white clouds move slowly across the blue sky. Occasionally I catch sight of sculpted, dark green hills, rising until their mossy heads actually melt into a long crown of mist. Wafts of air, warm and wet as a bathroom, heavy with the smell of damp grass, settle on us until they are blown away in a light breeze off the lake. From the position of the sun on my left and the warm, moist smell of tropical plants, I think we must still be heading north following the western coastline, the one bordering the DRC.

I wonder if Dr. Mayanja has raised the alarm yet. Mum might know I'm still alive if he has. She'll probably go to pieces when she finds out why, but at least she'll know. The thought makes me feel a bit better until I scratch my nose and Izzy's bracelet tickles my wrist.

The LRA beach the boats on a small cove around mid-afternoon. To the left and right, as far as I can see, steep cliffs drown under a cascade of heavy tropical plants and trees. Under the shade of a tree at the far end of the sandbank, a huge crocodile lies with its mouth open. It's not like the ones I've seen in zoos, that's for sure. The eyes seem to stand proud of a long upward-curling snout.

Mwemba sends the Sangoma off on some errand with three of the LRA kids. While he waits for them to return, he actually *runs* at the crocodile, shaking his gun. For a second I think he's going to shoot it, but he doesn't. I'm hoping the croc will turn on him, but it jumps at the noise and flies into the water with a loud splash. Its weaving body throws up sand, leaving a trail of curving gashes. When it has swum far enough away, Mwemba orders his soldiers to refill their water flasks from the lake. After they have drunk they bring us some. All the rations from the yacht are long gone, so the soldiers leave us a pile of grubby-looking fruit and berries. We eat the lot but it does nothing to lessen the stomach-cramping hunger pains we feel.

Marcus and Charis look in good spirits, considering, except that Charis's eyes are yellow and puffy. So are Jen's. Charis chucks her water over Marcus's filthy T-shirt and looks up at the towering hills. Marcus doesn't complain, even though his grafts are red and angry. I'm not even sure that the aloe vera has been helping him much. Sometimes he goes to scratch at the patches but stops himself with this pained expression on his face. I'm guessing they must itch like hell. None of us has the heart to talk about Izzy. I don't think any of us want to with the LRA soldiers watching our every move. It doesn't seem right.

"These hills remind me of Wales — minus the screeching

and the weird smell, mind," Charis mutters. She's right, the air is filled with screeching and cawing.

"Help me . . ." Marcus jokes, squirming in his damp shirt and rolling his eyes at me. "Every opportunity she gets, she throws water at me."

I can't laugh. I just can't.

"Don't think about it," Marcus tells me, suddenly serious. "This is how soldiers cope, Rio. If you let yourself think, everything falls apart."

"He's right." Charis's fingers buzz as she refills the flask and throws the contents over him. "You use the pain to help you survive."

Marcus shakes the water out of his hair, blinking and spitting, "Enough already!"

"Stop moaning! If you think that's wet, you should try camping with me in the Brecon Beacons."

To everyone's surprise, Marcus says, "I'd like that," a little too quickly.

Awkward. Now I manage a smile.

Charis doesn't seem bothered. She just rubs him on the back with her bionic arm and tells him, "No you wouldn't, Marky. You're too much of a wimp."

I drop onto the sand next to Jen. She's resting her head on her knees, sweating buckets and shivering. Ash kisses her on the head and sits on the other side of her. Her leg stinks worse than ever. When I stretch out next to her she moans, "I need a doctor. Today was my last antibiotic. What's wrong with these people?"

Mwemba is rummaging in a backpack. He looks across at us and his eyes narrow.

"Jen — not so loud." I'm worried he'll hurt her even more.

Ash takes a quick look to see where our guards are. "We have to make a move soon, ready or not," he hisses over at Marcus and Charis.

Charis nods.

Ash is right, but he's scaring me. "Don't you think there are too many of them, Ash? Or am I the only one here worried about the guns?"

"No. But look at Jen — she can't go much farther."

The Empty Child moves closer, so he clams up. That's when I notice something a little way up the hill, hidden deep in the greenery. *A telegraph pole with a wire attached.* I jab Ash with my elbow and hope he can follow my line of sight. We're not far from some kind of settlement, although I'm guessing Mwemba isn't taking us anywhere we can be found. Suddenly there's a whirring noise and this tinny little voice says: "BBC News with Jonathan Izard."

Mwemba is viciously cranking the handle on a small wind-up radio. It's so weird hearing a normal English voice again and imagining that guy sitting in an air-conditioned studio somewhere safe.

> *"The disabled teen adventurers whose yacht, the* Spirit of Freedom, *was thought to be lost at sea, have been seen alive and well in Tanzania."*

"*Well?*" Jen complains under her breath. "I don't think so."

"Unverified reports indicate that they may have been taken captive by the notorious Lord's Resistance Army led by Joseph Kony. Kony and his second-in-command, Moses Mwemba, are wanted by the international community for their brutal raids on innocent civilians. The rebel group is now largely confined to the jungles of the DRC. This from our correspondent in Dar es Salaam —"

Nothing about Izzy, though. I'm desperate to know that she's not still lying there.

"Thanks, Jon." A woman's voice. *"The authorities are remaining tight-lipped at the moment, so facts are sketchy, but if they have been taken by the LRA, Ash Carter and some of his team will have been well prepared by their military training. In the meantime, I'm told that the Navy SEAL team that has been working with several Central African nations to capture LRA leader Joseph Kony has been reassigned. Early this morning I spoke by satellite phone to the SEAL leader, himself an Afghan veteran, who is setting up base in Bujumbura."*

The radio cuts to a surprisingly clear phone line and an American voice. I like it, he sounds strong.

"Yes, ma'am. We're treating these guys like they're our own, and you can be assured that we're going to do everything in our power to get them home."

Then the presenter's voice again:

"That was Neema Swai, our correspondent in Dar Es Salaam, reporting. We'll bring you more on this breaking news story as it develops."

"Ash, did you hear that?" Marcus is too excited to worry about Mwemba. "They've got Navy SEALs looking for us!"

There's a hoarse, contemptuous laugh from Mwemba. "Let them look! They have been trying to find us for years. In the jungle — where we are going — they can be ten feet away from you and not see a thing." He shakes his machine gun. "We will kill them before they know we are there."

It's another hour or more before the Sangoma and the others drop out of the undergrowth at the edge of the cove. They have a coil of wire, a pile of mangoes, and more handfuls of that scary bark to hand out. The mangoes are overripe and messy, but they are the best thing I've tasted since we set foot on dry land. I'm longing to wash the stickiness off my hands in the lake, but as soon as we finish, the LRA kids force us to our feet and we're on the move again.

The cliff above the cove is too steep for Jen, so she is forced to clamber onto the Sangoma's back. She refuses point-blank until Mwemba aims his gun at her, screaming in her face. Then she just tosses her head and swings her bound arms around the Sangoma's neck like it's an act of defiance, and I get another glimpse of what Ash must have fallen for. The Sangoma smiles meaningfully at some of the LRA boys when he grips Jen's thighs. Poor Jen has to just sit there with her face pressed against the knot of his bandana, unable to move.

When we start climbing, the Empty Child takes some of Jen's weight from behind with a hand on her backside, shunting them up the steeper bits. She's quite strong considering how slight she is, because she's also giving the toddler a piggyback. The little boy isn't helping her much: Every time we duck under low branches he makes a game of grabbing a handful and hanging on until either they break or the girl tugs him free. The slopes are thickly wooded, so we have to zigzag our way up, the LRA soldiers hacking at vines and creepers with their machetes. Ash struggles with finding secure footholds, and a couple of times one of his blades actually gets pulled off by a root or something.

It is a huge relief when, after twenty minutes or so, we emerge onto this uneven, deeply rutted track. Cars have been along here; I can still make out tire prints. The trees rise above us on the other side until they are lost in mist. In places the road is muddy and swimming with water — it must have rained recently — and the humidity makes the air feel like I'm breathing molasses. The Sangoma sets Jen down and I rush over to support her. Walking is a lot easier here despite the mud, because there are dry, grassy bits right at the edge of the track where ferns and rubbery dark green leaves have shielded the path from the water. There is a line of weathered telegraph poles following the track, with a slack, vine-draped wire hanging between them. The air is alive with tiny bugs that bite us and swarm around the corners of our eyes. At least Charis, Jen, and I are able to bat them away. The guys have their arms tied behind their backs, so all they can do is shake their heads and blink.

All around us, the landscape shivers and rustles with life. I think, *This must be it — this is the jungle,* but when I see several of the soldiers run to either end of the track and keep the road covered with their guns, I change my mind. There's some way to go until they feel safe. Somehow I don't think there will be roads where we are going.

They stop us by a telegraph pole and one of the kid soldiers shimmies up it with the Sangoma's coil of wire over his shoulder. When he's at the top, he gently cuts into the cable with his machete. Then he bites at the end of the wire and lets the rest of the coil unwind and drop heavily to the floor as he twists the bare ends onto the section of cable he cut. The Sangoma forages in a backpack, pulls out this really old telephone with a dial, and fiddles about, connecting it to the coil. When he's done he listens to the handset a couple of times and then hands the thing to Mwemba, who pulls a grubby old printout from his back pocket and unfolds it.

That nasty, self-satisfied grin of his twists his mouth. "This," he says to us, holding up the phone, "is another reason your friends will find it impossible to trace us. Now, who is going to be your spokesman?"

18

A SH STEPS FORWARD. MWEMBA LIFTS THE RECEIVER and taps the cradle like he's doing Morse code as he reads the number from his printout. While he works it starts to rain, big slapping drops, and the ink begins to splatter and run. After a few taps I work out that he's actually tapping numbers. I try to memorize them — *five taps, nine taps, one tap* — and then I give up because I think I've missed too many and I'm not sure when he's leaving gaps. To be honest, I'm not sure what the point would be anyway.

By the time it connects we are all drenched. Mwemba pulls Ash to his side, water pouring in rivulets down their faces.

Rain hisses and shakes the bushes angrily. Seeing them together like that, I know who I'd follow: Ash looks superhuman on his blades, next to this twisted shadow of a human being. Izzy's death has hardened something in him. I wonder if any of the LRA kids see it, too?

"Listen carefully. My name is Moses Mwemba of the Lord's Resistance Army. If you want to keep your job, you will put me through to your newsroom." He waits. "This is Moses Mwemba of the LRA. Make sure you tell the world who I am . . . I assure you, this will not be a waste of your time . . . Hang up if you wish, but you will miss the best story of your career . . . It is your choice . . ." He says nothing for ages, and then, "A good decision. I have demanded five million US dollars in cash for their safe return. Tell the British Foreign Office to have the money dropped by parachute over the N5 road, ten miles north of Baraka, Democratic Republic of Congo, in twenty-four hours. If they fail to do so, the boy with no legs — Ash Carter — will die. If we see any movement on the ground, a second hostage will also die." Mwemba pushes the phone against Ash's ear. "Speak to him."

"Hello? Yes, he's for real — I'm Ash. Uh-huh, we're coping for the moment. Ask them to send antibiotics, tell them Izzy —"

Mwemba snatches the phone away before Ash can finish. "You have heard our demands." Then to the Sangoma while he tears the wires apart, *"Kusubiri hadi inakuja. Wewe kujua ambapo kupata yetu."*[12]

---

12. Wait until it comes. You know where to find us.

I'm guessing he's told the Sangoma to wait for the money, because when we start walking again the wiry witch doctor stays behind with two boy soldiers. The feather in the Sangoma's headband is wilting and matted by the rain, and for some inexplicable reason the sight gives me hope. If Mwemba is leaving him here, it means that this track can't be too far from Baraka or that road he mentioned. Maybe this dirt road *is* the N5, though I doubt he would give his position away that easily. When I look at Ash I know that he's working it out, too.

The soldiers force us onward again, watching the Sangoma and his guards melt into the bush behind us like shadows as the rain turns the furrowed road into a river. Water pours along the ruts and a tortoise races out of the undergrowth on tiptoe, faster than I would have thought possible. Ahead, our track weaves its way ever higher into the hills, sometimes dipping into deep hollows or twisting around a sheer drop. A white-hot fork of lightning actually hits the road ten feet from where we are standing. The crackling explosion is deafening and I'm left with spots floating before my eyes. The LRA soldiers shriek and chatter excitedly and they shove us forward, anxiously scanning the sky.

We walk along the track like the living dead, with our heads down. Soon we're all drenched and chilled to the bone. Only Marcus is enjoying the downpour. He throws his head back and opens his mouth, leans and twists so that every inch of his clothes and skin are soaked. At one point he whoops so loudly he scares the kid soldiers and we manage a laugh. I'm happy for him. Every now and again we pass sections where the trees have been cleared, and the views of the lake, even though they are amazing, are wasted on us because we're all so miserable. At least the insects have had to take the day off from biting us, and the clean water washes away some of the filth that has stained our hands and faces.

We don't stay on the road for more than a couple of hours, by which time the inky black rain clouds have moved out over the lake, leaving the dark green leaves around us wreathed in steam. When we reach a point where the ground levels off, Mwemba leads us away from the track through a patch of shoulder-high grass to our left. It gives way to ferns and more dense undergrowth, where the lead soldiers carve out a path whenever their way is blocked. It's confusing, because whichever direction you look, everything is the same. After a few twists and turns I'm totally lost.

It is quite late in the day when we stop in a clearing to rest. Most of the LRA kids who are not guarding us have put their weapons on the ground. The sun is a big bloodred ball touching the tops of the trees a little to our left. That means we must still be heading roughly northwest.

A few feet away on my right the Empty Child squats, feeding slices of mango to the toddler. He squeezes a wedge until the orange flesh oozes between his fingers and holds it out for me. I shake my head and he crams it in his mouth.

The Empty Child's relationship with Mwemba is bugging

me now more than ever. I see the LRA leader give her and the toddler a shifty glance full of loathing, but he complicates it by scrubbing at his forehead as if he regrets whatever it is he's thinking. It's like there's this love-hate thing between them. She won't ever look him in the face, but she's often the one nearest to him when we're on the move. It's like she is drawn to him even though she really wants to run away. Her body language, now that I think about it, is always tense until she can be on her own with the boy — like now, for instance. She sits apart from the others while we rest, making patterns in the dirt with the baby. I can't figure out how she can look after her kid on one hand and be so freaking heartless on the other. She's making my head explode, so I point at the toddler and ask her, "Is he really your brother?" They don't look alike, so I'm thinking maybe it's just some random kid she's picked up and just *calls* her brother. For all I know, she killed his parents.

She looks up.

Sign language it is, then. I point — "The boy" — then between them — "your brother?"

To my amazement she nods, and her eyes half close as she turns away. That's the first time she's even responded to me, but there still isn't a shred of anything remotely human on her face. The little boy eats with one hand and pulls with the other at the string of teeth, and then on a silver chain that I hadn't noticed before. It's tucked under her T-shirt. Whatever is on the end of it remains hidden by her collar. I find myself willing the kid to pull it out completely, I don't know why.

Soon I can begin to make out a silver rectangle, then a corner with what looks like . . .

The Empty Child slaps the toddler's hand away and pushes it back beneath her shirt. He giggles and looks at me.

"Is that a crucifix?" I ask her. Izzy was a Catholic. Surely if this girl is religious, she should have some kind of conscience? I wonder if it is hers or if it's stolen. Maybe she just thinks it's valuable.

She won't answer. The girl gives me the creeps, so I don't even know why I'm trying. As if she hears me thinking, she gets up and walks farther away, until she's half hidden by this plant with enormous wide leaves. I can see her hand, though, resting on her chest, and I can't be sure but I think her lips may be moving.

Suddenly there's a commotion in the trees at the edge of the clearing and this chimpanzee drops from a low branch, as bold as brass, and scampers over — all arms and legs — to investigate us. The nearest LRA soldiers scramble for their guns, but soon their alarm turns to laughter. The toddler totters over as fast as he can to see what's going on, and the Empty Child even pokes her head out from behind her bush. Mwemba doesn't bother to look up.

The chimp comes right up to Ash and Jen and pokes at Ash's blades, screaming and dancing before backing off warily. Charis clucks at it encouragingly to get it to come back, but it has lost interest in us. Split-Lip shoves one of his friends in the back and pulls the kid's machine gun out of his hand. He offers it to the chimp while the other boys laugh and make shooting signs. They're insane. They want the animal to take it and pull the trigger. Split-Lip seems confident that the chimp's not capable of doing it, and they're all laughing while it tries to figure out which end to hold. The toddler wants to touch its fur, but the Empty Child races over and scoops him up before he gets any closer and runs to safety with him squirming and squealing in her arms.

Seeing the danger, Ash hisses at us, "Find some cover!" but there isn't any near enough. It's too late anyway.

The chimp takes the bait, snatching the gun, and makes cooing noises while holding it upside down. Split-Lip lifts his up, showing the chimp how to grip the stock. Next thing we know, the chimp has flipped the gun over and the LRA kids are diving out of the way of the wildly swaying muzzle. The chimp folds its pink lips nearly inside out and bares its stained teeth in a smile.

Suddenly there's a rattle as the gun goes off, and dust devils patter around the feet of the soldiers. They scatter in panic. So do we. The chimp puts its eye to the barrel of the gun and shakes it, screeching. It sounds like laughter and the toddler joins in like it's some kind of game. Before anyone can get the gun back, the chimp grips it again and runs at some of the soldiers. Now the nearest LRA kids are *really* scared. They're squatting behind bushes, moving to keep out of the way of the wildly swinging gun. The other, more reckless ones are still finding it all hilarious.

Mwemba gets to his feet, angry, yelling at them to get the gun back. No one dares move. The chimp lets off more random shots, then, frightened by the noise, races in my direction, shaking the gun and screaming. The undergrowth is too thick to run into, so I shuffle backward on my backside until I'm stopped by the branches and there's nowhere left to go.

The chimp keeps running right at me, holding the gun across its chest, then stretching up and screaming at me so loudly it feels like my eardrums will burst. I'm cowering, scared witless, but suddenly the chimp falls silent. And hands me the gun.

I take it.

I look at it.

I clamber onto my haunches and let my finger fold around the trigger.

There's no time to think about what to do with it. The toddler wriggles and escapes from the Empty Child. He runs up to the chimp, screaming with excitement, with the girl hot on his heels. The chimp bares its teeth at the baby and screams angrily before scampering back to the trees.

I'm so torn I can hardly breathe. Even with my hands tied I can use this thing. The toddler runs over and throws himself at me. I feel his sweaty arms wrap around my neck and he buries his head in my shoulder. I stand up, with the kid still clinging to my leg, and point the gun at the girl. She stops dead in her tracks.

"Back off," I tell her quietly.

Almost imperceptibly, the girl shakes her head and looks back over her shoulder at Mwemba.

Ash and Marcus are on their feet and suddenly I am aware that all eyes are on me. Guns swing in my direction. Some of the kid soldiers start to move closer, but I lift my weapon and point it at the girl's chest. A bead of sweat tickles the side of my face.

Split-Lip's face has a smile frozen on it that turns to panic when he realizes what he's done. He looks frantically around at his friends for support as Mwemba bears down on him. His eyes are black and glassy, his face devoid of anything remotely human. He grips Split-Lip by the neck and frog-marches him closer to me. In a dangerous voice, he orders the boy, "Take it back."

When Split-Lip doesn't move, Mwemba fires a shot into the ground at his heels. The boy dances out of the way and walks over until he's shoulder to shoulder with the girl. "Give it to me," he demands, holding out his hands.

"I'll shoot her," I say, gripping the gun tighter.

"Do as he says, Rio!" Ash's voice is heavy, I don't know whether it's from worry or disappointment that the chimp didn't give *him* the gun. "Listen to me. Mwemba doesn't give a shit about any of these kids."

The girl looks at Ash and there's something on her face. It's like she's just woken up and has noticed he's there.

I waver.

"Guns aren't any use to us," Ash says. "Not now. Not here. They don't care who you shoot and you'll be dead before her body hits the dirt."

Mwemba smiles viciously at me. "Listen to your friend."

I'm caught in indecision for what seems like ages — then, reluctantly, I hand the gun to Split-Lip and watch his shoulders sag with relief.

The Empty Child shoves me roughly to the ground, and when the toddler tries to help me up she shakes him until he screams, then she hauls him away by his arm. Something in me snaps.

"Hey — go easy on him! He's just a baby!"

The girl turns her back on me, leaving me dazed and feeling like one more chance of escape has just passed us by. Will we get another?

Somehow Ash manages to elbow his way through the kid soldiers; he drops heavily to the ground next to me. "Nice try," he says, "but the timing was all wrong. You did the right thing."

"Mad bastards," Marcus mutters when we get back to the others, but he's trying not to laugh. "Wish I'd had my smartphone, though. Can you imagine how many YouTube hits you'd get?"

"Shut up, Marky," says Jen, who's throwing up again into a bush. "Rio could have been killed."

I look at her back and Marcus rolls his eyes at me.

The Empty Child seems to appear from nowhere with a flask of water for us. At first it looks like she's going to give it to me, but she seems to think again and throws it to Ash.

"Thank you," I say, but I'm talking to the back of her head.

She pauses for a fraction of a second. To be fair, I don't care now whether she listens to me or not. I'm too stoked by my discovery — the girl does have emotions! For the barest fraction of a second she was actually worried for me. There's a chink in her armor. Izzy's favorite word, *love*, has been growing in my mind lately and I can't shake it, however much I want to hate these sullen, horrible kids. It's like Iz has become my conscience — and I like it, because it feels like she's still alive, talking to me. If she was here, she'd be bugging me about trying to understand them or something, I know she would. Sometimes I wonder if the flutter I feel in my chest is her heartbeat.

I have to squat with Jen and make her drink. Sweat is pouring off her forehead and her pupils are wide. She takes a couple of feeble gulps and hands the flask back. I don't take it.

"All of it."

"For all we know, it could be this that's making me ill," she says weakly.

"It's the infection that's making you ill. Just drink it."

She's barely had a chance to finish when we're off again, into the bush. At the order of her leader, the Empty Child cuts our ropes, but only so that Charis and I can carry Jen between us.

By the time night falls we are all too exhausted to move. I'm almost asleep on my feet when we finally stop walking. On top of that, my battle-weary elastic band has finally given up the ghost and I'm being attacked by my own hair.

Ash grins at me as I wrestle with it. "Leave it alone. I like it like that."

"Yeah? You don't have to live with it." In the end I pull it back with my hands and make it into a fuzzy cushion.

No sooner have my eyes shut than I'm waking up again, and the sun has begun climbing into the sky, shrouded in mist. Then more walking until we cross a series of small hills and the ground starts to rise to another crest. That's when I see it, crawling across the horizon, dense and black beneath its thick, endless canopy. We all see it.

Jen drops to the ground, crying and shaking her head. "It's all over!" she gasps. "We'll never get out of there."

I squat next to her and hold her hands, trying to empty my head of the voices that are screaming at me: *No one will ever find you!*

Marcus and Charis lean against one another, ashen-faced, and the LRA leader turns to watch us. He's loving this. He even holds up his hands so everyone will stop, to let us take it all in. Only Ash stands there unbowed.

My mind is spiraling down into some dark, hopeless place, and I don't know if I'll ever be able to get it back. All this time I thought we *were* in the jungle — now I realize *this* is it. No wonder Mwemba is so keen to get to it. Once we're in there, we'll be lost to the world.

I can feel Ash's eyes on my neck before I even turn around. He rests his head between my shoulder and Jen's.

"It's tonight or never," he whispers, and my chest fills with ice.

19
DAY 16

JEN STUMBLES DOWN THE VALLEY SIDE BETWEEN me and Marcus like a zombie, and a couple of times we almost drop her because her knees give way. Her forehead bumps against mine. "I'm going to be next," she moans.

"No, you're not."

She gives me a bleak look.

Sometimes there is only room for one of us to lend Jen some support, because the deeper we go into the valley the more the bushes seem to close in on our path. It's like this thick bush is the guardian of the jungle, harassing us at every turn. When I touch Jen, she feels hot and clammy. She

shudders all the time, and the fetid smell from her leg is becoming unbearable. Occasionally she whimpers and bats a hand at it. Since we left Tanganyika it's been constantly swarming with flies. Charis and Marcus take turns to help keep them off but they give up after an hour or so because the insects are just too numerous. I'm worried sick about it, but I don't dare let it show on my face. Whenever the LRA give us water I wash Jen's leg with it.

Dusk comes early under our blanket of leaves. The ground has begun rising slowly now and Mwemba is like a man possessed, driving us on without a break. All the child soldiers can sense that safety is not far away. We march on, watching the towering green wall of the true jungle get closer and closer, until it is above us. As soon as we reach it he has Charis and me tied up again and assigns a guard to each of us. Two of them drag Jen along. All my energy is sapped now. I'm convinced that, one way or another, I'm going to die. Ash's words play over and over in my head. *It's tonight or never.*

When we finally plunge into the jungle I've never felt so lost in my life. Beneath the canopy *everything* closes in on you. Color is wrung from the world and everything is stained green. Sounds have this weird dead echo and the air is still and heavy. The light was fading outside. In here it has almost gone completely.

The lead soldiers hack and cut a path through the undergrowth, their machetes singing, until we hit on a narrow trail made by some jungle creature. A couple of Mwemba's boys have flashlights, one to light the way and the other to flash in our faces every now and again.

After what I can only guess to be an hour or so, Mwemba calls a halt. There are yellow lights ahead, bright against the endless green-black wall of jungle. I'm thinking that this must be their hideout but, deep down, I know that it can't be — we're not far enough in yet, and if it was their hideout, why would they have lights on?

Quietly Mwemba orders the LRA kids to gag us. Then they fan out and creep forward. There are about ten huts arranged around a clearing, surrounded by tree stumps. There is saw-dust everywhere, and piles of logs. A couple of the tree stumps have axes stuck in them, and a fire burns in the middle of the clearing, cracking and hissing whenever insects fly into the flames. Two guys are talking and there is music playing quietly in one of the huts, accompanied by the clatter of pots and pans.

When Mwemba waves at them, Split-Lip and a couple of his friends creep stealthily under the trees to the point closest to the fire. I catch the glint of Split-Lip's teeth when he looks back for a signal.

Suddenly I'm back at the clinic, desperate to help, thinking about those nurses again. These people don't have the faintest idea about the evil that lurks in the jungle shadows around them. The toddler is gripping the Empty Child's hem, sucking his thumb while he watches, and his wide brown eyes are full of flickering reflected light. When he spots the dog curled up by the fire he takes his thumb out and points.

He gurgles and shouts, *"MBWA!"*

One of the guys from the huts looks up and peers into the darkness. Angrily, the LRA leader lets out a weird, high-pitched trilling sound — it must be their signal — and gunfire spurts from where Split-Lip was hiding. I can't bear to watch, but I can't turn away.

The men seem to take forever to shudder and twist and fall to the floor, and the bastards keep on shooting them where they lie. I mean, they were just *talking* — what did they do to deserve this? *WHAT?*

Pots clatter to the floor and more people seem to emerge from everywhere, there must be at least twelve or thirteen of them, several women and a couple of kids. From the way they're dressed, I'd say they're poor but just *normal* people. They have no weapons that I can see. For all we know they could be refugees from all the fighting that goes on in this place. All of us are roaring into our gags, trying to warn them, but it's no use. I can only stand here groaning and crying like a lost child while the guns rattle on and on and on. Pretty soon it's all a blur because I just can't stop the tears. It is complete chaos — everywhere the mechanical rattle of the guns and the sickening sound of the impacts — and the radio playing happy, jangly African music for ages, until someone shoots that, too.

Then it's over.

The disgusting soldiers howl and screech like their team has just scored a goal. We're all too shocked to do anything but stand there staring.

While Split-Lip picks over the bodies for trophies, Mwemba and the rest of his boys walk through it all like it's just another day's work. They pull blazing sticks from the fire, throw a couple to the others, and torch all of the huts except the three nearest the edge of the clearing, which they leave untouched.

"*Kuondoka hakuna mtu hai.*"[13] Mwemba's command is chilling. I recognize the word *hakuna* from the song. *No? Nothing?* Then I get it — *hakuna mtu* — *no one.*

No survivors.

The LRA leader goes into one of the huts and drags a guy out. He's kicking wildly, scattering crumpled, yellowing magazines by the doorway, until the LRA leader shoots him in the head. Mwemba throws the body aside like it's just rubbish.

In almost no time, the groaning, pleading voices of the victims fade to nothing until all that remains is the roar and pop of the burning huts. Young voices chatter and grunt while they drag the bodies away and throw them under thick bushes.

When the Empty Child finally tears my gag off I shove her as hard as I can and scream at her. "*HAKUNA?*" I point with my bound hands at the bodies, and yell again, "*HAKUNA!* . . . *HAKUNA?*" until my voice totally gives out.

My last shove is so hard she almost falls over. But my rant is just noise to her. I don't even have any words to express what I feel. She just stands there pointing her gun at me,

---

13. Leave no one alive.

wide-eyed, not knowing how to deal with me because I'm not scared of it anymore. Her features don't even flicker. Ash keeps trying to pull me back by stepping in front of me and blocking my way with his shoulder, but I keep going until the girl loses her patience, lifts her gun, and fires into the air above my head. Then I turn my back on her in disgust and walk back to Jen, who has collapsed against a tree trunk. Her eyes are glassy and wide and she's shaking her head.

The others have been to Afghanistan, but that makes no difference. They are as badly affected by this as I am. Charis's nose is bleeding. She is wrestling with an LRA kid until her prosthesis cracks loudly and he hits her hard with the side of his gun. The soldiers' faces are twisted. Some look downright scared. They would love nothing more than to finish us off, but they know they would have to answer to Mwemba.

"Marky, NO!" Ash shouts in a vain attempt to stop a screaming Marcus from charging at Split-Lip, who easily side-steps him and shoots three rounds alarmingly close to his face. Marcus crashes into a tree trunk and Ash stops him from trying again, blocking his way with nothing more than his chest because their hands are still bound behind their backs. "*LEAVE IT!* Leave it, mate," he says as Marcus struggles to get past him. "It's no use."

Ash is right — the soldiers are so hyped they'd kill us by accident if we're not careful. After a second or two trying to barge Ash out of his way, Marcus gets it. He calms down, but barely. He shoulders Ash away angrily and falls to his knees, shaking his head and yelling obscenities at the LRA kids. All the while, the Empty Child's eyes flick from one to another of us, wide and disbelieving, like we're from some distant planet. We might as well be. These murderous children barely look human to me anymore.

When the settlement has been cleared two LRA boys shove me into one of the huts and stand guard by the door. I scan the room. There are a couple of reed mats and a camping stove on one side; on the other, cooking pots and a couple of boxes of neatly washed and folded clothes. There's a shelf stacked with French books and several yellowing copies of some newspaper called *Le Monde*. At the back of the hut there is a kind of bamboo ladder with clothes drying on the rungs, and toys scattered around it, looking like they were just being played with. I try not to think about it.

Split-Lip and the Empty Child drag Jen inside next and leave her by the back wall. I just want them to get their filthy hands off her. All the LRA child soldiers have these vacant half smiles on their faces, and the whites of their eyes are bulging, like they're all stoned. It's even scarier because of the night shadows and the angry orange glow of the burning huts. The rest of the LRA soldiers stand by the pile of bodies in silent expectation as Split-Lip hands them strips of that bark, like it's some kind of reward.

As soon as we are alone in the hut, I slide over to Jen and gently push her hair out of her face. Her eyelids are heavy;

she's barely conscious. She just looks up at me with tears streaming and says, "I want to go home."

I hug her as best I can. "I know, babe. So do I."

"You love him. Don't you?"

Neither of us can cope with listening to the noises outside, but her change of subject still takes me by surprise. It's as if we're still on the yacht. It throws me — I don't know what to say.

She doesn't wait for an answer. "I've seen the way you look at him."

I drop to the floor next to her, still unable to answer. After what we've just seen I can't even go there: It's hard to believe that she's even thinking about that right now. I worry the infection is making her delusional.

Jen closes her eyes like she needs to sleep — she doesn't say anything else. She manages a weary smile just as Ash and Marcus duck through the doorway. I've never been so happy to see them. A few seconds later, one of the kids shoves Charis in. There's blood all over her mouth and chin, and Marcus hurries to help her as she stumbles over the threshold.

Charis steadies herself against his shoulder. "Thanks, Marky." Her voice is dead.

"Anytime . . ."

She tries to work the fingers of her prosthesis, but part of the socket is split. "Well, that's *fantastic*, isn't it?" Fortunately the split doesn't seem to have broken all of the electronics. With a bit of adjustment, three fingers hum open and shut. It still works.

To our amazement Ash's guitar twangs outside and some of the LRA kids start singing as if nothing has happened, like they're on a freaking camping trip.

"Can you believe that?" I say.

"Right now?" Ash comes to sit with me and Jen. "I think I'd believe anything."

His eyes meet mine briefly and I'm relieved to see something other than disappointment in them when he looks at me. I have this intense yearning . . . an urge to fall against his chest, bury my head, and hide. I know I'd feel safe there. Instead I just say, "Those kids are seriously warped. I used to pity them. Right now I don't think I'd care if they all died."

Izzy's voice pops into my head as I'm speaking. What was it she said? It was only a few days ago, but it seems so long now that I can barely remember. *Try something different. Love those who hate you. Like Madiba did.* I want her to shut up and I feel terrible for wanting it at the same time.

I've tried, Iz. I can't do it.

It must be after midnight by the time the crackling fires have burned themselves out. Outside, the orange light and floating red embers have given way to darkness. The sweet smell of smoke is everywhere and it stings my eyes. For most of the time we've just been sitting here in silence, unable to move or do anything other than listen. Judging by the crashing that has been going on, the thatched roofs must have caved in one by one, and I'm guessing that mud walls don't burn too well because when Marcus peeped out he told us they were still standing. He thinks some of the LRA kids have been dousing the flames.

Suddenly Ash nudges Charis with his shoulder. "We need to get out of here now," he tells us, "while we can still find our way. We should head northeast for Bujumbura. That's where the radio said those SEALs are setting up shop. Marky — go see how things lie."

"Right." Marcus heads for the door, watches for a moment, and then nods over his shoulder.

I'm still trying to get my head around the fact that Ash knows which direction to head in. I haven't thought to look at the stars since night fell. Meanwhile he's been looking out for us every second, and he knows that this is his moment to act. Suddenly Ash is taking charge, and after what just happened I'm ready to try anything to escape, even if we die trying. Ash is battered and bruised, his hair is matted, and his stumps are obviously agony, but written on his face is enough strength to carry all of us another hundred miles. My heart swells. Jen is right: I do love him.

Ash looks at us and there is fire in his eyes. "Charis?"

"Yes, Cap'n?"

"I think now is as good a time as any, don't you?"

"About bloody time." Charis smiles and works her shoulders until she can pull her stump out of the prosthetic socket and tug her ropes free. Next, she scoots over and unties me so that I can slide the knife out of my waistband and cut Ash's ropes. Being free to move on our own terms is such a relief. I don't think anything has ever felt so good. If I survive this, I'm not sure anything will ever feel as good again. While I'm working, Charis goes over to the doorway and helps Marky loosen his ropes until he's able to tear them off and rub his wrists with a long sigh. Now that he's got the use of his hands again, Marky glances outside and makes some of those finger signs you see in the movies. My guess is he's telling Ash that our two guards are on the left of the doorframe and there are six LRA kids some way off to the right. The rest loses me.

Ash throws his rope angrily onto the straw mat as soon as I've cut the last strand. "The back of the hut is against the jungle," he tells us. "Looks like the walls are just mud, so all we need to do is make a hole big enough to crawl through, and we're out of here." He scrambles over to the far wall to help Charis untie Jen.

"Ash," I whisper, "what if they catch us?"

His voice is gentle. "What do we have to lose?"

Nothing.

I stop to check on Jen, but she looks like she's asleep. Her breathing is shallow and her eyes are moving rapidly beneath the lids. When I shake her, she wakes but doesn't seem to know where she is for a while.

Ash joins Marcus at the door for a few minutes, watching the LRA kids. When he's satisfied that he has seen enough to make a decision, Ash gets us all together. His face is set like stone. He's in control again.

"Keep watching, Marky. They're all high on that weed they chew," Ash explains. "We need to be quick."

I'm nearest the back, so I start to clear a space.

"Here . . . I've got an idea." Charis, slipping her prosthesis back onto the stump. "I've still got plenty of battery power left, because I've hardly had to use this." She adjusts something on the side of it, and it buzzes as she opens out the fingers. "Rio, help brace my elbow." Charis arranges the fingers into a claw, pressing them against the mud wall.

I push hard against her elbow while she makes the fingers close, and huge chunks of mud crumble through them and fall to the floor. The motors make a labored, grinding noise — is it too loud? Ash smiles at me reassuringly from the doorway, his face illuminated by the dying light from the fires. I think fear is making it seem louder. It's hard at first, but we find a rhythm once the first few handfuls have crumbled away. We do it again and again until the metal fingers are scratched and bent. It seems to take ages, but eventually the hand suddenly breaks through the wall and I almost shove the whole thing through. We pull it back and start again.

While we work, Ash pulls off one of his blades and digs away some of the looser chunks. Pretty soon we have a hole big enough to get your head through, and there's nothing out there but dense black jungle.

20

THE NEXT HOUR IS THE LONGEST OF MY LIFE. IT
seems to take forever to widen the hole. A couple of times,
at the sound of booted feet outside, Marcus waves his arms
and sends us all scattering to our positions. They're false
alarms, though. All the while my heart is pounding constantly, willing the hole to get bigger.

Eventually, by taking turns, we make it big enough for
Ash to get his shoulders through. He's got the widest torso, so
if he can get through, then we all should be able to — with
a squeeze. I'm dripping with sweat, breathless, and covered
with mud, but there's no time to take a break.

"Shh!" Marcus waves his arm at us from the doorway. He's heard voices again.

One of them is definitely Mwemba. Suddenly, covering up the hole and brushing off the dirt is a life-and-death thing. I'm trying to stop my hands from shaking but when I try to wrap Ash's rope back on his wrists, I fumble and drop it. Panic makes me clumsy when I try to pick it up again. In the end Ash shakes his head and takes it off me. I've left him no choice but to drop against the wall, holding it behind his back. Just before I do the same thing, I grab one of the reed mats and slide it up so that it covers the hole. To my surprise, underneath one end is an old machete.

I can't let the soldiers find it. There's no time left to think. I grab the handle and throw it behind the hanging laundry, cringing at the metallic clunk it makes. Charis and I had our hands tied in front, so we scramble like mad to get back to our places, arranging the ropes round our wrists so we at least *look* as if we're tied up. I'm just managing to sit down with my arms crossed when the door flies open and Mwemba bursts in.

I'm shaking like a leaf. Mwemba's bloodshot eyes scan the room, slowly, purposefully. Next thing we know he's yelling at one of his boys, *"Kuangalia yao kila saa!"*[14] and then he ducks back out.

We all look at one another with total relief. I don't need a translator to figure out what he just said, either. He's telling the LRA kids outside the door to guard us closer than ever.

---

14. Check them every hour!

Ash is thinking the same. He throws his ropes off. "We have to do this — *now* — while we're only an hour or so from where we entered the jungle. Marky, you go first. Make sure the coast is clear."

Marcus doesn't need to hear any more. He pulls the mat down and slides out. Pretty soon, all we can see of him are his legs, wriggling until they disappear completely. Next out is Charis. She just leaves her bionic arm by the hole looking like some weird, half-finished construction project. The metal joints are all twisted and we've run the battery so low that the fingers barely close. Her legs slide out when Marcus pulls her from the other side. I retrieve the machete and shove it out to them. When I get to my feet I turn to look at Jen, and I'm hit with this terrible realization.

I grab Ash's arm and hiss, "Ash, wait." I look to see if Jen is listening. Her eyes are open but she looks out of it. "What about Jen? She can barely walk. They'll catch us."

"We're not leaving her."

"No." I feel like I'm drowning, but I have to say it. "*You* are leaving *us*. I'm staying here with Jen."

His voice almost breaks out of a whisper. "*What?* Don't be crazy, Rio. No way!"

"I mean it. Get help. They won't hurt us if we're the only two hostages left. They need us too much. Besides, another day and you're dead, remember?"

Ash pushes his hair back. His eyes are searching for answers. "I'm not leaving you, Rio. Either of you."

"But this is the best way, don't you see? If you manage to escape, you can bring help. If we all get caught, we won't have achieved *anything*. You three were soldiers. If anyone has a chance at survival, it's you lot."

Charis pops her head back through. "Er, guys . . . we need to go."

I *so* don't want this, but I can't see any better way. "Please?"

"She's right." It's Jen, breathless and fighting for every word.

Dropping to his haunches, Ash strokes her forehead. "Like I said, I'm not leaving you."

"But you left me ages ago, Ash," Jen gasps. "I'm cool with it. You should both go. And I want you to know, before you leave, that *I* stole your letter. Rio took it off me, that's why it was in her bag."

"What?" Ash's face is pale.

A tear rolls down Jen's cheek and she's shaking like a leaf. "I lied, Ash. I'm so sorry."

He stands up, running his fingers through his hair. "And you're telling me this *now*?"

I push him toward the hole. "You need to go, Ash."

"I'm so sorry," he tells me. "All this time . . ."

"You too, Rio." Jen won't look at either of us, even when I go and stand next to her. "Just go. I'll be fine."

"No. I'm not leaving you alone." I grab her hand and hold it tight.

"Fine," Ash mutters. I've forced him into a corner and he has to take the lead. It's what he does. "I'll go. But as soon as we get help, I'm coming back."

"No, Ash." I look into his eyes, holding them until he gives in. "If you care about us at all, don't come back. Just send help." He's not moving, so I reach out and give him another push. *"Go!"*

After standing there opening and closing his fists for what feels like an eternity, he finally drops to his knees and crawls out, and the last we see of him are his blades.

Suddenly I'm finding it hard to breathe. My mouth is dry and I feel like everything good has just been sucked out of my life through that pathetic hole. I stick my head out and watch Ash clamber up on his prostheses, silhouetted like some African predatory animal. Marky and Charis are there waiting for him.

When Ash has explained why Jen and I aren't coming, there's a brief soundless argument, Charis and Marcus flailing their arms at Ash. For a moment all three look like they might return, but they stop when I shake my head: They *have* to go. Charis blows me a kiss and she and Marcus reluctantly melt into the tangled undergrowth. Before Ash follows, he turns to look over his shoulder and raises his hand briefly. Then he's gone.

I crawl back inside and pull the mat back up over the opening, trying desperately to stay strong — for Jen.

When I get back to her side, Jen says, "Thanks," quietly, and weeps into my shoulder. "Do you think all this — what's happening to me — is punishment for what I did?"

"Jen — it's *not* punishment. Besides, I completely forgive you."

Jen groans quietly through her tears. "I hope *Ash* will forgive me."

I pull her to me and hold her tight. "He will."

"I know what he meant — why he wrote what he did in the letter."

"You don't have to talk about this."

"I think he told his mum he was going to break up with me, but when he got blown up and I was there every day with him in the hospital, it all became too difficult. He didn't want to hurt me. So he just pulled away. And now? Let's just say that sometimes you can see that two people are meant for each other . . ."

I watch her watching me, and neither of us can speak. The truth has finally come out, but I don't feel any better about it.

After a while Jen says, "This probably sounds stupid now, but can we still be friends?"

"It's not stupid."

"You haven't answered my question."

"That's because I thought we already were."

"But I've been —"

"Trust me." I peep out the door to see where our guards are, in case they're listening, but they're still too busy getting high off that stuff they chew. "Compared to these maniacs, you haven't been *anything*."

Jen's energy is all spent. She closes her eyes.

It's boiling hot in our hut, and the air is so heavy and thick with smoke that it's painful to breathe. So how come I feel like I'm freezing? I strain to see if I can hear the others outside, but they've gone, leaving a gaping hole in my chest every bit as big as the one we made in the wall. There's nothing but jungle noises and fire out there. It's just Jen and me now, alone.

21

HE GUARDS CHECK ON US MAYBE AN HOUR AFTER
Ash and the others escaped. Jen's too ill to be moved so,
when they return with Mwemba, the LRA leader grabs my
arm and tries to drag me out of the hut. He screams in my face,
spraying me with foamy spit, and I cling to the doorframe
like I'm possessed, terrified about what he's going to do to
me. Mwemba tears me off the doorframe like a rag doll and
throws me into the clearing. That really hacks me off. It's like
the straw breaking the camel's back: Finally he's treating me
like one of his victims, like he did those nurses, and Izzy, and
the loggers whose jumbled, bloody bodies are not even cold
yet. Something in me snaps and I scramble back to my feet,

swearing at him and yelling until it feels like my throat has burst.

"*Come on then, you* freaking *coward! Come on . . . !*"

I don't even know why I think it's a good idea to say that. I feel in my waistband for the paring knife but I'm shaking too badly. I fumble for the handle and drop it. Mwemba strides toward me while I'm trying to scramble away, kicks the knife out of reach, and hits me so hard on the side of my head with his pistol that my ears ring and the world dissolves into a huge, fizzing white spot.

It's the shock that brings me around. I'm cold and wet, spitting blood and wondering why my left ear is ringing. Wherever I am, it's so humid I can barely breathe, and everything smells of stale sweat and damp grass and I can actually *taste* mud. As I take a few shuddering breaths there is the rattle of a bucket being put down and the screeching and rustling of night creatures in the undergrowth. Then the pain kicks in, and when I try to lift a hand to feel the hard swelling on the side of my head, the noises shrink to nothing and then back again. I can't do it. My hands are tied behind my back and my wrists are slippery with sweat, rubbed until they are raw meat. Even small movements are agony because they make my arms slide together, smearing salty sweat and grit into the wounds. Something tickles my left wrist — a bracelet. I never wear bracelets.

I give up trying to work anything out for the moment, and manage to lever myself onto one elbow, choking back the burning, bitter acid that rises to the back of my throat. My stomach groans painfully. Then I discover that I'm lying on a mud floor next to a toppled chair, and I'm in a puddle of water that shimmers with blurry orange circles of light and shifting shadows. There's a pair of boots near my feet, and I follow the legs up to see that a tall, thin guy is standing over me, his head tilted to one side. I can't make out his features yet, everything is blurred, but I feel his boot tuck under my knees and flip my legs over so that I roll onto my back. I'm blinking, trying to get my eyes to work again. *Where am I?*

When he's had an eyeful, the guy straightens up and spits his words out with disgust, in a thick African accent. "Wake up, English bitch!" He waits, kicking the soles of my throbbing feet.

I can see now that Boots is wearing a green-and-brown combat jacket. His shoulder-length hair is twisted into thin, tight braids and it droops across his bulging red eyes when he bends closer again. Memories are starting to nibble at the back of my head. *They all have bloodshot eyes. Why is that? Izzy — Izzy's dead! The others have left me here!*

My soaked, sweaty hair is moved aside with the barrel of the pistol he used to hit me. Then warm fingers stroke the tears from my eyes. The guy is so close now I can feel his breath tickling my face. It smells *disgusting*. His voice changes. It is deeper, softened with false kindness, but it is more dangerous now than ever.

"Rhiannon . . . Rio? Something to drink? If you tell me, it will be better for you. Why don't you tell me where the others are heading, eh . . . ?"

I can't move. I can barely breathe. I don't want to die. But I can't tell him what he wants to know, either. The longer I stay silent, the farther Ash can get from here.

My tormentor goes to the door and yells something in his own language. I think he's calling someone. He waits, listening, and then disappears. While he's away I try to push the mush out of my head by shaking it and squeezing my eyes shut until they hurt. Dribbles of water and strands of hair tickle the side of my nose insanely and I can't scratch. Instead I shake my head some more and snort like an old man.

Mwemba — that's the guy's name. This is bad. This is really bad. How is this even happening to me? And what have they done with Jen?

Suddenly the room begins to swim and everything around me starts moving of its own accord, shifting in and out of focus. My stomach is contracting painfully and that bitter, burning sensation is back in waves, but my mouth is too dry to swallow. Somehow I manage to lever myself upright with my elbows, trying desperately to hold on to the contents of my stomach.

Cautiously I twist myself even farther until I can sit upright and get a good look at the room. It is small and round, a mud hut with branches and leaves twisted together to make a tall, conical roof. The mud wall is lined with neat piles of magazines, arranged like herringbones so that the piles won't collapse. By the door some are scattered and bloody, trampled and stained in the last, frantic struggle of whoever lived here. Anorexic supermodels grin at me from their torn, flapping pages. There's even a faint smell of perfume from a grubby scratch-off card: JLo Glow, the same one Jen wears.

Suddenly I remember. *The logger being dragged from his hut. Mwemba shooting him in the head.* On the far side of the room, a few splintered shelves are scattered with shards of crockery, and below them is an old TV with a cracked screen, still sitting in the wheelbarrow that transported it here. The back has been taken off and there are bits of circuit board on the ground nearby. A line of plastic cola bottle tops sit on a ledge behind it, full of screws.

On top of the gutted TV is a photo of a middle-aged African woman grinning at me from beneath a huge, colorful headdress. It's a wide, genuine mother smile. I think I might even grin back if smiling wasn't so painful. Can't think why the TV would even be here, though. There aren't any plugs — we're in the middle of nowhere. Then I put it all together: the magazines, the bottle tops, and the TV, and I get this picture in my mind of the family. Dad's interested in technology, in taking things apart to see how they work. He's hoping to sell enough hardwood to afford an old TV, maybe even use this one for spares. Mum's got her magazines; she's all up to date with the royals, William and Kate and the Queen.

Was . . . were . . . they're all dead now.

A flickering yellow light is coming from a battered old oil lamp suspended from one of the blackened branches that holds up the reed roof. It sputters and chokes, hissing almost as loudly as the crickets outside, and it rattles under constant attack from huge moths and night insects. The floor is alive with those that have already beaten themselves senseless. As my eyes focus I can see that the room I'm in doesn't have any windows. And it's still dark outside.

A familiar voice barks.

Mwemba — and he's heading back.

Fear rattles through my chest and I fight to control it. A shadow appears at the door, rests its hand on the frame. "Well? Do you have anything to say to me?"

I stay silent, shaking with fear.

Mwemba stomps back into the room, crunching the swarming insects under his boots like he hasn't even noticed they were there. He stands between me and the light so all I can see is his outline, framed with a sickly yellow aura. I blink away tears — the light is painful. The girl, wearing baggy cargo pants, takes her place at the door to watch. She leans a shoulder against the frame and the barrel of her gun clunks heavily against it. The Empty Child, the girl that never leaves Mwemba's side. Her lifeless, dull eyes look right through me as usual. She's insane. This girl hacks innocent people to bits and doesn't feel a thing. It is pitch-black beneath those half-closed eyelids.

That naked toddler that follows her around grabs a tight handful of her pants and stares past them at me. He smiles, playing peekaboo with me. When the boy gets no response, he totters over and grabs my nose. His little hand is all grubby and sweaty, and his stubby fingers explore my nostrils and mouth until I shake them away. A few strands of my hair flop over my face and he lifts them gently so he can place a kiss on my cheek. With an innocent chuckle, unaware that this is anything other than a game, he runs off and out of the door, doing that flailing toddler thing, evaporating into the gloom.

"Miss Cruz," Mwemba snarls eventually, "I do not have the whole night . . . Are you going to tell me which direction your friends are going, or must I find out the hard way?"

Back to earth with a bump, and I am grateful to the kid. He's detached me from this reality and made me understand something — *I have all the power.* I'm going to run away to some safe place inside my head and hide, because Moses Mwemba can't follow me there. All he can do is hurt my body. I don't even need to think about my answer. Nothing he can do to me now will ever make me talk.

I actually smile at him as I say, "Go to hell."

Mwemba stays calm, but suddenly I understand something. He's scared! He's lost half his hostages and he knows Kony will have his nuts for earrings if he can't get them back. The warlord's nostrils widen. He comes and kneels by me, caressing the side of my face. Every time I snap my head away he yanks it back, squeezing my cheeks like putty.

"You could make things easier for yourself, pretty girl. I will find the others anyway — you know that, don't you? — north, south, east, or west, whichever way they went. It is just a matter of time. This jungle is home to us. We know it like we know our own skin."

The way he speaks — slowly, deliberately, emphasizing odd words — his touch — they make me feel claustrophobic.

I can't breathe. I squirm and snarl like a wild animal through my pinched lips. "Get . . . off . . . me!"

Suddenly he pulls the chair upright, grabbing my hair and yanking me onto it, panting with the effort. His disgusting hands are all over me, and I kick and struggle while he ties me to the chair.

"How long do you think they will last, Rio?" he huffs, fighting with me. "There are animals out there. Dangerous animals . . . You will help your friends if you tell me."

His scare tactics are useless. I know where I'd rather be right now — out there with them.

"Why are you even bothering to ask me?"

"I'm asking you because I am a good soldier." Mwemba taps the side of his head. "Intelligence. I cannot see in the dark. What good is it to me if I track them to the edge of the jungle tomorrow and have no idea which way they are going? I will just waste time. Now, are you going to tell me what I need to know, or not?"

And all the while the Empty Child just stands there in the doorway, watching her leader at work. Suddenly it gets to me, I mean *really* gets to me. I yell at her. *"What are you looking at?!"*

She doesn't leave. No, that would be far too easy. I can't be sure, but I think her eyes flicker slightly — I probably imagined it, though.

Mwemba turns to her. "Go! Get me a bag. And bring *iboga* — bring some roots." Then he looks at me and smiles secretively. The smile fades when he realizes the girl still hasn't made a move. He runs at her, chasing her outside, his fists raised. "I told you to *go!*" he yells, and there is a hollow thud when he manages to land a blow.

For some reason the girl hasn't jumped to do what Mwemba says. That scares me. She always does what he says. I want desperately to cry, but I can't let myself, so I close my eyes and imagine that I'm far, far away from here. Somewhere safe. Somewhere beautiful.

The whale shark moves so slowly, like nothing in the world will ever bother it, and Ash is swimming toward me. He is going to tell me something — something good. There is a glint in his eye. He's close, so close, and we are totally alone — out on the ocean. I love it here. I am lifted on the surge of water from the shark's tail and we watch it slip by. When Ash turns back to me his eyes meet mine. The whole of the Indian Ocean is reflected in them. He opens his mouth to speak. "I've been wanting to ask you something, Rio . . ."

When Mwemba returns he's looking pleased with himself. He's been away for what feels like ages this time. There is something behind his back that he does not want me to see when he squats in front of my legs. Seconds later a group of malnourished soldiers begins to gather in the doorway, murmuring excitedly. That's not good.

I feel a pang of sadness when Mwemba shifts and knocks the mum photograph off the corner of the TV. The glass shatters and it just lies there, facedown. Mwemba grins at me again, breathing in deeply through his nose. He says something to the guys at the door and they all laugh.

Chicken dey merry, hawk dey near. One of Gran's crazy West Indian sayings that makes sense to me now. I'm so scared.

While they just wait there for, I guess, the Empty Child to return, pain begins to creep back into the sores on my wrists and face. I throb just about everywhere. I try to ignore it, and start singing my own version of that Muse song, "Uprising," under my breath. Somehow I feel strengthened by my pathetic, whispered rebellion.

For some reason Mwemba is still not making a move. He's got something horrible planned for me, I know it. When there's more movement outside the hut, my heart sinks. *This is it, then.* I sing my song faster, louder, so he knows he's not going to scare me so easily — and to annoy him — but he just watches me intently.

The soldiers part at the doorway when the Empty Child returns. She's pulling short strips of bark off some twigs, and stops when she reaches Mwemba's side. He holds out his free hand without taking his eyes off me for a second, and the girl drops a bundle of roots into it.

"Give the bark to the boys."

Whatever he is holding behind his back rustles.

My heart is racing and I'm all clammy. I'm desperate to get away, but I can't move the chair. It just lifts on its back legs, and if I tilt it any farther, I know I'm going to fall over.

Mwemba asks me, "You know what this is?" while he folds up a small root several times and puts it into his mouth. It's the stuff I've seen them chewing on the way here. All I know is that it makes them go manic, like they could do anything.

And the girl is handing it out to the soldiers like bubblegum. I shake my head.

"We call it *iboga*!" Mwemba laughs as he starts chewing, his pupils widening. "This is the root. It is the strongest part of the plant."

The others whoop and cheer. They can't wait for the show to begin, and I'm the main attraction.

The girl looks over her shoulder at me.

"In a small dose, it heightens *pleasure*," Mwemba continues ominously. "It is a shame the Sangoma is not here to enjoy some. The Bwiti witch doctors use it to give visions. It will help *me* to enjoy the spectacle. In large doses, however, it is not so . . . nice."

His words make me shudder. He still has a handful.

"Now, Rio. Tell me. Where did your friends say they were going? Why have they left you here on your own?" He stands up, totally wired, turning the remaining pieces of bark over in his palm. "You don't owe them anything."

"I owe them the chance to get away from you!"

"That is not going to happen."

"No? You haven't found them yet!" I'm defiant and he hates it. But he hides it well. He smiles again.

"It is just a matter of time."

And still he holds back from whatever it is he has planned for me. I am shaking violently, but I'm determined to endure whatever it is without giving them a thing. Then I hear this scrunching sound, like someone crumpling a plastic bag. It's coming from whatever Mwemba is holding behind his back, and it sounds angry.

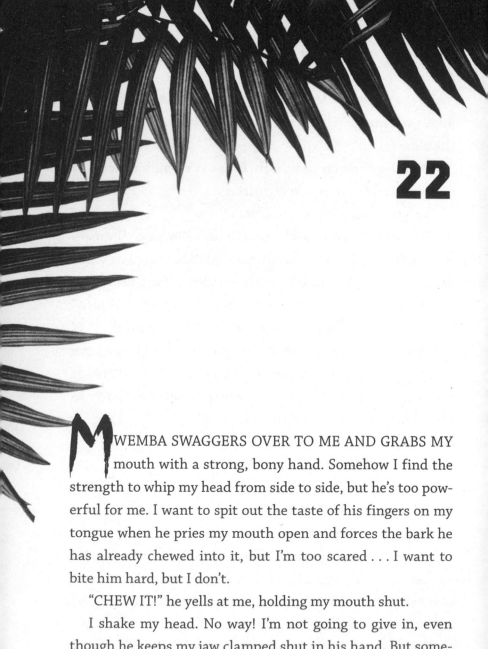

22

MWEMBA SWAGGERS OVER TO ME AND GRABS MY mouth with a strong, bony hand. Somehow I find the strength to whip my head from side to side, but he's too powerful for me. I want to spit out the taste of his fingers on my tongue when he pries my mouth open and forces the bark he has already chewed into it, but I'm too scared . . . I want to bite him hard, but I don't.

"CHEW IT!" he yells at me, holding my mouth shut.

I shake my head. No way! I'm not going to give in, even though he keeps my jaw clamped shut in his hand. But something is beginning to happen to me anyway. I get this strong,

unpleasant taste, all bitter and earthy. Then my tongue starts to tingle and go numb. When the tingling sensation stops it's like everything is being amplified. I can hear the still, stale air inside the hut, shifting like it's a rushing wind, and the walls seem to be alive with tiny, squirming black microbes.

"That is good," my tormentor says quietly, looking into my eyes. "Very good. Let *iboga* take you."

Somehow my will to fight is being sapped. My mouth is filling with saliva and I have to swallow to stop myself from choking on it. I'm still fighting, but it's getting harder and harder, and I lose count of the times I have to swallow. By the time Mwemba releases his grip I can't even let the soggy ball of bark fall from my mouth. It rolls out when I ask him, "Why are you doing this to me?"

"The poison will do wonderful things to you. Things you will not be able to endure. Then you will *beg* to talk to me, won't you, Rio?"

Poison?

As he speaks he pulls a heavy plastic bag from behind his back. I don't know if it's the drug or my imagination, but I could swear it is moving. He places it on the floor and waves for the Empty Child to pull my wet T-shirt up. She pulls the hem over my head, bunching the damp fabric behind my neck. All my resistance has sapped away, and she tugs me around like I'm a doll. Mwemba is spinning. Everything is coming in and out of focus, and when I whimper he just hisses and bares his teeth at me in an impossibly wide grin. The girl is like a huge black bat at his side, beating her big, leathery wings. When she has finished and all I have covering me above the waist is my bikini top, Mwemba kicks the chair over so I'm on my back. He tells the girl to hold my shoulders while I'm still winded from the fall. Then, when she is in position, he tears open the writhing bag and tips the contents onto my skin.

I scream. I'm covered with huge black scorpions. I don't know whether they are really that big or if it's the drug, but their spiny legs are like needles digging into my skin, and Mwemba flicks at them with a stick if they try to escape. He's making them angry so that they begin to arch their segmented tails. They scurry from side to side over my rib cage while the room seems to grow and shrink around me.

When the first agonizing sting hits between my ribs I convulse with the pain. It spreads like razor-sharp needles, and I'm convinced my skin is turning black and scaly as I squirm and fight. The pain is like nothing I've ever known. It's eating me alive. It burns like fire. A second scorpion is scurrying up to my face, chased by Mwemba's twig, clacking its thick, sharp pincers.

The guys in the doorway are laughing. One minute they're human and the next they're a pack of hyenas snarling and biting at each other's flanks. Suddenly this huge African mask is right in my face — grinning — and when it speaks, its lips don't move. I'm hallucinating.

"Where are they, Rio? You want it to stop?"

I *do* want it to stop. I want to tell him they're heading for Bujumbura, because then, maybe, he'll take the scorpions away.

But there's this fire inside me that won't go out. I see Izzy's face and I know that Mwemba can't get at *me*. I'll die first. And I'll go to my grave glad I died so that Ash could live, knowing that he loves me, too. So I laugh dementedly and spit at Mwemba in Gran's best Jamaican accent: "Want all? *Lose* all!"

Mwemba curses.

A second excruciating sting sinks into my neck. I swallow my screams until they are just a raw rumble in my neck and I watch the scorpion retreat, leaving its sting behind to swell like a balloon until it must be the size of an apple. Half of this is my imagination — I know it is — but it's *so real*. It's the drug. I try to pull the sting out, to get at it with my hands, but I don't seem to have any. All I see is Mwemba's face in mine, his gums bloodred, his teeth long and sharp, and he's snarling like a wild dog. Then, as I'm arching my back to scream, the girl releases my shoulders. I twist free violently and the scorpions slide off me before Mwemba can catch them.

"Fool!" Mwemba's voice. "Why did you do that? Look what you have done!"

None of it matters anyway. The fire swells to a crescendo in my throat until I explode in a rainbow-colored scream, and then I'm suddenly free of it all, floating away from some broken and twisted body covered in scurrying insects, tied to an old chair, sprawled on the mud floor at my feet.

There are no dreams this time. No memories to curl up in and hide. My body burns when they douse me with cold water and I wake up to more pain and misery. The drug is making me hypersensitive to everything and so, *so* dizzy. Bizarrely, I think it may be helping with the pain, because I can bear it now. It feels like I am watching myself from a distance and all the sounds are muffled. Even the yellow light doesn't burn the backs of my eyes anymore. Squinting to focus, I can see that the Empty Child is standing next to Mwemba and she is holding a long, sharp machete. I can hear the edge of the blade singing to me like it has just hacked someone's bones. That *has* to be my imagination. When she looks up I can see that her left eye is swollen and half closed, but it glistens through the slit like it has found some life at last. I can tell that Mwemba is mad, really mad. Is this the endgame now?

He pulls my head up by my hair and his voice is flat. "You stayed for your friend, no? The girl who cannot walk."

I don't answer.

"It was very noble. Very *kind*. You did not want to leave her alone with us?"

The threat in his words sends a shiver through me. I'm looking at the girl's machete and remembering. I'm remembering what these people do.

"You would hate for anything to happen to your friend, wouldn't you, Rio?"

My voice almost breaks. "Don't you dare! Leave her alone! You can do what you like to me."

Mwemba laughs. "You think I just want to hurt you? You are strong. Very strong." He smiles. "I admire this. It would make you a good soldier if you were not also so very stubborn.

A soldier needs to be strong, but he also must learn when he needs to employ a different tactic to achieve his objective."

He sounds different. I tell him, "You'll never find out where they are!" but my words feel like they are crumbling into dust the second they leave my lips.

The LRA leader is looking too pleased with himself. He's found a way. Some new way to make me speak.

Mwemba looks at the girl. He grabs her forearm so tightly that the skin forms deep folds around his fingers as he sneers, "Tonight I will teach you both what makes a good soldier, eh?"

The Empty Child might as well be a statue; she doesn't even register the pain she must be feeling, or try to pull her arm away. She could be thinking *anything* behind that mask she wears.

Suddenly Mwemba lets go as if she has burned him.

The fight is leaking out of me. I don't even believe myself when I tell him scornfully, "You can't teach me anything." I know my words are so much hot air.

"Oh? You really think so?"

"Yeah. Because you're a maniac, and when Ash brings help . . ."

"Help? There is no help in the jungle, Rio. And I *will* convince you to give me what I want. Do you know why?"

I shake my head.

"Because you care about your friends. You care about them too much . . ."

My spine feels like it has turned to ice.

". . . and I still have one of them here."

I look at the girl's machete. "What are you going to do?"

Mwemba laughs at me.

"I still won't talk."

"No? Then I will do what I want, and afterward, yes — yes, you will talk." He turns to the girl and his words are calm, matter-of-fact. "Bring me her friend's hand. We will start with that."

"NO!" The scream surges out of me.

"So. You are ready to talk to me?"

I'm consumed with a terrible mixture of fear, guilt, and anger. Ash and the others *have* to escape, it's our only chance. It is pitch-black out there and it will take them ages to get anywhere. I'm appalled to find myself weighing whether the freedom of all of us is worth one hand. Have I bought them enough time? It doesn't feel like it. I should just cave, surely, but I don't know what to do. *I just don't know what to do!* While I'm dithering, I lose my opportunity.

Mwemba thinks my silence means I'm still holding out. He waves his hand and his voice is barely a whisper when he tells the girl, "Go and do it."

Before I can protest, she's gone. I let out a hoarse scream in frustration, straining at my bonds. I hate her for not waiting. I *hate* her for only needing a whisper.

"No! PLEASE!" I beg. "You can't!" Tears stream down my cheeks. "I'll talk!" But even as I say it I know it's too late. He's not going to change his mind. He's not even going to answer me, because he actually *wants* this. Mwemba wants to crush me completely. Black thoughts threaten to overwhelm me. All this is *twisted* and the worst thing is that Mwemba has left me feeling like it's my fault. Like I'm doing this; I'm the only reason Jen is going to lose her hand, and I could have stopped it if I hadn't taken so damn long to decide. My heart pounds wildly. It feels like it's going to burst. Tears stream down my face and I whisper, "I'm begging you . . . Stop her."

Mwemba is just watching me, enjoying seeing me in distress. He picks up a battered old shortwave radio and fiddles with the dials. It clicks, then it hisses and screams, spitting out French, Russian, and then English. Mwemba looks at me and then checks his watch.

"I'll tell you anything. You win. Please, please . . . just stop her."

"In good time. This is your first lesson, Rio. No pain, no gain, eh? Is that not what you sportspeople say?" He chuckles at the proverb, payback for the time I quoted Gran.

"I'm begging you." I bite my bottom lip and resist the urge to yell at him. Instead I roar and struggle and kick vainly at the legs of my chair and cry, "*Help me!* Somebody *please* help me!"

"No one will help you, Rio. They don't even know where you are."

Outside, a scream splits the night.

A human scream.

Jen.

It burrows into my bones until they vibrate with it and I can't cover my ears to block it out. It doesn't ever seem to stop, and I can't help the tears of guilt and shame that run in hot rivers down my cheeks in response. These people are butchers.

Suddenly there is silence.

After a second or two, the bush creatures screech and howl in response. Mwemba laughs at me and hatred burns my heart to a cinder.

The Empty Child appears back at the open door with a filthy, bloody rag. It is heavy, still dripping blood through the fibers. She brings it to Mwemba, who takes it from her and holds it up to my face with a smile. "You see? Now I think you will speak. Or shall we take the other hand?"

I bite my bottom lip to stop myself from saying anything that might give him an excuse, and end up whimpering pathetically. How will I ever live with myself? How will I ever face Jen again? I've destroyed that girl. It's like this trail of disaster follows me — missing all those clues on the yacht, messing everything up for Izzy.

"Please," I ask him, consumed with guilt, "don't do anything else to her, I'm begging you. Untie me. They're going to head for Bujumbura, to the Americans."

"A wise decision." Mwemba goes to the door and shouts for his men. "Untie her," he tells the Empty Child, and disappears from sight.

Outside the boy soldiers bark and trill like wild animals when Mwemba emerges, eager to get started. He's taking a search party to look for Ash and the others and, thanks to me, he knows exactly where they are heading. They won't have got far during the night — it was too dark — and Mwemba has a huge advantage because he knows this place.

When the Empty Child comes over, I badly want to kick or hurt her, but I know that would only put me at more risk, so I sit still while she cuts the ropes at my wrists with her machete. She leans toward me like she's got something to say. I start to pull away, blind with fury, but she touches me, and there is something about her touch that disarms me — the way she is looking at me — her eyes are burning. I've never seen them like that, so I stop.

The girl bends until her lips are alongside my ear and her breath is hot and loud. It's like she wants to say something — something important — but she can't. I can feel her shaking with the effort. She takes so long over whatever it is she's trying to say that I think she's going to think better of it. Then, for the first time since we were taken, the Empty Child finds her voice and whispers into my ear, so quietly I can barely hear her.

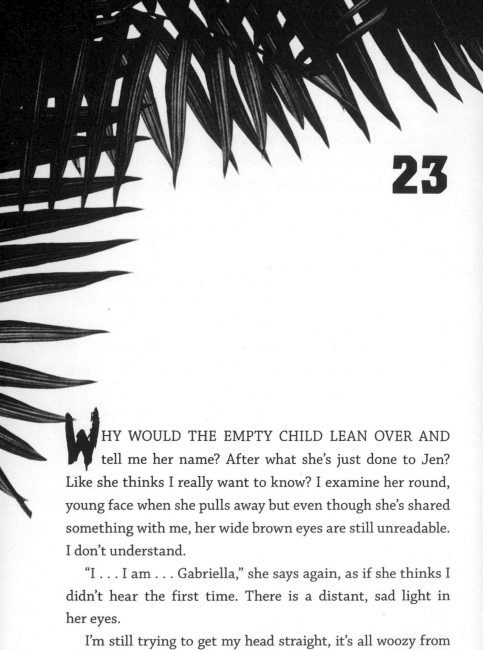

23

WHY WOULD THE EMPTY CHILD LEAN OVER AND tell me her name? After what she's just done to Jen? Like she thinks I really want to know? I examine her round, young face when she pulls away but even though she's shared something with me, her wide brown eyes are still unreadable. I don't understand.

"I . . . I am . . . Gabriella," she says again, as if she thinks I didn't hear the first time. There is a distant, sad light in her eyes.

I'm still trying to get my head straight, it's all woozy from the *iboga*. My whole body burns with pain and I have a splitting headache. I don't care about her. All I want right now is to see Jen. She might be bleeding to death. She might already be dead.

My lip is swollen and I can taste blood. Behind me, Gabriella picks away at the remaining ropes that bind me to the chair, and as soon as I feel them loosen I yank myself free and stagger to my feet, grabbing for my T-shirt.

"Look. I don't care what your freaking name is. Take me back to Jen!" I demand, pulling the T-shirt back over my head and throwing the rope at her. She doesn't catch it. It just hits her chest and falls to the floor.

The toddler runs over and starts playing with the end of the rope, while she just stands there like a moron. Something weird is happening to her, though, because she strokes the boy's rough, round head. Seeing her finally care for the kid makes something snap in me. Why couldn't she care for anything else? How can the same person do that and chop someone's hand off without blinking? My heart twists, black with hatred, and when Izzy slips into my head telling me, *She was a girl once,* I block her voice out. Right now I wish "Gabriella" was dead. I'm even thinking how to do it.

"So you just going to stand there watching me or what?"

She looks away, hoisting the toddler onto her hip.

"Then take me back, you heartless bitch."

I can smell Jen's leg from outside. There are LRA kids guarding every side of the hut now, the few who remain. I can see one posted at the back, sitting cross-legged by the hole we

My mind is spinning. I drop down beside her and look at the doorway. "I know you did." My eyes fill up. Nothing is making sense! I hated the girl so badly just now I could have killed her if I had any kind of weapon. Why would she suddenly change like this?

Jen waves her fake stump. "The girl . . ."

"Gabriella. She said her name was Gabriella." I'm still trying to take this in.

"I know. She came back with this blood-soaked rag and told me I have to bind my clenched hand with it and wear it all the time from now on if I want to stay alive."

"She did?" I'm still twisted up inside like a knot. "Well, she's right. If Mwemba finds out about this, we're all dead."

"Rio, why do you think she's helping us?"

"I don't know. I just don't know."

Outside, the sky is beginning to glow in the east. I wonder how far the others have got. I can only hope I've won them enough time to get clear of the jungle and then some, but I'm scared that they'll be found and brought back, and nothing will have changed.

I'm left alone, sitting beside Jen, to worry while the sun rises and the heat goes from stifling to unbearable. Outside I can hear Gabriella's feet slapping against the hard mud floor as she does whatever it is she does in the mornings. Jen slips in and out of consciousness; her body is fighting the infection and losing. I look at her and find myself thinking — selfishly — that if this carries on much longer she's going to die and I'll be left here, all alone.

One of the LRA soldiers brings some water for us and I attempt to swill and spit the bitter taste of the *iboga* from my mouth before I allow myself to give in to the desperate desire to drink any. It takes an iron will, but I just allow myself a few gulps. Then I lift Jen's head to help her drink. She swallows it without even waking. Afterward I do my best to give her a bath with what remains, cleaning that putrid burn while she can't feel the pain and trying to cool her fever. She groans a bit as I work, but the wound looks better when I finish, and doesn't smell quite so bad. There's a terrible problem with flies, though. They're swarming over the bloody rag, and I constantly have to wave them away. I want to sleep so badly, but I daren't. I have to stay alert, for both of us. There's been no sign of the girl — of Gabriella — since dawn.

Just before midday there's a commotion outside and I recognize one of the voices. It's not Mwemba. It's the Sangoma. In a way, I think I'm almost relieved because it means Mwemba is still looking for the others and there will be no bad news. Despite what Ash said, the military might have dropped something, too, the ransom. Could it all end?

The toddler appears by the door of the hut and runs away chuckling when I make encouraging noises at him. For a second I have this image of myself holding him hostage, threatening to throttle him unless they let us go. But I can't do it. When he comes back, he's hiding behind a handful of Gabriella's pants with an injured expression on his face, like he read my mind or something.

She throws a package of berries and fruits wrapped in a leaf at me. My hands shake as I tear it open and shove handfuls onto Jen's lap and into my mouth. I'm so famished that I almost miss the brown paper bag that dropped with it. To my surprise, it is a blister pack of pills.

Antibiotics.

The Foreign Office must have heard Ash's request and dropped something. The Sangoma has brought it back. I pop one pill out of the pack and slip it between Jen's lips, forcing her to wash it down with a last mouthful of water. She almost chokes on it, but finally swallows. While she does I have this daydream: Ash is safe. He's telling the American lieutenant to come for us and refusing to be left behind, running back to get me on his amazing blades. I imagine him sweeping me up into his powerful arms and carrying me away from all of this.

When the girl turns to leave, I say, "Gabriella . . ." and she stops in her tracks at the sound of her name. My voice is breaking with the effort, but I manage to say, "Thank you — for looking after Jen."

To my surprise she spins on her heel. "I did not do anything for *you* — or your friend! I did this for *ME*." There is anger in her voice.

The gratitude withers inside me and turns to pure acid. "Fine!" I spit back. "I don't know why I felt the need to thank a murdering, self-centered little psychopath like you anyway!"

"Do not judge me!"

"I wouldn't waste my time! You *disgust* me."

Gabriella looks at me, blinking. Then she wails bitterly, "I disgust myself!"

A tear rolls down her cheek.

I'm floored.

Her words hang in the air. We just stand there looking at one another for ages until the fire in her eyes dies and she tells me quietly, "You should have run away while you had the chance. Mwemba does not want money. He wants people to know who he is, not to hide in fear like Kony does. He will do something *very* bad before they catch him."

"Why don't *you* run away from him? You don't have to do this."

Gabriella doesn't want to listen but she's torn. She stands there like before, just waiting and thinking, like she's never going to speak again. Suddenly I'm aware that what I said was completely stupid. Of course she has to do this. These people will kill her if she ever tries to run, if they ever find out about Jen.

My voice is softer when I ask her, "Where did you get the hand anyway?"

Nothing.

After a long time just standing there examining the ground, she tells me sullenly, "There were many bodies. It was not hard to find one."

I can't help it, I shudder at the thought. A kid her age should never have to . . .

Gabriella leaves me with a parting shot. For the first time, I hear the child in her voice, distant and filled with a desperate sadness. "I am lost. I can never be like you."

Yet for some reason she's helping us. I'm so confused about her. I want to cry but I know that if I let myself, I may never stop. And Izzy's voice won't stop bugging me. *Love* . . . I hear it as clear as if she were in the hut with us, too.

"Gabriella, come back!" I call after the Empty Child, softly, but she doesn't answer me. As soon as she sets foot outside there are more excited voices in the clearing. It sounds like the search party is back. They are chattering triumphantly. One of them is definitely Mwemba, and he's heading this way.

Next thing I know, Ash is thrown through the door.

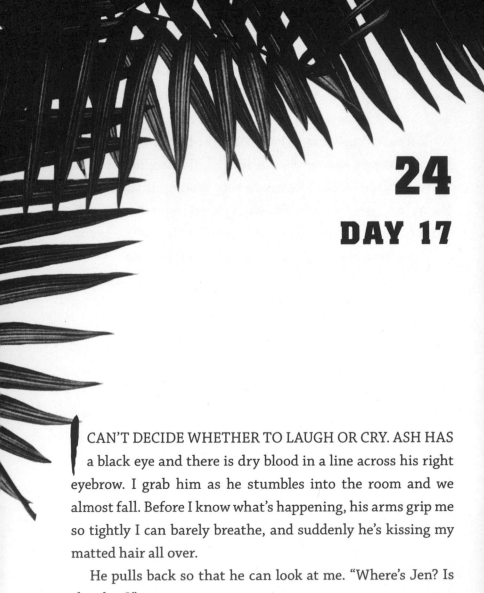

24

DAY 17

I CAN'T DECIDE WHETHER TO LAUGH OR CRY. ASH HAS a black eye and there is dry blood in a line across his right eyebrow. I grab him as he stumbles into the room and we almost fall. Before I know what's happening, his arms grip me so tightly I can barely breathe, and suddenly he's kissing my matted hair all over.

He pulls back so that he can look at me. "Where's Jen? Is she okay?"

I point to where she's curled in a ball up by the laundry ladder. She's asleep. When he finally lets me go I ask him, "The others?"

He puts his finger to his lips and we sit in the middle of the room. "We split up," he whispers into my ear. "I told them to head south while I went north toward Bujumbura."

"Why did you . . . ?" Then I realize I've been an idiot, and now I'm mad at him. *"Ash!"* I rub my eyes. "You did that on purpose! Telling me you were heading to Bujumbura. You *wanted* them to find you."

He smiles. "It worked, didn't it? There's no way the LRA will waste any more time going after Marcus and Charis now. They'll be able to get help."

I'm so worried. "But now *you're* back. I didn't want you to come back. Mwemba said he'll kill you."

He pulls me against his chest to stop me from talking. Then he lifts my face gently. "Maybe — but that's all changed now. He's lost too many bargaining chips. Besides, I told you there was no way I'd leave you and I meant it. What did those animals do to you?"

I can't deal with that yet. It's still too raw, so I just say, "When they found out you had gone, Mwemba . . . hurt me."

Ash can't speak for a second. "Rio. Oh, Rio. I'm so sorry."

I can't bear to see the pain in his eyes. "It's okay," I tell him, "I *wanted* you to go — really. To escape."

The next time he speaks, his voice is heavy with emotion. "I'm never going to leave you again, Rio. *Never*, I promise."

I let my head fall against his chest and we just stay locked in each other's arms for ages. It feels so warm and safe I can almost shut everything out. We're back on *Spirit* after the swim. He's going to tell me . . .

Suddenly Ash says, "The girl — she didn't tell Mwemba!"

"What are you talking about?"

"That we'd escaped."

I pull away. "She *saw* you?"

"Yes — just as we were leaving. I turned around and it's like she had some sixth sense or something. She was holding her kid's hand, by the fire, and her head was turned toward us. There wasn't a flicker of surprise or anything. She just walked away and let us leave!"

Now I have two reasons to be grateful to that girl. "Something is going on with her, Ash. I mean, why is she helping us all of a sudden? Her name is Gabriella and she can actually *speak*! She risked her life to save Jen's hand."

"Jen's hand?" When Ash looks at Jen and notices the bloody rag, all the color drains from his face. Scared that he will do something rash I put my hands over his mouth and whisper into his ear, "It's okay — what I mean is — it's not real." And I tell him what happened. When the tension drops from his shoulders we just stay there for a while watching Jen sleep.

After a few minutes Ash says, "So the girl, Gabriella, really is a friend?"

"I don't know. What I *do* know is that, even if she is, we need to be very careful around her. She's too close to Mwemba."

"And she's pretty twisted — don't forget what she did to those nurses at the mission."

We're silent for a while, both thinking about Gabriella. Then I shake the pack of pills. "She gave me these — so with any luck we can get Jen back on her feet in a few days."

"Rio . . ."

We stop talking when we hear the sound of someone approaching. A few seconds later, Mwemba enters carrying a duffel bag. He throws it on the ground and unzips it. It is *full* of money. "This is what your family think you are worth," he sneers at Ash, "just seven hundred fifty thousand dollars of their own money."

I don't care about the amount. All I can think is — *they did send a ransom*!

"They *beg* me to spare you, because the British government will not pay anything and this is all they could get in the time they had." He waves at his soldiers to get us up. A couple of them shake Jen awake and haul her to her feet. I'm worrying that the bloody rag will come off, but it stays put. One of them grins when he sees it and I want to slap his face.

"It is very touching," Mwemba continues, "but all this will buy them nothing. The world *will* hear about Moses Mwemba and the LRA."

"Africa is changing, Mwemba," Ash snaps back. "Nobody cares about you. In ten years' time you will be nothing more than a bad dream. When all this is over they'll lock you up and throw away the key."

The warlord's eyes are full of hate, and I can't believe it when he digs a lighter from his pocket, grabs a handful of bills, and sets them alight. He drops the flaming bundle into the bag just before it burns his fingers, and lets the whole thing burn.

"They will care," he says with a deadly smile, "if they want to deal with me — because my Africa does not give a damn about you or your money."

I'm truly shocked. Gabriella was right: None of this has been about the ransom! What does the guy want? Just publicity?

As black smoke billows higher and higher around the hungry flames, the soldiers shove us out of the hut and into the dazzling sunlight. My heart sinks when I see that the LRA kids have loaded up all of their stuff again. Weariness settles around my heart like a lead weight. Without speaking, Ash and I support Jen between us and, with a loud, confident shout, Mwemba leads us onward, plunging along narrow, overgrown paths ever deeper into the green twilight beneath the steaming canopy.

There is nothing but endless, hazy green shadows as far as the eye can see. Thick, mossy vines hang from impossible heights and the jungle floor is alive with insect life. Swarms of small black flies attach themselves to the sweat patches on the soldier's backs. Since Ash and I are exhausted, two of them have been dragging Jen on a makeshift stretcher thrown together from logs and old brown palm leaves. She is conscious most of the time now, but still very weak. Mwemba doesn't seem to care about me giving Jen her meds when she needs them, but the Sangoma scowls and shakes his pouch of bones to scare me. I can hear the constant hum of swarming insects on my back, but I'm too tired to do anything about it. The air feels like all the freshness has been wrung out of it. It is so heavy it seems to part like a curtain when you walk through it. There's no wind and the chattering and screaming wildlife echoes around you from all directions.

As soon as we'd set foot under the canopy, I felt lost; now I feel like I'm a fish swimming through a stagnant pond. Every movement is a huge effort. The one thing that gives me hope is when I look across at Ash. His blades barely make a sound, flexing slightly as he walks. He must be mentally done in after last night, but he doesn't show it. If anything, he looks more alert than ever.

When Ash returns my look, my heart flutters and I feel so grateful that he came back, grateful and guilty at the same time. Ash looks at me again and inclines his head, and I realize that he's signaling. He's telling me to watch Mwemba and the lead LRA kids. They're walking along, hacking vines and enormous ferns and pushing them out of the way. He wants me to try to make a mental note of every cut or disturbance, as they slash their way forward. It's like a trail — our passport out of here. So I follow his lead and watch the pale, fresh cuts and the discarded leaves, but when I look back over my shoulder to double-check, it's almost impossible to see any difference because the whole jungle floor is littered with fallen branches. Right now everything in me wants to give up, but seeing the way Ash copes in spite of it all gives me the strength to keep trying.

Whenever there is the smallest gap in the canopy, the ground is thick with chest-high grasses, straining for light. The LRA kids become more and more talkative as we walk, and I'm certain it's because they feel safe. They are *that* sure that no one is going to find us in here.

Our route climbs relentlessly toward higher ground. Other than at night the LRA don't even bother to tie us up now. A couple of times we have to cross quite deep ravines and Ash slips badly on his blades. They seem to come off more often now, and he's in pain where they rub, but he suffers in silence. We have to help carry Jen sometimes, but the antibiotics are working so well that by our third day in the jungle she's well enough to walk a fair way unaided. A couple of times she stumbles and almost loses the bandage that hides her counterfeit injury.

Walking is exhausting even for me, and there is precious little food to go around. We've been living off roots, nuts, and berries, and strange, twisted brown fruits ever since we left the loggers' settlement. The LRA child soldiers keep all the best pickings for themselves and we get the crud — literally. It gives me diarrhea, which is *beyond* embarrassing, because our guards insist on staying close by if we need to go. Hunger makes us all snappy, including our captors. The only one who seems to enjoy being in the jungle is the Sangoma, who has a spring back in his step and finds a new, brighter feather to chant over and stick in his bandana. This morning, he clambered up a tree and came down with a honeycomb crawling with angry bees. He and Mwemba ate it, Mwemba taking his share off the blade of an evil-looking knife while the Sangoma shoveled it into his mouth with sticky fingers, insects and all.

Since Gabriella revealed her name, I can barely get her to look my way. There's never any chance to be alone with her and I'm not even sure she wants it. She won't even let the toddler come near us now. I'm so frustrated. The only thing that keeps me trying is that glimpse of rebellion she has shown. I want to work on it. Mwemba, for his part, can be rough with her, but he is almost superstitiously wary of her at the same time. The fact that he tries to ignore the girl is probably a good thing for us, because he doesn't seem to notice anything different about her.

Mwemba occasionally makes us stop while he tries to get news on his radio, but all he gets is static. Today, though, we have climbed to the top of a steep, thickly wooded slope and emerged into this tiny grassy area. There are weird barking sounds coming from somewhere up ahead and they echo through the jungle. Nobody seems too bothered about them. Mwemba is cautious and spends some time checking out the clearing. He is just about to give the order to move on when there is a crashing in the jungle just ahead. Trees shake close to the edge of the clearing and there is a deep, rapid slapping sound.

"What *is* that?" Jen stands up weakly to look.

The LRA soldiers are looking in all directions. Weapons rattle everywhere and they point them at the undergrowth, running for cover behind vines and tree trunks. They grab us, push us to the ground, and stand over us with their weapons at the ready. Only Gabriella seems unmoved. She hauls the toddler onto her back and watches the trees quiver.

For a second or two it all goes quiet except for the static on Mwemba's radio. He switches it off, signaling at the Sangoma to go ahead and investigate. The Sangoma pokes at the bushes with his gun and then disappears through a thick patch of ferns.

Silence.

Suddenly the crashing starts again, loud and angry. There is the rattle of a gun going off wildly, more slapping sounds, and the Sangoma emerges screaming from between the trees — followed by this enormous black thing.

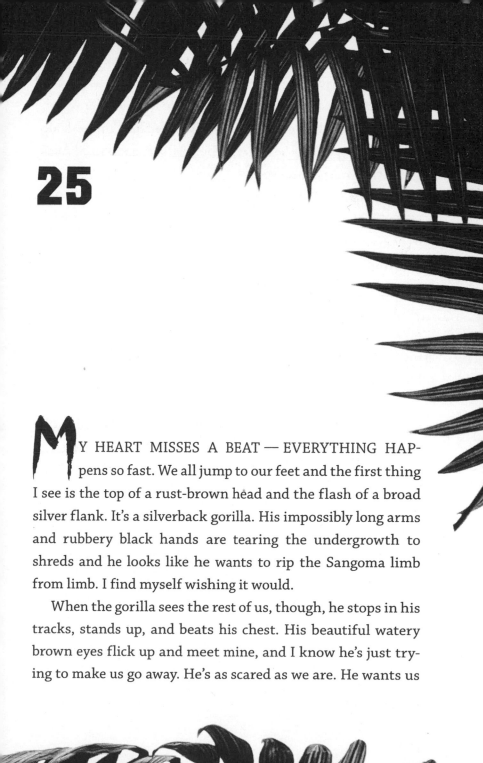

25

MY HEART MISSES A BEAT — EVERYTHING HAP-
pens so fast. We all jump to our feet and the first thing
I see is the top of a rust-brown head and the flash of a broad
silver flank. It's a silverback gorilla. His impossibly long arms
and rubbery black hands are tearing the undergrowth to
shreds and he looks like he wants to rip the Sangoma limb
from limb. I find myself wishing it would.

When the gorilla sees the rest of us, though, he stops in his
tracks, stands up, and beats his chest. His beautiful watery
brown eyes flick up and meet mine, and I know he's just trying to make us go away. He's as scared as we are. He wants us

to see what he's capable of if we are hostile. Suddenly I'm thinking, *If only Iz was here. She'd love* this. Then, as I watch, I'm amazed to see that the gorilla is wearing a leather collar.

A couple of the nearest LRA soldiers decide it's a good idea to fire their guns in the air, and the gorilla drops to his knuckles, turns around, and runs.

"KUACHA!"[15] Mwemba, yelling at the shooters to stop. *"KUACHA!"* He waves his arm at them. *"Unifuate."*[16] They run to him and disappear into the forest after the silverback.

I find myself yelling, "Don't hurt him! Don't you dare hurt him!" and Ash has to calm me down. When I snatch my arm out of his grasp I notice that Gabriella is next to me. I plead with her, "Don't let them hurt him," but she turns her back on me. In the end Jen pulls at my other arm and we fall to our haunches and wait, watching the shuddering trees fall silent.

We don't have to wait long. There is the rattle of automatic gunfire and more jarring impacts in the trees. Leaves fall like snow, and a raw, animal barking and grunting shatters the peace, followed by primates screaming. I cover my ears but I can still hear more gunfire. In the stillness that follows, there is a gut-wrenching howl and another, single shot. Jen and I are both crying by now. They had no need to do that.

It must be another fifteen minutes before Mwemba emerges, grinning all over his sick, twisted face. Between the four of them it's taken this long to drag the dead gorilla back.

---

15. Stop!
16. Follow me.

They are sweating like pigs, each of them hauling on one of the silverback's limbs. The poor thing is covered with dark crimson blood, and its watery, wild eyes are closed forever. Mwemba guts and skins it where it lies, ignoring the clouds of flies that swarm over his arms. Soon the ground around him is slick with blood and crawling insects. When he's finished he slices huge slabs of meat off its flank, which he and some of his guys eat raw. I'm surprised to see that Split-Lip won't touch it. Then Mwemba chops the head off, making this big thing of showing it like some warped trophy to his soldiers. There's a scattering of nervous laughter. Gabriella has taken the toddler as far away from the scene as she can get, and she's playing with him behind a tree so he can't see what's happening. I tap Jen's shoulder and point.

"That's weird."

Ash looks, too. "She doesn't want him to see the blood."

"She didn't seem that bothered when they were killing *people*," I say.

Jen's struggling with the smell, she looks really gray. Her leg is still angry and crusted, but it is much better. It's the bound hand that is the problem now. She constantly tugs and twists at it with a furrowed brow, desperate to stretch her fingers, but there's no chance of that.

"Don't even attempt to get your head around them, Rio," she says. "They're a bunch of psychos."

Mwemba must see how upset we all are, because he throws the gorilla's head at us as a joke. Jen screams, but the head falls short, landing with a dull thud. I can't tear my eyes from it, though. Neither can Ash. The bloody collar fell off in the air and is lying in the grass just a few feet away. There's a small black box on it, and I'm closest.

I look at Ash and whisper, "Are you thinking what I'm thinking?"

Ash nods, slipping off one of his blades and rubbing his stump. "GPS tracker?" He hands me the blade, and says loudly, "Hold this for me, would you, Rio? My legs are killing me."

Nobody looks, they're all too interested in Mwemba's kill. Keeping my eyes on our nearest guards, I take the long, curving prosthesis, slide it through the grass, and hook the small foot through the loop of the leather collar. I pretend that I'm checking the carbon fiber blade as I draw it back up the slope. Then a quick flick, and we've got the collar. It's covered in warm, sticky blood.

"Do you think it still works?" I shoot a quick look over my shoulder and find myself staring Gabriella square in the face. She's still some way off, but she's watching us intently. I put my finger to my lips. For whatever reason, she does nothing, and for the first time I *feel* something, some connection. Iz was right. The LRA fighters are just kids, especially Gabriella. There's something about that girl that I just can't put my finger on. Something hidden behind that wall of steel she puts up.

Ash notices she's looking, too. It takes a bit of work, but eventually he manages to twist the box free of the collar and slip it into his pocket. When he's finished he beckons to Gabriella. She doesn't move. Patiently, he smiles at her and beckons again.

"You're wasting your time . . ." I begin, but she's already getting to her feet and walking over. I can't believe it. "Hey! What have you got that I haven't?"

"Charm, charisma, good looks . . ."

Jen mutters, "Give me a break. Don't tell me *she's* got a thing for you, too."

When Gabriella arrives, she just stands there.

Ash tells her, "I want to thank you."

She squats, tugs up a handful of grass, and starts braiding it.

"For letting me go. You're not like the others, are you?"

I take a look over at Mwemba. He's noticed that she's here, but he doesn't make a move, so I nudge Ash to let him know.

"I'm Ash, this is Jen, and this . . . this is Rio."

Gabriella's voice is as flat as ever. "I know your names."

"Good. I just thought that if we're going to be friends we should be properly introduced."

To my utter astonishment, Gabriella looks up and meets Ash's gaze. She seems shocked, and glances away. When she looks back in my direction she's blinking like she might cry or something. *No way.*

Whatever it is, it's brief. She sucks in a deep breath, then whispers so quietly that we can barely hear her. "You cannot be my friend. No one can be my friend. It is too dangerous."

"Too late," Ash tells her with another heart-stopping smile. "The deed is done." Then he asks her softly, "Where are you from?"

"Maracha. It is in Uganda."

This is amazing. I ask her, "Do you have any family there?"

Her head drops and she shakes it. "They are all gone."

"But these guys are your family now?" Ash wonders, waving at the other fighters.

A shrug, then she shakes her head. "They are not my family —" Something ignites behind her eyes, makes her rethink whatever she was about to say. "I do not have one. Kony owns me. They do not trust me because, when we get back, Kony will force me to be his wife."

Now Ash looks lethal. "We have to get you out of here," he hisses. "When we escape, you're coming with us."

Gabriella's eyelids flicker, but she won't look up at either of us. "I cannot."

We look at one another and I tell her softly, "Gabriella — you're not old enough to get married."

She looks at me like I'm an idiot. "I will not have a choice." Gabriella is closing down and straightening up. My stupid comment has confused her.

Interview over — and Iz is on my shoulder saying, *I told you so. Just children — broken.* I understand now that I can't see my captors in black and white — with the exception of Mwemba and his creepy Sangoma. There's no hate left in me for the others, in spite of what they're doing. It's like my eyes are suddenly opening and when I look around all I can see is *children* — disturbed, deranged, frightened children. They laugh with Mwemba over his kill, but fear is always behind their eyes. Everything they do is about survival — it has never been clearer. None of them should be here. What I thought was a lack of emotion in Gabriella is something else. Everything in that kid has shut down; all she is doing is protecting her heart, because she thinks that the moment she allows herself to feel, her whole world is going to fall apart. Worse than that, it could all be over for her. The thought leaves me feeling raw and even more helpless. I remember her shocking words — *I disgust myself!* A sharp, shooting pain grips my chest, and I let out this involuntary gasp. It's as if I can feel my heart snapping in my chest like a twig.

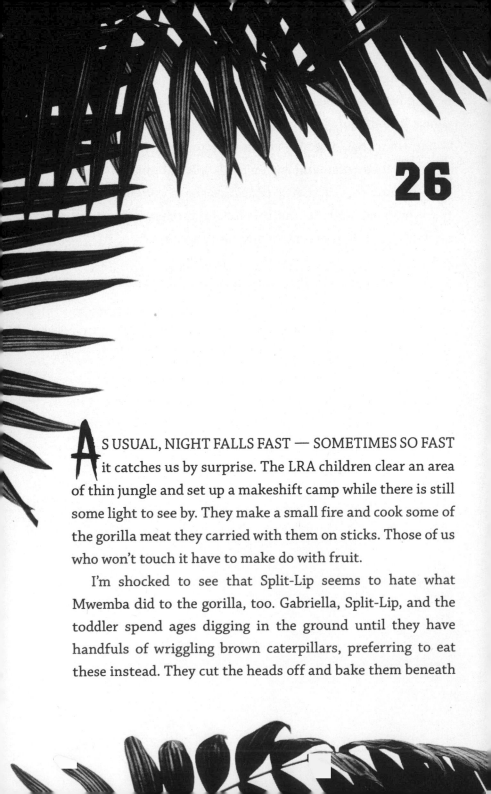

26

AS USUAL, NIGHT FALLS FAST — SOMETIMES SO FAST it catches us by surprise. The LRA children clear an area of thin jungle and set up a makeshift camp while there is still some light to see by. They make a small fire and cook some of the gorilla meat they carried with them on sticks. Those of us who won't touch it have to make do with fruit.

I'm shocked to see that Split-Lip seems to hate what Mwemba did to the gorilla, too. Gabriella, Split-Lip, and the toddler spend ages digging in the ground until they have handfuls of wriggling brown caterpillars, preferring to eat these instead. They cut the heads off and bake them beneath the fire wrapped in thick leaves. When they are ready, the toddler plonks his hot little body on my lap and chews a handful of them. He offers me a few, but I'm not *that* desperate, even though my stomach growls so badly it hurts.

Ash tries them, though, and makes the baby laugh by making faces. They're almost having fun, and I swear that by the time Ash has finished, Gabriella is on the verge of smiling.

Jen is fiddling with her bandaged hand without thinking, and I jab her because Mwemba has seen Gabriella talking to us again. He jumps to his feet and thunders over, grabs the girl by the arm, and shakes her hard. Her head drops and she tries to pull away, but his grip is too tight.

"*Kuja na mimi! Unafanya nini?*"[17]

"*Hakuna, Baba.*"

Mwemba drags her to her feet, slapping the side of her head, and throws her back toward the main group of soldiers.

"*Kuja na mimi!*" The tone of his voice gives me the creeps. He *so* doesn't want her anywhere near us, and I hope he's not questioning her loyalty.

Whatever was growing in Gabriella's eyes at Ash's antics instantly dies. She stumbles but holds her ground, seeking out the little boy.

Something rises in me, and I'm scrambling to my feet and facing the LRA leader before I have any idea how crazy I'm being. I reach for Gabriella's hand and pull her and the baby

---

17. Come with me! What are you doing?

behind me, and I'm shaking like a leaf when I tell him, "No! Leave her alone."

Mwemba just stares at me. I'm guessing he's not heard that word much. He laughs, looks past me at Gabriella, expecting her to shove me in the back or something, but when she doesn't move, his hand drops to his pistol holster. When he speaks his voice is full of danger. "Do not cross me. The girl is mine. She will do as I tell her."

I watch his eyes widen when Ash gets to his feet next to me, and then Jen. We're like this kamikaze human wall between him and Gabriella. I'm sweating, thinking, *This is it. This is where we all die.* Ash tells Mwemba, "She's a child. They're all children. What's wrong with you?"

I'm playing nervously with Izzy's bracelet, and the picture of St. Christopher carrying the baby on his shoulder flashes in the firelight. Izzy once told me that St. Christopher is stooped because the child is so heavy. She said that St. Christopher doesn't grasp at first that the child is heavy because it's Jesus, and *he's* carrying the weight of the world. It had never crossed my mind before, but the image reminds me of Gabriella and her baby brother. She's been carrying that kid for miles. For some reason I can't explain, I think Izzy, or God, or whoever is out there, wants us to carry the girl — to take some of her load. So I take a deep breath and tell Mwemba, "If you want her, then you're going to have to kill all of your hostages."

Ash and Jen look at me as if to say, *What the hell are you doing?* Around the fire I can see one or two faces looking this way. The Sangoma is loving it. It's not going to be much longer before all this tension goes boom. Mwemba stands and watches us with those glassy red eyes, fiddling with his gun. Suddenly he draws it and points it at my head.

Everything in me turns to jelly, but I stand my ground and look him in the eye. If I'm going to die, at least I'll go knowing that I stood up for something. Like Izzy wanted to.

"You do not think I will pull the trigger?"

"Rio . . ."

I barely hear Ash's voice. I just stare right into those angry eyes, ignoring the cold metal against my forehead, and, don't ask me why, but all my fear melts away. It's totally crazy, but for the first time in days I actually feel *good*. "Go ahead." I tell him, "Do what you like. You don't scare me."

Mwemba's grip on the gun tightens and he pushes the barrel into my forehead. I stand my ground.

Suddenly Gabriella moves around us. She places her hand on his arm and lowers his gun. Her voice is soothing when she speaks. "*Hakuna, Baba,*" she says again.

Mwemba snatches his arm away from her as if her hand is burning his flesh. For the first time I see doubt in his eyes. After a brief standoff he throws up his arms and walks away, angrily demanding, "*IBOGA!*"

We're all just left there watching.

I can't believe it. *We won!* My legs give way and I steady myself against Ash. Then I'm thinking, *Hakuna, Baba?* What was that? I know *hakuna* is *no,* but *baba*?

"I swear, if I ever get out of here . . ." Ash mutters.

I stop him. "We promised Iz, remember? No revenge."

"Iz was something else," Jen agrees.

"Don't talk to me about Iz!" Ash spits at us. His neck is taut with the effort of holding himself back. "There's revenge and then there's justice. I'm sure Iz would agree. And don't ever try to play mind games with that twisted bastard! Do you know how close he came . . . ?"

"I'm sorry."

Whatever he was going to add just comes out in a hissing breath. He turns his back on me. He picks up a stick and pokes at the ground with it until it snaps. Then his shoulders sag and he leans forward. "That was reckless, Rio. *Really* reckless."

"I know. Something in me just snapped."

"She's right about Izzy," Jen chips in. "Iz would have done exactly what Rio just did, and you know it, Ash."

He looks up at her and then turns to me with a grimace. "Okay — I get it. Just don't do anything like that again. Ever . . ."

"I won't, I promise."

Gabriella is still there, watching us blankly. She turns to leave without a word. I don't know what I expected, really. I reach out and take her hand. There's something I need to know.

"Gabriella."

She won't turn her head to look at me.

"What does *baba* mean?"

The girl's eyelids close and her mouth opens slightly, like she might tell me. When she looks up I swear her eyes start to fill, but no tears fall. She squeezes them shut to stop it and her voice is hoarse as she barks at me, "It means nothing. *Nothing!*"

Progress — she's angry. Seized by a sudden realization, I follow up with, "Those nurses at the mission — I don't believe you killed them. Did you? Did you even *help* to kill them?"

Gabriella hangs her head and clams up. It's like she *wants* us to think the worst of her.

Ash says, "You were just cleaning that machete, weren't you? For someone else . . ."

She won't look up as she tells him, "I watched them die. It is just as bad. I always watch them die."

"No," I tell her. "No, it's not the same. You watch because you want to find a way to help. I know you do. Tell me if I'm wrong."

But she won't listen to me. Lifting her arms like she's fending off blows, Gabriella runs off into the gloom without saying another word, her head in her hands. She finds the darkest place she can, where she thinks we won't see her face, but even from this distance I can see her shoulders shudder and heave.

"That's one seriously damaged kid," Ash mutters.

I hardly hear him. She's just given me a flash of inspiration, something important. "Yes — but Gabriella is the key for us, Ash."

"The key to what?"

"To helping the LRA kids." They're talking quietly and some of them throw quick glances to where Mwemba sits with his back against a tree, chewing strips of *iboga*.

Ash looks at me like he thinks I'm nuts. "Don't even go there, Rio. We need to concentrate on staying alive, on getting out of here. We're not social workers."

For the second time Jen backs me up. "Rio's right, Ash."

We both look at her.

"Stop acting like a soldier and see them as people — not enemies. How many of these kids do you think really *want* to be here?"

He's quiet, thinking.

"And they all have guns. We have to help them break free. If we can get them on our side . . ."

Still no answer. I give Jen a grateful smile. "Gabriella is definitely the key, Ash. I thought they were all scared of her — even Mwemba — but it's something else. Maybe they pity her for some reason, like she's the one who has suffered the most? Or maybe they see that she's the only one who hasn't given in to it all, and they want to be like her. Whatever it is, if we can get her to open up, I think they will follow that girl. We might even have a chance of turning them against Mwemba and the Sangoma."

Ash shakes his head, but he's smiling. "You're right. Both of you. Crazy, but right. What have we got to lose? The only question is how?"

I tell him, "That's where Iz and her beliefs come in. Nobody's ever shown Gabriella love before. Or if they have, it was a long time ago. If you ask me, she's been watching us look out for one another and she wants to be a part of it. We need to be her friend."

We sit there for ages after that. Gabriella's toddler is still squatting by Ash's feet, eating. Ash tickles him in the ribs and steals a couple of his caterpillars while he giggles. As I watch the pair of them I think about the GPS tracker we found. I wonder if gorillas wander very far from their home territory. If they do, then it's useless. And what if it doesn't even work? What if whoever attached it in the first place stopped monitoring it years ago? Maybe they only check once a month. Or less. I have to stop my train of thought before depression sets in again.

Jen's nose wrinkles at the sight of Ash and the kid eating grubs, and I see how much better she looks. "I'm so hungry," she tells me, "but I'd have to be on my last breath to eat *those*."

Even without makeup and covered in grime, Jen looks beautiful. I haven't told her, but the Sangoma has been keeping an eye on her, especially now that she's starting to get some life back in her face. She notices the direction I'm looking in and shudders.

"Is he still watching me?"

"Uh-huh. I didn't think you knew."

"He gives me the creeps."

I don't answer.

The Sangoma knows we've noticed. His mouth just widens into a twisted yellow grin.

made. Jen is lying against the wall where I left her, her eyes closed. A blood-drenched old rag has been twisted over the end of her right arm.

I have this flashback to the marina, thinking how perfect she looked back then. How perfect she *was*. All those things feel like a lifetime ago. Izzy was alive then.

"Get out of my way." I push the Empty Child hard and she hits her head on the doorframe. I'm not sorry. Right now I'd love to *really* hurt her more, but I don't waste my time.

Jen's eyes open.

I'm so relieved that black spots gather on the edges of my vision. My eyes fill with tears and I almost faint. I don't know how I stay upright. She's still really weak from her ordeal and the infection in her leg. I can hardly speak when recognition lights up her face. It's my fault they did this to her. Why did I wait? I should have just told Mwemba what he wanted.

Suddenly she's trying to sit up and her face is creased with worry. "Rio, what did they do to you?"

"To *me*?"

Jen lifts her bloody stump and smiles weakly. Her voice drops to a whisper. "Don't worry. This isn't real."

"What? What are you talking about?" I look over my shoulder, but the Empty Child has gone.

"That girl came in here with her machete. I was scared to death at first, but the girl's got a voice! She just told me to scream. She told me Mwemba wanted her to chop my hand off, so I screamed all right. I screamed like hell."

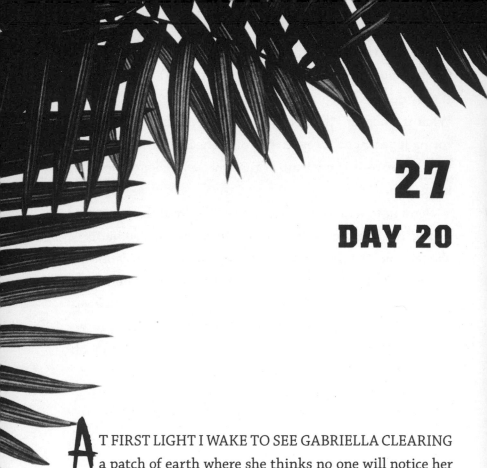

27

DAY 20

AT FIRST LIGHT I WAKE TO SEE GABRIELLA CLEARING a patch of earth where she thinks no one will notice her and drawing on it with her finger. The toddler is on her hip. When she has finished she straightens up and takes a battered old hand grenade out of her pocket.

I can't believe what happens next.

Gabriella throws the grenade, then hops and steps over it, whispering something, her breath jarring as she lands. The toddler giggles and Gabriella puts her free hand over his mouth to silence him.

Hopscotch.

With a grenade.

I'm assuming she knows not to pull the pin.

Soon we're packed up and moving again, crossing a couple of steep ravines, and then the ground slopes downward for ages. Mwemba and the Sangoma seem to consult a lot, and every so often the Sangoma throws his bones on the ground and chants over them. Neither of the LRA leaders seems very happy. They've been talking normally up to now, but when we move on they begin communicating in whispers. The LRA child soldiers are getting jittery, too.

"What do you think that's about?" Jen asks me in a whisper.

I shrug — haven't got a clue.

Ash is as sharp as ever, he's been watching them closely. "I think they were expecting to find something — or someone. Look . . ."

When we pass the place where they were debating, you can see spots where the vines have been cleared. Someone's even made a small seat out of branches in a tall tree overhead. "I think there should have been lookouts up there. If you ask me, they're worried. Whoever was here has bailed."

As if in response to Ash's words, our guards close in around us. For the first time in days, they tie us up.

Ash has been walking with Gabriella's kid in between his roped arms. He's got this rough beard now, and the humidity has made his hair wavy. Since he was recaptured I've wanted to ask him again about our swim — what he was going to say. I want to know in case we don't make it out of this, but I can't bring myself to ask in case it was nothing or something stupid.

Every now and again, Ash points out things and names them, waiting for the toddler to gurgle a response. So far the boy has learned *blades*, *tree*, and *sky* in English. He laughs every time any of us say them.

Watching the two of them makes me daydream about being back home with Ash, doing normal stuff, but my thoughts are interrupted when Gabriella's quiet voice breaks in from behind.

"When I was a young girl I wanted very much to go to school," she says, "but I had no money. We were too poor."

Those last words were filled with longing. I look over my shoulder to where she's walking with her machine gun slung across her hips. I tell her, "Where I come from, school is free — everyone goes."

Her jaw drops. "You are very fortunate. If I had been at school, I would not have been taken."

"How did it happen?"

"When I was twelve years old, I lived with my grandmother. She was teaching me how to cook *matoke* when they came."

"*Matoke*?"

"It is green banana mash. I think you would like it. It is very good. The soldiers ran into our house. They killed my grandmother in front of me, then made me finish the cooking so that they could eat." Gabriella's voice chokes to a halt.

I can't help it — when I turn to look at her again, my face is wet with tears. I can *feel* the grief, the waste of her childhood, hanging in the humid air between us. To my surprise, a single tear rolls down Gabriella's round cheek, leaving a thin, pale streak.

To give her a breather I change the subject, even though I want to hear more. "I miss my mum, too. We live together. Dad ran off when he found out she was pregnant. Gran made him marry her, but he stuck it out from a sense of duty and then left when I was about his age." I nod at the toddler. "I've only ever seen him a couple of times since, usually because Gran *makes* him get in touch. What about your dad and mum? What happened to them?"

"Mama died from malaria when I was five years old. My father" — she turns her face so that I can't see it — "he died also."

"But . . ." I point at the kid on Ash's shoulder. "Didn't you say he was your brother?"

"The child *is* my brother."

"And you are how old — fourteen?"

"I am almost fifteen years old, I think. I do not count the years."

"And he's about two, so he would have been born just after you were taken — and you said your mum died when you were five. So how can he be your brother?"

Gabriella doesn't answer, so I'm left wondering if she's just decided to make some random orphaned kid her brother. Of course, there is another possibility . . . but I dismiss that thought. It's too horrible, more horrible, even, than everything that's happened. She would only have been twelve, could she conceive at that age? Maybe. I wouldn't blame her for lying about it, and it would make sense of why she cares for him. Maybe it's what helps her to cope, having a child to love.

As we're walking on in silence, Jen pipes up. "Last night," she says to Gabriella, "you called Mwemba *Baba*. What is that? A mark of respect?"

Just like when I asked before, the word is like a shutdown switch.

"No," is all she'll say, before pulling away again.

As the jungle shadows lengthen and begin to shift we enter a large area of packed mud where the undergrowth has been hacked away, but the jungle canopy higher up still covers it, hiding it from prying eyes. There is a rough, hastily constructed platform next to a fire, which is beginning to die, although it is still smoldering. A small, sturdy hut has been made from branches and thick, twisted vines, covered with makeshift thatch. Whoever built it was not expecting to have to leave anytime soon. All around there is evidence that people were here: discarded fruit, nutshells, and boot prints. This place was deserted in a hurry, and not very long ago.

The veins in Mwemba's forehead look like they could burst if they throb any more. He runs to the platform and screams at the top of his voice: *"KONY!"* Then he screams it again until he is hoarse: *"KONY!"* The sound of that word reverberates around the jungle, and birds take flight far above our heads.

Suddenly Mwemba lunges at the Sangoma and grabs him. "Where have they gone? Consult the spirits."

Beads of sweat roll from the witch doctor's temples and he's actually trembling. The Sangoma's gravelly voice breaks when he speaks. "Kony has betrayed us. We must get out of here. There is no time."

Something is going badly wrong. The LRA kids are looking everywhere, and they're *really* on edge. Ash drops the toddler to the ground and we look around, but all we can see is jungle. Suddenly Mwemba barks at the LRA kids nearest us: *"KUSHIKILIA KWAO!"*[18] and they force us to our knees.

Jen screams and yells, "Get your hands off me!" There's an angry crack in the new skin that was forming over her burn, and it's weeping. One of the soldiers pokes her in the back with his gun when she reaches down to rub it.

When they try to subdue Ash he fights back, and it takes *five* of them to control him. During the struggle, one of the LRA kids kicks the back of his knees and knocks him off balance. He goes flying, and the GPS tracker falls out of his pocket when he hits the ground. It bounces a few feet and then stops. Just behind his back, Gabriella stands motionless, her eyes wide and black, staring at it.

The Sangoma notices where she is looking. He picks the little black box up and turns it over in his hand. "You knew about this," he tells her. "You were near them when the gorilla was killed."

---

18. HOLD THEM!

Gabriella doesn't deny it.

"He is right. I saw you with them." Mwemba's face turns thunderous.

The three of us are kneeling in a line with our heads bowed. This time I know there will be no way out. Nobody is coming. My heart is pounding so badly it feels like my chest will explode.

Suddenly Mwemba marches over, grabs Jen, pulls the filthy rag off her bound hand, and holds it up by the wrist. She gives him the finger with it, smiling at the shock on his face.

"Thanks!" She pulls herself upright, trying not to shake too badly and failing. "I've been *dying* to do that."

Gabriella raises her gun at Mwemba and the toddler hides behind her leg.

Her threat doesn't even faze the LRA leader. Mwemba launches himself at her, grabs her by the arm, and pulls her until she is standing in front of me. Her hands are limp, so he lifts her gun and shoves it against her chest — hard — forcing her to hold it ready. When he speaks, his voice is black with hatred. "*Kuwaua.* Kill them."

Nobody moves. The LRA kids in front of me are all looking to see what Gabriella will do. I'm guessing the ones behind us are, too.

"*KUWAUA!*" Mwemba screams, grabbing Gabriella's gun and shooting it at the ground right in front of me. I jump a mile and almost lose my balance. Dirt is spitting up from the ground and the automatic fire seems to go on forever. There are actual bullet holes puncturing the earth by my knees. If I fall forward even an inch, I'll be dead. I can even feel the wind from the bullets. Then it stops almost as quickly as it started. Mwemba places the gun back in Gabriella's hands and twists it in them until the smoking barrel is aimed right at my face.

Now Mwemba's voice gets deadly dangerous. He unclips his pistol. I think he's going to shoot Gabriella if she doesn't do what he says. "*Kuwaua,*" he hisses.

"It's okay," I tell her, blinking away the tears. "It's not your fault."

Gabriella is crying, too. She spits "*HAKUNA!*" right in Mwemba's face and throws the gun back at him. It clatters to the ground. "They are my friends! I will *not* kill them!"

Her toddler screams and begs to be lifted up. He stands there with a handful of her pants leg in one hand and sucking the thumb of his other, watching everything through those huge brown eyes.

"*Binti.* That is precisely why I *wanted* you to do it." Mwemba flicks the safety catch off his pistol and is about to put it to Gabriella's head when the Sangoma, turning the GPS box over in his hand, walks between us and hisses at Mwemba, "We do not have time to wait for her to kill them. This area is too exposed —"

The Sangoma stops talking, instantly.

This black hole just *appears* in the side of the witch doctor's head and he crumples to the ground.

Mwemba's jacket is sprayed with blood.

We're all just frozen there, hardly able to believe our eyes, looking at the Sangoma's twisted body as a sticky, dark puddle begins to ooze out from behind his head.

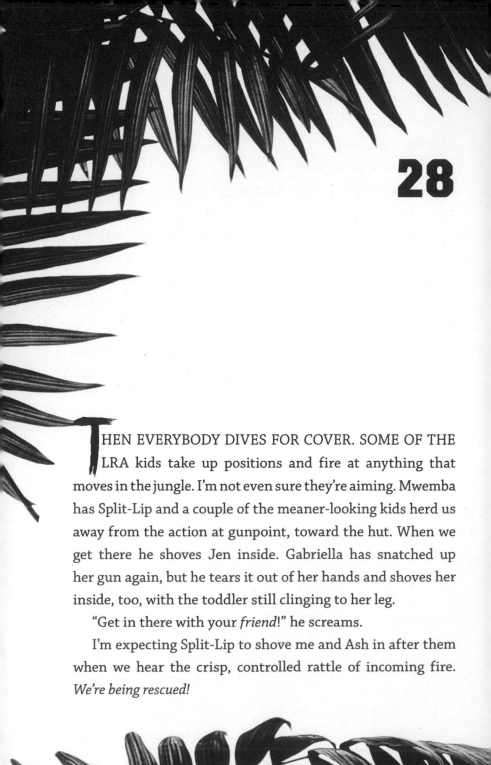

28

THEN EVERYBODY DIVES FOR COVER. SOME OF THE LRA kids take up positions and fire at anything that moves in the jungle. I'm not even sure they're aiming. Mwemba has Split-Lip and a couple of the meaner-looking kids herd us away from the action at gunpoint, toward the hut. When we get there he shoves Jen inside. Gabriella has snatched up her gun again, but he tears it out of her hands and shoves her inside, too, with the toddler still clinging to her leg.

"Get in there with your *friend*!" he screams.

I'm expecting Split-Lip to shove me and Ash in after them when we hear the crisp, controlled rattle of incoming fire. *We're being rescued!*

Mwemba barks orders at his fighters, grabbing a burning log from the fire. Before we know what's happening, a full-scale gun battle is raging in the jungle behind us. Mwemba wedges the burning log in the makeshift door and pushes it shut.

"If they try to get out, shoot them," he tells a couple of his boys. Then he waves his machine gun at me and Ash. "You two are coming with me."

Just as he's turning he cries out, "Ai!" and clutches his ankle.

I look down just in time to see the tail of a long green snake wriggling away from the blazing door, into the undergrowth.

Mwemba swears loudly and waves his gun at me and Ash again, as if what just happened changes nothing. He is *deranged*.

"It's over, Mwemba!" Ash rants at him. "Give it up. Surrender and you might get out of this alive."

"There will be *no* surrender. I am not interested in staying alive."

Split-Lip looks alarmed, like this is news to him.

"After today," Mwemba continues, his eyes gleaming, "the world will know my name."

From behind the door we can hear Gabriella pleading desperately as the dry wood crackles and goes up like a torch. "*Hakuna, Baba . . . Hakuna . . .*" The little boy starts wailing, too. The whole thing is like hell. The fire roars and black smoke curls upward. I feel the dry, withering heat begin to scorch my face.

"Silence!" Mwemba yells, and actually shoots at the blazing door.

"Jen!" Ash looks as though he would put the fire out with his bare hands if he could.

"Ash! Help us!" Jen's fingers poke through the gaps in the sidewall, and I just manage to touch them before I'm pulled away. The toddler's wail cuts right through me. All the while Jen is pleading for help and Gabriella just yells, *"Baba!"* over and over.

"You can't just leave them in there to burn!" I rage uselessly at Mwemba.

He's deaf to all of it. He waves Gabriella's gun in Split-Lip's face. *"Go!* Go back to the fighting! Make sure the Americans know they will die for coming here."

Split-Lip hesitates, his eyes flicking to where we stand, lit by the flames. "But where will you take them?" he lisps. "If the hostages are no longer here, they will kill us all."

"I said GO!" Mwemba fires in the air so that Split-Lip has to duck. He turns and runs. "You two — kneel before me." Mwemba watches us kneel in the dirt, and the barrel of his gun against the back of my head is hot. "Do not try anything you will regret," he tells Ash. "Your girlfriend will not live to tell the tale."

"It's not me you need to worry about." Ash nods at the place where the snake bit him.

Mwemba stamps his foot and shakes it. "A snake rarely wastes any venom on the first strike."

I'm starting to choke on the thick, wafting smoke and the heat on my neck is getting unbearable. Gabriella's voice is farther away, as though she has moved to the back of the burning hut. It's just a whimper now, and I imagine her and Jen crouched against the back wall, shielding the boy with their bodies.

"*Baba! Baba . . . !*" she cries, more weakly now.

"What are you going to do with us?" I ask Mwemba. If the Americans are really here, all this seems pointless now.

To my surprise, Mwemba just laughs at me. "What I should have done many years ago. I am going to die, and you will die with me, and the world will remember the name of *Moses Mwemba*."

I'm determined not to cry, but I'm so scared I can barely breathe.

The battle is raging in the jungle in front of us now, too. The desperate, undisciplined clatter of the LRA guns is more scattered, and I try not to think of how many of those children lie dead or dying out there. Then, like a bolt out of the blue, it dawns on me: why Gabriella has always been by Mwemba's side, and why he's been different with her. Why she kept calling *Baba* from the hut . . .

"You're Gabriella's father."

I feel the barrel of the pistol drop slightly.

"Surely you can't just *leave* her to burn."

"What?" Ash shifts his weight, and I can tell he's itching to take action. "He's doing that to his own child?"

"*Dada* is Swahili for *sister*," I tell him. "It's what Gabriella's baby brother calls her. *Mama* is *mum* and *Baba* — I'll bet you anything that *baba* means *dad*."

"This does not concern you!" Mwemba growls, and the barrel of his pistol clunks painfully against my skull again.

Now Ash rants at him, "How can you do this? Let her burn alive? Your own daughter!"

Mwemba's eyes bulge red as he screams at Ash, *"I said silence!"*

Everything in me yearns for escape, for someone to come and douse the flames that scorch my back. Gabriella and Jen have fallen silent, and I try not to think of what is about to happen to them. I catch American voices now, echoing through the undergrowth, calm and controlled. There's no doubt in my mind that Ash is thinking of ways to turn on Mwemba, but I know he won't — afraid that if he makes a move the guy will shoot me first. As if sensing that we might try something, Mwemba changes position, putting me in between him and Ash. With his free hand, he is constantly wiping away beads of sweat that stick his braids to his face.

Ash's voice croaks above the roaring flames: "I'm going to kill you, you bastard."

Mwemba laughs, and when he speaks his words are slurred. "You think that death frightens me? You think I have not stared death in the face more days than you have breathed on this earth? Death does not scare me. Kill me if you can. I will welcome it."

"Why are you doing this?" I plead with Mwemba. "It's all over now."

Fixing me with his bloodshot eyes, he answers with grim conviction. "Kony does nothing but hide. Soon the Lord's

Resistance Army will disappear from the earth. Thanks to me — *only* to me! — the whole world will know who we are. *I* did this. I did this for him, and he thanks me by running away like a coward. You Westerners are so soft. You think this life is all there is, buying your televisions and your cars and your computer games! This is God's judgment. This is what the LRA is for, to be the hand of God. *I* am God's judgment on *you*."

There's nothing else to say to him. He's a madman. So I lean against Ash's arm, and think again of Iz, and *long* for this nightmare to end. My life is over, and I never even had the chance to live it.

We kneel in silence, waiting. The flames consuming the hut crackle louder than ever, showering us with smoldering embers, choking us with thick black smoke. I'm so sick about Gabriella and the baby and Jen that I haven't even noticed Mwemba's gun barrel has dropped from the back of my head. Ash jabs me with his elbow, and my heart leaps when I follow his gaze.

Mwemba looks like he's trying to fight the poison from the snakebite but losing — there's blood oozing from his nose. Ash shifts his position slightly, and I swear he doesn't make a sound, but Mwemba's head shoots up like he's been stung. He looks around like he's seeing things for the first time, wiping the blood from his face and steadying himself against a tree trunk. He looks at his sleeve briefly, swaying wildly, and then lifts his gun again. It's not even near my head. On our knees, Ash and I back away slowly.

"You need medical treatment," I tell him, watching the barrel of his gun swing wildly toward Ash. It sweeps around in search of the sound of my voice. It's freaking me out. All it needs is for his finger to twitch on the trigger . . .

Ash moves slightly. He gets to his feet as if he is going to make a grab for the gun, but Mwemba suddenly snaps to attention and shoots where he thinks he sees us. His shot is a mile wide, thank God.

"Do not come near me!" When he speaks, Mwemba's tongue is black.

Silently Ash helps me up. We are all wreathed in billowing smoke. The fire has almost consumed the roof of the hut; any second now it will collapse. Suddenly Mwemba loses his balance and crashes backward into the undergrowth. He pulls himself up to his knees before we can take advantage of the situation, aiming his gun back in our direction. Mwemba fights to lift his eyelids, but he must be seeing double, because his gun isn't quite pointing at either of us. Ash signals for me to go round to the left — he's going to try to get Mwemba's gun.

As if he's telepathic, Mwemba fires a couple more rounds at us and we have to dive for cover. I'm scared that he's going to try again, so I grab Ash's arm and whisper, "Leave it, Ash!"

Mwemba's gun flails around and his arm moves at every sound, swinging that black muzzle wildly in every direction. Suddenly he swears angrily and staggers into the jungle, yelling incoherently and shooting at anything that moves. I don't wait to see where he's going. Ash and I grab a couple of large fallen branches and run to use the ends to bash the smoldering doorframe away from the hut. The end of mine catches light from the embers, and I have to jump out of the way when the door comes crashing down in a shower of sparks and glowing charcoal. Smoke pours out of the opening, and it's a while before we can see Jen and Gabriella lying on the floor against the far wall. We both try to get in, but we can't. We're beaten back by the flames.

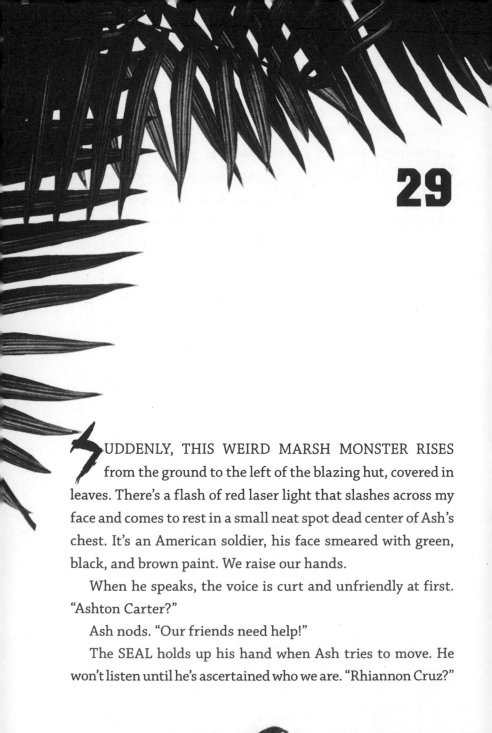

29

SUDDENLY, THIS WEIRD MARSH MONSTER RISES from the ground to the left of the blazing hut, covered in leaves. There's a flash of red laser light that slashes across my face and comes to rest in a small neat spot dead center of Ash's chest. It's an American soldier, his face smeared with green, black, and brown paint. We raise our hands.

When he speaks, the voice is curt and unfriendly at first. "Ashton Carter?"

Ash nods. "Our friends need help!"

The SEAL holds up his hand when Ash tries to move. He won't listen until he's ascertained who we are. "Rhiannon Cruz?"

"Yes," I choke, and all the time I'm thinking, *I'm free! Why me?* If only they'd come earlier, they might have saved Jen and Gabriella.

"US Special Forces — you're safe now." The American lowers his weapon, alert to danger but waving us to him. While we approach he presses a button on his gun. "Lieutenant, I got two hostages on the northeast access."

Ash doesn't wait for him to finish — as soon as the SEAL lowers his gun he's ripping the remains of his T-shirt off and shouting "I need water!"

Realizing that there are more hostages inside the burning hut, the SEAL throws his water bottle to Ash.

Ash tears the lid off and pours it over his shirt. Holding the wet cloth to his face, he runs inside.

The SEAL is too heavily armed — I'm guessing he can't go in without all his bullets and grenades exploding, and he's not prepared to ditch his weapons just yet. He crouches and peers through the door, but he can't see much through the smoke that's pouring out. "How many?" he asks me.

I tell him.

He relays the information, his eyes fixed on mine, but I don't read any hope in them.

"Help is on the way — hold tight."

My heart skips a beat. *Help* is taking too long.

Suddenly Ash bursts out of the doorway in a ball of smoke. He's got Jen under one arm and Gabriella with her child under the other, sheltered beneath his steaming T-shirt.

The girls collapse on the ground, coughing but alive, and the SEAL rushes over to give first aid.

"Yes!" Ash drops to his knees and roars at the canopy. "YES! Thank you!"

Then he jumps up and throws his arms around me. He stinks of smoke and sweat, but I don't care. Neither of us does. I'm looking up at him and he's looking down at me. We're both drunk with relief and grief and hope, unable to move. He smiles, looking at me like I'm made of glass, and pushes my hair back from my face. I stop breathing, and just looking at him calms me, slows my racing heart. I don't know how long we stay there, but he closes the gap between us, then lifts my hand to his lips to kiss it and locks his fingers in mine. There is such seriousness in his face — the same look he gave me when we were swimming. I'm unable to do anything but watch his hazel eyes on mine.

Suddenly all the noise fades. He's holding my face in his hands and kissing me on the forehead and my nose and eyelids. I breathe him and he breathes me, and then he kisses me like I have never been kissed in my life.

When we part there's one question I have to ask. "Ash, what were you going to say?"

"Come again?"

"When we were swimming — I have to know. What were you going to tell me?"

Ash's eyes twinkle at me. "Really? *Now?*"

I hit his arm. "Yes!"

"I . . . I was going to ask — do you think it's possible to see someone for the very first time and know . . ."

"Know what?"

Ash exhales. "Know that you've just discovered the only person who can make you feel completely whole."

Lieutenant Ben Jackson Jr. is leaning against the wooden platform when we finally meet him. The air is full of ash and the sweet smell of burning wood. When he sees us walk up with his colleague, the lieutenant lifts his baseball cap, runs his fingers through his hair, and then flicks it back on. There's an amazing tribal tattoo around his arm, just visible under his short sleeves, and I notice that there's a pale band around the ring finger on his left hand. I'm just thinking, *He's a real looker*, when I feel Ash's arm slip possessively around my waist.

Soldiers are everywhere, many of them African, wearing NATO armbands. To my surprise, nearly all the LRA kids are seated in the center of the clearing, disarmed and looking more like children than ever. I can see Split-Lip near the edge, his head bowed. When I look back to where the hut stood, there is just a smoldering, blackened clay ring filled with glowing timbers where the roof caved in. Flakes of ash still lift from it and hang in the air.

Jackson holds out his hand to Ash and rewards us with a charismatic smile. "Good to see you both alive and well. I didn't realize the British Army issued upgrades," he jokes, admiring Ash's blades.

Ash takes his hand and laughs.

The lieutenant's eyes are warm and friendly. I know that

he's not going to give us any crap, so I ditch the formalities and just ask him.

"What happened to Izzy, did they —"

"Yes, ma'am. They found her. Your friend's body was air-lifted to our base. I'm so sorry we didn't get here sooner."

Before I can ask him anything else I feel this familiar little arm wrap around my calf. It's the toddler. I look down. His blackened face is streaked with tear trails. The boy tries to tell me something, but I can't understand what it is through his gasping sobs, and when I pick him up and turn around Gabriella is there. The SEAL who found us is guarding her closely. She smiles and I pull her stiff, thin body into a hug with my free arm. She doesn't know what to do, so her hands stay clamped firmly by her sides.

I kiss her forehead. *"Thank you."*

The lieutenant is taken aback. "Isn't she one of the insurgents?"

"Yes and no . . ." I say.

"So, which is it?"

"Gabriella . . . helped us."

Jackson seems unconvinced, but he lets it drop for the moment. "I can't leave without Mwemba. You guys were the last to see him, right?"

Ash's voice is flat and precise. "Yes."

Jackson claps him on the arm. "Good. Show me."

"Do not hurt him," Gabriella says. "Please, sir, take him alive."

I'm shocked. After all he's done to her?

"I can't guarantee that. He's a dangerous man."

"Then let me go to him. He will listen to me."

"Can't do that, either." The lieutenant orders three of his men to move out.

I hold Gabriella's hand before we leave. "I'll do what I can," I tell her. "I promise."

There's no sign of Mwemba by the hut. His trail looks like it will be easy to follow, though: It flails through thick jungle for quite a ways until it breaks out into one of those grassy clearings where there are too many rocks for the trees to take hold. Jackson silently orders his men to fan out, and we hold back as they take up their positions.

Suddenly something rattles out in the grass, and bullets whip and thud into the trees around us. The SEALs don't reply yet. Two of them slide on their bellies and melt into the grass.

Mwemba's disembodied voice yells, "You will not take me alive!" He is delirious and his words echo all around us.

More shots fly in this direction — too high, though — and Jackson orders some brief covering fire.

Mwemba's voice rants again, breaking with emotion. "Come and take me if any of you are man enough! What are you? GET AWAY FROM ME!" He seems to be hallucinating. His voice suddenly changes to a rasping hiss. *"I will not be humiliated . . ."* Then silence. As we wait and watch, Mwemba rises slowly from the long grass and just stands there, holding his gun limply while he sways from side to side. His face is drawn and stretched in agony.

"Sniper One, do you have a target?" Jackson murmurs into

his neck mic. "Okay. Hold your fire." Then he shouts, "Moses Mwemba! Drop your weapon!"

Mwemba's grip tightens, like he's going to shoot his way out.

Suddenly Gabriella comes crashing out of the trees to our right. *"No! Do not shoot!"* Her voice is hoarse from the smoke and she runs through the grass, throwing herself in front of Mwemba, stretching her arms out wide. He looks at her, but his eyes are unfocused. "He is my *baba*!" Gabriella wails. "My *baba*. He was not always bad!"

I can't believe it. After all that guy has done, she still loves him. He's her dad.

"*Baba,* put down the gun," Gabriella pleads, turning to him. Mwemba just stares at her with his jaw wagging, like he can't believe she's there, blinking wildly. For the first time since this whole ordeal began, it looks like he hasn't got a clue what to do.

"Do you still have a target?" Jackson hisses into his collar.

I tell him, "Lieutenant, you can't — not while Gabriella's there!"

He raises his palm to shut me up. "If we can take him alive, we will."

"*Baba*, please . . ." Gabriella is actually tugging at the gun, and it looks like Mwemba is letting it fall. He looks so tired, and the venom is making him twitch. Gabriella twists to adjust her grip and as she does, Mwemba's face hardens. The muscles in his arm go taut.

30

IT HAPPENS SO QUICKLY. MWEMBA SWINGS HIS GUN up with practiced ease and, as he does, there is the soft splutter of automatic fire from somewhere in the long grass. Mwemba staggers backward.

Gabriella screams. She tries to hold him.

The gun flies out of Mwemba's hand and his lifeless body crumples to the grass.

A weird, deathly silence descends, broken by jungle creatures scattering in panic. Without thinking, I run through the clearing to Gabriella. A Navy SEAL rises from the grass, covering me with his gun. When I reach her she's lying across

Mwemba's body and she's crying like a baby, a high-pitched keening as if all her emotions are locked up so tightly that her grief can only leak out one breath at a time.

I drop to her side and hug her tight, rocking her, until all the pain that wracks her slender body has shuddered to a halt. I feel like I don't ever want to let her go.

"You're my friend," I whisper into her ear, desperate to let her to know she's not alone anymore.

Gabriella sobs. "I don't deserve . . . anything. Why are you saying this?"

"Because I care about you, Gabriella. We all do."

She shakes her head. "It drove him mad . . ." she sobs. "It made him *angry* all the time, so *angry*."

"What did?"

Gabriella turns her exhausted, empty eyes on me. "Baba and Mama were taken by the LRA when I was five years old. Mama hid me in the bush and my grandmother found me after they had gone. She took me to live with her. I did not see my parents again until . . ."

I wait a moment as she gulps in breath and wipes her face on her arm. "Until you were twelve? When the LRA came to your village and killed your grandma? But you told me your mama *died* when you were five."

"I *lied*!" she wails. "I did not want you to keep asking questions. I thought Mama *was* dead. I lived with my grandmother for seven years, until the LRA soldiers killed her and took me to Kony. Baba had not seen me since the day he had been taken — he did not know who I was, but Mama *did*. She could never forget. She screamed when she recognized me. Mama knew what the LRA would do to me. She tried to help me escape but we were captured. When we got back, Kony punished my father. He said that Baba could not control his own family, therefore *he* would. Kony made my father give Mama to him."

"Oh, Gabriella . . ."

"If Mwemba did not agree, they would have killed him. Because he did, Kony made him his general. That is how they control people."

It is like someone has hit me in the chest. I can't breathe. "The boy is your half brother. He's *Kony's* child, isn't he?"

Gabriella nods.

I can't think what to say. "Where's your mama now?"

"Mama died in childbirth. Baba gave the boy to me. He is God's judgment on all of us."

We're silent for a while. Gabriella's head is full of images that I can only guess at. What must be a lifetime of tears won't stop falling. After watching Ash distracting the toddler for a while I ask her, "Why doesn't your little brother have a name?"

Gabriella hangs her head. "I did not want him to have one. Whenever I look at him I remember what happened."

"It's not his fault," I tell her softly.

"I swore to myself he would not have a name until we were free."

"You are free now," I tell her.

"No," she says, looking at her father's body. "I do not think so. I do not think I will ever be free."

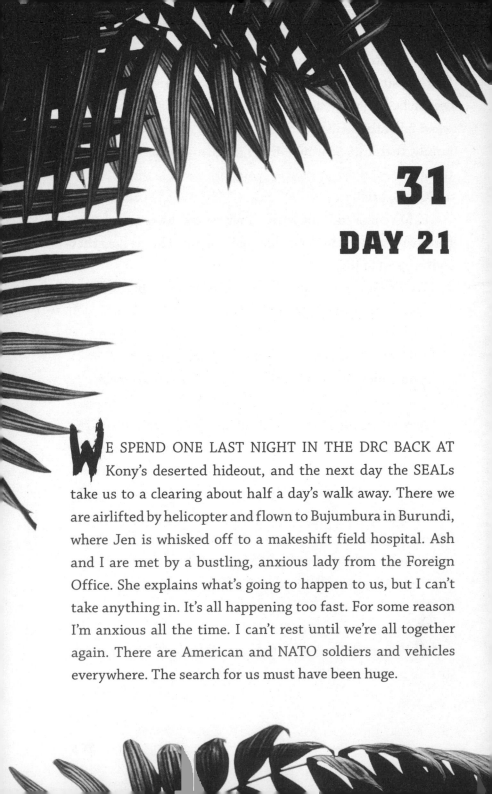

31
DAY 21

WE SPEND ONE LAST NIGHT IN THE DRC BACK AT Kony's deserted hideout, and the next day the SEALs take us to a clearing about half a day's walk away. There we are airlifted by helicopter and flown to Bujumbura in Burundi, where Jen is whisked off to a makeshift field hospital. Ash and I are met by a bustling, anxious lady from the Foreign Office. She explains what's going to happen to us, but I can't take anything in. It's all happening too fast. For some reason I'm anxious all the time. I can't rest until we're all together again. There are American and NATO soldiers and vehicles everywhere. The search for us must have been huge.

I first catch sight of Marcus and Charis in one of the command tents, talking to a couple of African guys. I'm amazed to see that Charis is holding Marcus's hand. Her other arm ends in a folded sleeve.

She drops Marcus's hand when she sees us, screaming, *"Rio! Ash!"* and flies into our arms for a group hug. When we let go we're all crying like babies. Charis takes a step back so that she can look at us, her face illuminated by this wide, infectious smile. "We couldn't believe it when they said they found you all alive!" She laughs. "Where's Jen?"

"We heard that they got all of you, but nobody's told us if she's here," Marcus explains.

I tell him, "As soon as we touched down they took her off to the hospital to check her leg."

Marky whoops loudly, punches the air, and does a little jig around Charis. Laughing, Charis pushes him out of her way and introduces us to the African men who are with them, Gibbs and Moto. It turns out they were the ones who first discovered Charis and Marcus limping down the hill toward their research hut. They looked like a pair of zombies, apparently.

"Especially me," Marcus laughs. "Gibbs nearly wet himself. I don't think they'd ever seen someone with my unique good looks before."

"It was also getting dark," the man named Moto says dryly.

"We are running a trial, reintroducing gorillas to the jungle. Every male is tagged, and we plot their locations daily on a virtual map," Gibbs explains. "When the Americans came to pick up your friends we had begun to notice that Jenga, one of the males, was outside of his normal territory. This is very unusual."

"We took them back to where we last saw you, the loggers' encampment," Marcus tells us, "but you were long gone."

Charis adds, "And soon afterward, Gibbs called the lieutenant."

"Yes. I went looking for the females and found the head of Jenga — the primary male. When we discovered the collar without its GPS tracker, we knew one of you had picked it up."

"Don't you just love all these guys in uniforms?" says a voice by the door.

"Jen!"

She's on crutches and there's a clean white bandage around her leg. She's with this young African soldier wearing a Red Cross armband. I almost bowl her over when I go to hug her. She avoids Ash, but she's not quick enough to stop me from throwing my arms around her. At first Jen's a little stiff, but after a couple of seconds her head falls against mine. I kiss her cheek.

"*Please*," she laughs at Ash over my shoulder. "You two could *seriously* use a shower."

I stand back to look at her. She looks amazing. "Where did you get the makeup?" The girl looks like she's just been made over for a *Vogue* cover shoot.

Jen jerks her thumb over her shoulder. "You think all these soldiers are guys? Well, duh. I just wanted to feel like *myself* again. Oh, by the way, this . . . is Joseph." She won't look Ash or me in the eyes when she says his name.

Joseph clears his throat and turns to leave. "I should be getting back to the hospital." He pauses in the entrance, looks back at Jen with a pair of *smoldering* eyes, and asks, "I was wondering . . . can I see you again before you leave?"

Jen looks at Ash briefly and her smile falters. "No. I don't think so," she says.

Joseph nods but he's embarrassed. "If you change your mind . . ."

"I won't," she says sadly, "but thanks for asking. It's not you."

Joseph looks puzzled and leaves — awkwardly.

Ash looks at me. He reaches out to touch her. "Jen —"

She steps away. "It's okay, Ash. I'm fine, really. Rio's amazing — and I'll get over it eventually. I just don't know if *we* can stay friends. It will hurt too much. You understand, don't you?"

"Of course I do, I just wish —"

"Then let's just leave it at that. It may change, but right now all I want to do is get out of here. I'm sorry."

Ash and I don't see her again after that.

"Jen requested a flight back to Cape Town and, as far as I know, has asked to be reunited with her family there," Charis tells me the next day when I ask if she's seen her. "She wanted me to tell you she was sorry but she couldn't face saying good-bye."

We don't admit it, but we both know the reason. I wish she had said good-bye, though, because there's a big black hole in me and I don't know how to deal with it. The military psychologist puts it down to separation anxiety after spending the last few weeks looking out for each other under extreme stress. Perhaps that also explains why I seem to be getting more and more anxious by the day. I can't rest until I find out what has happened to Gabriella and the LRA boys. I ask anyone who looks remotely official what is going to happen to them, but all anyone will tell me is that they are being "processed" by the Ugandan authorities. Whatever that means. When I ask if I can see them I just get strange looks and "We'll see what we can do."

Back home in the UK, whenever I ask the Foreign Office about Gabriella, no one will tell me *anything*. Now that I'm free it's like nobody wants to deal with me. Mrs. Carter manages to find out from the American embassy that Gabriella is going to be repatriated to Uganda, and that the Americans are trying to find a teen refuge where she and her brother will get the help they need. I hope they do. They have been on a journey. Gabriella has carried that kid for miles, probably saved him from all sorts of horrors, and I can't help but wonder — has she been saving the child, or has the child been saving her?

A couple of weeks after our rescue I get the news that they succeeded in finding somewhere for them in Entebbe, Uganda, but the place doesn't have Internet. I try calling. I'm so nervous I nearly put the phone down before anyone picks it up.

"Gabriella *Mwemba*?" A middle-aged woman's voice, very stern. The line goes quiet so long I'm about to ask if she's still there, but just as I open my mouth, the woman says, "She was here, but she left after only one week."

"Do you know where she went?"

"No . . . I am very sorry."

"Why did she leave?"

A disapproving "That girl is *very* disturbed" is all I get. I have to bite my lip so I don't say something I'll regret. I mean — what did they expect? They're a refuge, for God's sake, surely they have experience looking after disturbed people. I'm gutted.

"If you hear from her — would you let me know? *Please?* It's very important. Tell her Rio called."

I don't know if they ever do. There is no phone call, even though I spend days jumping up every time the phone rings. Over the next few months I manage to trace Gabriella to a few more Ugandan care homes, but I'm always too late. At one of them she even had run-ins with the staff and she ran away again, taking the little boy with her. I hate to think of her on the move, friendless and with nowhere to call home. She needs to know that there are people who care about her. But by the New Year the trail has gone completely cold. It's like she never existed.

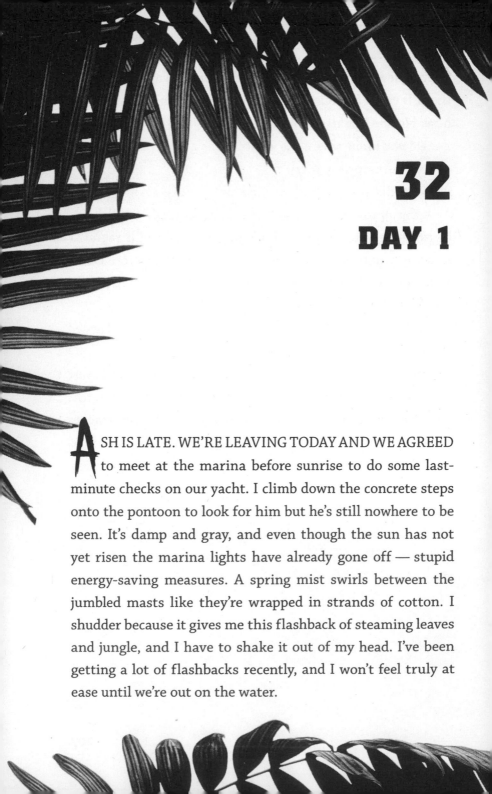

32
DAY 1

ASH IS LATE. WE'RE LEAVING TODAY AND WE AGREED to meet at the marina before sunrise to do some last-minute checks on our yacht. I climb down the concrete steps onto the pontoon to look for him but he's still nowhere to be seen. It's damp and gray, and even though the sun has not yet risen the marina lights have already gone off — stupid energy-saving measures. A spring mist swirls between the jumbled masts like they're wrapped in strands of cotton. I shudder because it gives me this flashback of steaming leaves and jungle, and I have to shake it out of my head. I've been getting a lot of flashbacks recently, and I won't feel truly at ease until we're out on the water.

Beneath the mist, the sea is black and calm, sloshing lazily against the floats. I walk a short distance along the pontoon to see if there is a light on anywhere. Perhaps Ash has gone on ahead to the boat? The thud of my deck shoes on the boards is eerie, emphasizing my growing feeling of isolation. I tell myself not to be stupid. No one is going to creep up on me. I check the boards for foreign objects and take a peek over my shoulder. Since we got back I've been paranoid that it's going to happen again. That someone is going to snatch me away from here and I'll be powerless to do anything about it. I used to love my own company. Now I need to see people — lots of people — just to feel safe, and it's messing with my head.

I want the old me back.

I need to know that I can be independent again. That's why I'm not going to let this stupid anxiety get the better of me. It's also why Ash and I are going to sail around the world, this time setting off from home here in Weymouth. We want to face our fears together, to prove to ourselves that we could have done it. I've put my Women's Laser Radial Olympic training on hold and, after we announced our intentions to the local press, a boatyard owner donated a forty-foot yacht. Mrs. Carter has helped us to kit it out. It's far from the *Spirit of Freedom* but I love it. No bells. No whistles. This yacht will need *sailing*. They even painted a new name on it for me yesterday, *Izzy Lionheart*.

I swallow the rising panic and force myself to walk onto the junction. *Don't be stupid*, I tell myself. *This is England, not Africa. What's the worst that can happen?*

It doesn't help.

Our yacht is moored halfway up one of the aisles and I can tell before I get close that Ash isn't up there, either. Now I'm really starting to lose it. Something must have happened to him, but what? I worry that I've gone too far and turn to look back the way I've come. My heart jumps.

There is a hooded silhouette just standing in the darkness at the end of the pontoon — a strange, deformed-looking shadow. It seriously freaks me out. All I can think of is the Sangoma's yellow smile. I frantically scan around to see if there's anywhere I can run but the marina is deserted. There's only one way out and the shadow is standing in it.

"Who are you?" I yell, fumbling for my phone. The screen lights up as I swipe it. My hands shake badly and I can't remember how to get the number pad on. "I'm calling the police!" Terrified that I'm taking too long, I look up.

The shadow doesn't answer. For a moment it looks like it is caught in indecision, like it may just turn and go back up the steps. Then a part of it seems to wriggle away, bouncing onto the boards with a loud thud and a throaty laugh. A small boy runs at me out of the gloom. He's dressed in wrinkled, oversized jeans and a thick winter jacket. He stops in his tracks when he sees the fear in my eyes. Behind him, the other shadow steps forward, too, its footsteps so light on the pontoon that they barely make a sound.

I can't believe my eyes.

Ash drops to the pontoon behind them and grins at me.

The figure pushes back the hood of her unbuttoned coat and the first watery dawn rays illuminate a worried, round face. She is openly wearing that silver chain around her neck now and there's a bent old crucifix dangling from it. Her hair has grown and she's wearing a colorful dress that's about two sizes too big, secured with a wide, glossy belt. She looks beautiful.

"Rio," she says, smiling uncertainly. "It is me."

ACKNOWLEDGMENTS

I would like to thank Moto for being the accompaniment to my African journey both in real life and in my imagination. The sound of his homemade marimba echoing across the valley as I walked down the hill to the farm in Zambia is one of my enduring memories, as is the kindness and hospitality of all the Africans I met. The LRA, in my experience, are not at all representative of typical Africans and I would hate for my story to leave that impression, hence this note. The Africans I met were generous to a fault — like the laborers who shared their precious Nshima with me, like Patrick who had nothing yet still offered me a precious bag of groundnuts. They are ingenious like the farm workers who allowed me to record their amazing singing, whose accompaniment was a guitar strung with chicken wire because they could not afford strings. They are intelligent like Michael, whose encyclopedic knowledge of the world was gathered from reading and re-reading secondhand magazines in a foreign language, and like Mwiza, a dedicated investigative news journalist at just eighteen. Thanks, guys, for showing me the real Africa. Thanks, too, to all the wonderful listeners across Africa who shared their lives and experiences with Debi and myself. You are truly inspiring.

I'm also indebted to my family and friends — to Stee, Anna, and Josh for some great, insightful feedback, and to

Colin, who always seems to see things that I don't. To my amazing editor-chickens Imogen Cooper and Rachel Leyshon for their patience and dedication to carving something likely to float out of the jumble of raw materials I presented them; and to Helen Jennings for trimming the rigging just before it hit the water. For those all-important final tweaks, Laura Myers showed patience above and beyond the call of duty, and Tina Waller — what can I say? Thanks for all your hard work from the day you first championed *Torn*, and *congratulations . . . !* For my American readers, once again I am deeply indebted to Siobhán McGowan for her amazing insights and attention to detail. Just like Rio getting those few extra knots out of *The Spirit of Freedom*, she has ensured that *Taken* will slice its way across The Pond with accuracy and elegance.

Thanks also to Wing Commander Nick Carter, consultant in trauma rehabilitation at Headley Court Military Hospital, for sharing details of an inspiring Arctic sailing trip he undertook with some very brave amputees.

Finally — shiver me timbers — to Debi, my own first mate, without whom this particular yacht would have sunk without trace long ago: Thanks for all the splicing, knotting, and trimming, and for helping me navigate this thing from concept to launch.